/ renew by

LOVE BITES

ALSO BY ADRIENNE BARBEAU

Vampyres of Hollywood
(with Michael Scott)

There Are Worse Things I Could Do

LOVE BITES

[VAMPYRES OF HOLLYWOOD II]

ADRIENNE BARBEAU

THOMAS DUNNE BOOKS ⚕ *New York*

ST. MARTIN'S PRESS

This is a work of fiction. All of the characters, organizations,
and events portrayed in this novel are either products of the
author's imagination or are used fictitiously.

THOMAS DUNNE BOOKS.
An imprint of St. Martin's Press.

Based upon the characters created by Adrienne Barbeau and
Michael Scott in *Vampyres of Hollywood*.

www.thomasdunnebooks.com
www.stmartins.com

Library of Congress Cataloging-in-Publication Data

Barbeau, Adrienne, 1949–
    Love bites / Adrienne Barbeau. — 1st ed.
        p.   cm.
    ISBN 978-0-312-36728-2
    1. Motion picture producers and directors—Fiction.   2. Vampires—
Fiction.   3. Hollywood (Los Angeles, Calif.)—Fiction.   I. Title.
    PS3602.A759L68 2010
    813'.6—dc22

                                                    2010021688

First Edition: September 2010

10   9   8   7   6   5   4   3   2   1

For Billy, Cody, William, and Walker —
the blessings in my life

ACKNOWLEDGMENTS

Without Julie Smith—author, teacher, mentor, and all-round great new friend—this novel would be a novella. She guided me every step of the way and I couldn't have done it without her.

I am indebted to all the wonderful people who helped me get these words on paper: to my always supportive husband, Billy Van Zandt, for knowing what works; to Meg Bennett, for her wisdom and advice; to Wyatt Harlan, for her brilliance and patience; to Glenn Casale and Brian Williams, for a peaceful place to write; to Eva Long and Sally Fallis, for reading the early words; to Officer Tony Lee of the Beverly Hills Police Department; to Sgt. Mitchel Grobeson, LAPD Retired; and to U.S. Marshall Scott Samuels, for the facts and details, even if I didn't always incorporate them.

Huge thanks to Karyn Marcus, Elizabeth Curione, and all the folks at Thomas Dunne Books, and to Erin Brown, who showed me how to pull it all together.

This is the third time I get to thank Jane Dystel and Miriam Goderich and everyone at Dystel & Goderich Literary Management. Without you, there wouldn't have even been a first, and I am forever grateful.

LOVE BITES

CHAPTER ONE

I am nearly five hundred years old. My skin is flawless, my butt is tight, and my tits don't need help staying up. Unless you impale me, dismember me, decapitate or drown me, you can't do me much damage. I've been stabbed, scalded, and stretched on the rack, and I have survived. I've been burned, flayed, and shot, and I have survived. I've lived through the Thirty Years' War, the French Revolution, and the Spanish Inquisition. The Taiping Rebellion, the Boxer Rebellion, two world wars, and a couple of scathing movie reviews from the *L.A. Times*. And two weeks ago, with a little help from my personal assistant and a hunky Beverly Hills cop, I managed to do away with the mother of all evil, leaving me the most powerful vampyre in North America. I'm not saying I'm invincible, but I've got a pretty good track record when it comes to dealing with danger.

So why was I so terrified to drive over the hill to Studio City to have Christmas Eve dinner with the parents of a man I barely know?

He looks like a cross between Springsteen and the model they use in all those paintings of Christ. Melt-in-your-mouth attractive.

Water-in-the-desert attractive. Good-looking enough to get me going just staring at him, and that doesn't happen very often, believe me. The last time was Nureyev, in the sixties. It's the cheekbones. I like the ones you can cut paper on.

His name is Peter King, and he's a detective with the Beverly Hills Police. Early forties. Divorced. We met two weeks ago when he was assigned by his Captain to investigate the murders of my business partner, three of my stars, and an employee of my film company, Anticipation Studios. Yes, five murders, all connected to me. I am Ovsanna Moore, writer, producer, and star of seventeen blockbuster horror films, several less than successful ones, and a few that went straight to DVD. In the film business, I'm known as a Scream Queen. In my private life—my very private life—I'm known as Ovsanna Hovannes Garabedian, Chatelaine of the Clan Dakhanavar of the First Bloodline. A vampyre.

A fairly powerful vampyre, when you consider my clan includes most of the A-list Hollywood stars, past and present.

Peter King knows what I am. And he'd asked me out just hours after he'd discovered my secret. I found that intriguing. I like a man who's not put off by an extra set of teeth. I was intrigued enough to accept his invitation.

So there I was, standing in my dressing room on Christmas Eve, throwing clothes on the floor as fast as I could try them on and get them off again. I'd already eliminated a Costume National suit and my Diesel jeans. What should I wear to meet the family of a man I'd already fed on but barely knew? I was so nervous, if I'd had a gag reflex, I'd have been on my knees in front of the toilet.

Meeting his parents, for God's sake? On Christmas Eve?

I'd just taken my Carolina Herrera smoke suede pants off the hanger when the fowl started honking.

Someone was in my yard.

I rely on a gaggle of geese to sound an alarm. It's an idea I borrowed from Louis XVI, and I swear it's more effective than my high-tech security system. Like Louis, geese are territorial, and when they're upset, they're loud.

This time they were making a hell of a racket.

I let my senses sharpen. I am of the Dakhanavar clan—vampyre elite—with extremely honed sight, smell, and hearing. When I choose to, I can hear conversations taking place half a mile away. I stood still and listened.

I heard the geese.

I heard the koi in the pond. The waterfall hitting the stream. The neighbor's cat cleaning herself out on the street. And more fucking geese.

But I couldn't hear the intruder.

Maybe I had Marcel Marceau in my yard?

I couldn't smell him, either, which meant he wasn't human. Humans give off a distinctive scent specific to their tribe. What I did smell, over the goose shit and honeysuckle, was something pungent and feral.

I dropped the hanger and the pants on the floor and moved through my bedroom into my office. Whoever it was had had to scale the two-foot-wide, twelve-foot-tall stucco wall that surrounds my property—he wasn't there by accident. I unsheathed my fangs but kept my claws in so I could use the computer to bring up the security cameras trained on the grounds.

I hit the keyboard and my forty-five-inch monitor split into eight screens, giving me a 360-degree view of my property. I could see the guest cottage, the pool, the squash court, the front drive— nothing there save honking fowl. They had spread all over the yard, which they didn't usually do, and had completely abandoned their resting place by the waterfall. Which was where I finally saw movement: behind the thick bougainvillea on the far side of the stream.

You remember those scenes in *Angel* where David Boreanaz was standing on one side of the room and suddenly, without being seen, he was somewhere else? That's what vampyres do. We transport ourselves so quickly that we become momentarily invisible. Something having to do with the speed of light. In the movies we call it "space-shifting." I don't do it very often; I don't have the need. My lack of practice was evident in the several seconds it took me to get to my yard. I've got to get back in shape.

The smell near the water was overpowering, like burning manure, and I knew for certain whatever was there wasn't human. Or female. No bitch on earth gives off that kind of stench. I dropped my fangs, let out my claws, and studied the ground as everything took on the glowing clarity of my vampyre vision.

The sound of his claws pushing off the cliff fifteen feet above me brought my head up, just in time to see him hurtling down on me from the waterfall. I threw out my arms to deflect him, and my nails sank into his fur. He was some sort of wolf, three times the size of a Grey, with rabid orange eyes and a coat so black that it disappeared against the darkening sky. I could feel it, though. A coarse, grimy undercoat, thick enough to act like armor, and then the outer pelage, as sharp as porcupine quills with razorlike edges. His muzzle was wide and long, overfilled with an extra set of yellow fangs that peeled his lips into a Jack Nicholson rictus and sprayed me with white foam. A Tom Savini wet dream. With foul breath.

I met him in midlaunch, and we went down in the water. He had me pinned beneath him with all four paws. The stream was only inches deep. I'd spent thousands of dollars lining it with broken tourmaline granite. The fucking rocks were making mincemeat of my back. If I'd known I'd be playing Little Red Riding Hood, I'd have bought moss. At least I was nude; having to bleach my own blood out of my suede pants would have left me doubly pissed.

He shifted his weight to his front paws, pressing my shoulders deeper into the rocks, and tried going for my neck with his fangs. I couldn't throw him off. He must have weighed 250 pounds. I held him back with both hands, my claws slicing through his pelt into his flesh. His muzzle was inches from my face, snarling and slashing from side to side. His breath was rancid, infected, like the stench of a sewer. I couldn't get close enough to get my mouth on him. Feral saliva dripped like acid in my eyes. I wedged a leg under his belly and gashed it with my claws. I tried again for his bowels, but he trapped my leg with his hind paw. Blood from his belly poured down on my breasts, pooling between them and sliming down through my legs into the water.

We struggled like that for minutes, holding each other at bay in a thrashing embrace. I was snarling; he was growling; the geese were honking. He was stronger than I was, in that position, anyway, and if I couldn't do something to get out from under him soon, the only Peter I was going to be spending Christmas with was a guy in a robe with the key to a gate.

In the distance, I heard a siren and realized the silent perimeter alarms had been tripped. The security company I pay an arm and a leg to was sending its armed guards. I wasn't sure how much help they'd be. If I couldn't kill this thing, I doubted anyone else could.

The beast heard the siren seconds after I did, just as the car's flashing lights turned the sky red outside my gates. There was a screech of brakes and voices shouting, and then the thing was off me, racing to the wall, scrabbling up and over, taking the twelve feet like it was a bunny hop. He disappeared into the wilds of Bel Air.

I closed my eyes and retracted my claws. My fangs slipped back inside their sheaths. I wasn't worried about the security guards finding me naked; in all the trips they've made to the house over the years, they've never managed to have the right password with them or the right set of keys. It would probably take them half an hour to get in. By that time, I'd be presentable and apologizing profusely for the false alarm.

So I lay there in the water for a moment, watching my flesh mend itself in the lowering light, and thought about what had just attacked me.

It was a wolf, all right, but not your North American garden variety. He wasn't a timber or a Grey. He was a were, and as soon as I'd touched him, I'd known what kind.

Werewolves come in several varieties. You've got humans who like using magic or a talisman (most often a wolf pelt) to shape-shift at will. They're called boxenwolves or hexenwolves. I've seen a couple wearing their talismans around their necks, hanging out at the Magic Castle. That's the landmark mansion on Franklin where you can have dinner and watch magicians entertain. The last time I went, Phyllis Diller was doing jokes about her husband, Fang, and the boxenwolves in the audience were eating it up. But they never let on that's what they are, and nobody would believe them anyway.

Then there are humans who don't have any control over their shape-shifting; they've been cursed by a devil or a demon, and when the full moon comes up, they're possessed. The French call them loup-garoux; online they're beta-wolves. Remember Joan Crawford?

And then there are humans who think they're wolves and act like wolves and sometimes have the ferocity of wolves without doing any shape-shifting at all: lycanthropes. Like Joe Eszterhas.

This werewolf had never been human. He might be able to shift to human shape, but that was where the similarity ended. He wasn't a boxenwolf or loup-garou or lycanthrope. This beast was a true were.

Werecreatures come in almost as many varieties as vampyres. They *are* vampyres, actually, although not purebred. The *nogitsone* in Japan, werefoxes in China, the *boudas*—hyena people—in Morocco, apemen in Sumatra, *santu sakai* in Malaysia. You think about an animal and somewhere on earth there's probably a werecreature inhabiting that form. Weres are a breed born from the coupling of Lilith—the Night Hag—and an ancient Akhkharu serpent. They're a vampyre hybrid that can only change into a specific beast shape, and they're nothing but evil.

Who, I wondered, was this were, and why had he just tried to finish me off?

CHAPTER TWO

Did I want to jump her bones? I didn't even know if Ovsanna had bones. I knew she had blood because some of it was mine. I'd let her feed on me to save her life, right after I'd discovered she's a vampyre.

I'd found that out when I'd followed her and her assistant to a mansion in Palm Springs, thinking they were leading me to a serial killer the media had dubbed the Cinema Slayer. The killer who'd practically shut down the town and sent every A-list star running for the hills.

The Cinema Slayer was there, all right, but he wasn't your average everyday serial killer. I stumbled into a coven of monsters and weirdos the likes of which I never believed existed, lorded over by a Bette Davis look-alike in a *Whatever Happened to Baby Jane?* outfit. Baby Jane's name was Lilith. *The* Lilith, Ovsanna said, who claimed to be Adam's first wife, before Eve. Ovsanna called her the Night Hag and said they were related by blood. That's when I realized Ovsanna was more than just a movie star.

So I asked her out. Which surprised me as much as it surprised her. Having a vampyre spend Christmas Eve with my parents had never been on my short list.

This all happened two weeks ago. We'd been standing in the rubble, staring at the fireplace, which was the only structure that had survived the explosion, when out of nowhere I thought about my mother's house on Christmas Eve, and how much fun we always have, and how last year was the first time since I'd divorced Jenny that I'd been there alone, and how that *hadn't* been as much fun. The next thing I knew, I was asking Ovsanna to come for dinner.

It was only after the words came out of my mouth that I considered the ramifications. And the implications.

The ramifications I could deal with. As far as I was concerned, the case that had brought us together was closed, so I wasn't breaking any departmental regs. Of course, the Captain might not see it that way—he didn't know yet that the killer was dead—but my conscience was clear. That was one. And two, I was sure Ovsanna didn't want her true self exposed any more than I wanted to expose her. No one would believe me anyway. There's no such thing as vampyres, right? Three, I'd known her only two days by then, but when you've been a cop as long as I have, you learn to trust your instincts, and my instincts said she wasn't a threat. So what was the worst thing that could happen—she wouldn't eat my mother's food? Ma's served food to actors for twenty years; she knows they're all nuts when it comes to worrying about how they look. She wouldn't take it personally.

The *implications,* on the other hand, I should have taken seriously. Since when did I bring a semistranger into my parents' home for a visit, let alone on a major holiday? What did this mean? I'd dated Jenny for nine months before we ran the family gauntlet, and even then I'd only started with my mother.

Ovsanna was having a major effect on me, fangs and all.

I wondered if she could control my mind. Didn't Dracula do that in one of those movies? Maybe she'd put a spell on me right from the beginning. From the first time I'd interviewed her. Maybe she's got bad breath and body odor and I can't tell because she's messed with my senses. Do vampyres have magic powers? I mean, apart from the transformation and teeth thing?

I'm a detective. I'll do a little detecting and find out.

CHAPTER THREE

I called Peter to tell him I needed a little more time to get ready. I didn't tell him why. I didn't want him to think I was battling monsters on a weekly basis. And I definitely didn't want him thinking I needed him to save my life again. I should be able to take care of myself.

But until I knew who this werebeast was and why he was after me, I didn't want to involve a man I was hoping would stick around. I knew from past experience that creature attacks and romance don't mix. I lost Lord Byron that way. As fascinated as he was with my Armenian heritage—he even learned to read our language so he could write about us—once he saw me take on a werebeast, he turned tail and disappeared. It didn't matter that I'd sliced and diced the were to bits and made sure no leftovers remained.

Peter didn't seem to be afraid. In fact, from the way he'd asked me out, I suspected my genus was an attraction.

We'd been standing in front of the charred remains of Lilith's house in Palm Springs. The gelatinous ooze drying on my boots was none other than one of my former lovers, a famous film star and one of my clan—the Vampyres of Hollywood. All the life-threatening wounds I'd sustained at the hands of the Night Hag had healed almost instantly, but I was covered with ash and mud, my leather pants were shredded, and my hair looked like a used Brillo pad. Not the kind of thing to inspire a dinner invitation. Or take home to mother.

"Do vamp— Do . . . do you . . . celebrate Christmas?" he had asked. Why he'd thought of Christmas, or me and Christmas together, at that moment is beyond me—maybe because the fireplace chimney was the only thing left standing?

"Are you asking about vampyres in general? Are we Christian—is that what you want to know?" I couldn't keep from smiling; I swear he was actually squirming.

"No, no. I mean, well, sure, I'd like to know that, too, sometime. There's plenty I want to know, but not right now. This definitely isn't the place. No, I mean, you . . . do you have plans for Christmas Eve?"

"Nothing specific. I'll probably go to the office for a few hours." I unstuck a blob of drying *dhampir* from my jeans—it looked like part of an ear—and threw it into the ash.

"Come have dinner with us." He had such a nice smile.

"Us?"

"My family. My mother and dad. And a couple of sisters and brothers. Do something normal after the horror you've just been through. We start in the late afternoon and go all night. It'll be very casual and a lot of fun. No paparazzi, I promise—not even an Instamatic."

I laughed. I didn't know what to say. Was he asking me out on a date?

"My mother's a great cook. Do you like to eat Italian?"

I looked down at my former lover's crust on my boots. *He'd* been Italian. Rudolph Valentino. I should never have turned him; his blood had been as disgusting as his personality became. "Uh, Peter . . . I'm not much on eating. Or drinking, for that matter. I can explain it all to you another time, but I don't think—"

"Look, you don't have to eat. You're an actress—no one expects you to eat. No one expects you to do anything normal. You can do whatever you do when you're at any kind of party. You must have something you do to keep your secret. It's not a sit-down dinner anyway, we all just fill our plates and hang out. No one will notice. Just come. You and Maral, if you want."

That was nice of him. Maral is my personal assistant. She's worked for me for nearly ten years, and we're rarely apart. She makes sure of that. Just days before, Peter had been investigating her, wondering if an incident she'd been involved in when she was younger had anything to do with the case he was working on. He'd cleared her of suspicion, but she'd been pretty snotty to him since. She was going to be even nastier when she found out he'd asked me to his parents' house and she couldn't go. Her mother was having trouble with her younger brother, and she'd begged Maral to spend Christmas with them back home in Louisiana. Maral doesn't think of it as home anymore—as far as she's concerned, her home is with me—but she couldn't disappoint her momma. She was flying to the bayou early on Christmas Eve.

I accepted his invitation. From the moment the day before when I'd accidentally cut him and had had to tend to his bleeding hand, I'd been seduced by the sight and smell of his blood. Watching him deal with everything we'd been through since had only heightened my estimation of him. He seemed like a good man. Honest. Capable. And he didn't take himself too seriously.

He had offered me his wrist when I needed it. Now, once again, I could feel the Thirst coming on me. This time it had nothing to do with need and everything to do with attraction.

I put the suede pants back on the hanger. Time to show a little leg.

CHAPTER FOUR

I carried all the presents out to the car, went back and grabbed my jacket, and locked the house. It was a beautiful night, crisp and clear, with a quarter-moon showing. The wintersweet had its first spicy-scented blooms. I stood for a moment just to take it in. I had plenty of time. Ovsanna had called to say she'd been delayed. She didn't say what had happened, but I got the impression she'd had to chew some-one out.

I left SuzieQ's gifts on her doorstep. Her shades were drawn, which meant she was still asleep. She works nights. She'd said she might stop by my mom's later in the evening, but I wasn't counting on it; she's flaky when it comes to social engagements. She's been my tenant for the past five years, renting the guesthouse in the back of my three-bedroom Beverly Hills bungalow. Over the years, she's become a good friend. My closest friend, probably, now that Jenny was gone.

SuzieQ is an exotic dancer. She dances with snakes—that kind of exotic dancer—and she's really good at it. She keeps them in cages in her big front closet, which sort of freaked me out at first, but I guess I've gotten used to it. She barely bothers to close the door anymore when I go over there.

I hoped she'd like the gift I'd bought her. It was a signed first edition of some coffee table book she'd been talking about. *Dancing Women.* It set me back $135. Plus, I'd gotten her a turquoise cashmere sweater. I knew she'd like that.

There was no traffic on Sunset, so the drive to Ovsanna's took ten minutes. She lives high up on Stone Canyon Road in Bel Air, in a pretty magnificent Spanish estate. The gates alone must have cost half my yearly salary. They look like the Moors designed them a couple of centuries ago.

I had the code to the gate (thanks to a paparazzo named Steady Eddie who'd been hanging around Ovsanna's during the Cinema Slayer case), but it's against my cop nature to let on everything I know. Plus, I didn't want to start the afternoon with Ovsanna thinking I'd been spying on her. So I pressed the button on the intercom and waited for the massive iron barriers to swing open.

She was standing outside the front door when I pulled up. She had her back to me and was staring into the darkness. What a great ass. It was just about perfect. Then she turned around and smiled, and my heart started pounding. I mean really. I could feel it. She looked fantastic. All that black curly hair and pale skin and those dark eyes. She was wearing a clingy, cream-colored dress made out of some sweater material that stopped just above her knees. And legs. Great legs. This was the first time I'd seen them; she'd had on jeans the day I'd interviewed her and leather pants the day of the . . . well, whatever we were calling what happened in Palm Springs.

"Hey," I said, scintillating conversationalist that I am. "How are you?"

"I'm fine," she answered. "Merry Christmas."

"That's right. You're right. It's almost Christmas. Merry Christmas to you, too." Boy, we were off to a brilliant start. "Are you ready?"

She had a tall gift bag in one hand. "I wasn't sure what your parents might like, so I took a chance. . . . Do they drink wine?"

"They're Italian, Ovsanna. At least my mom's side is. They drink wine like you drink—"

Oh shit, I thought. This could be a long night.

CHAPTER FIVE

Peter's parents' house was charming. On a corner lot, with a huge pepper tree shading the driveway and a white picket fence all around it, covered in climbing rosebushes. The fence wouldn't keep out a wolf—hell, my twelve-foot wall hadn't—but I didn't think there was much danger I'd been followed. Still, I needed to keep my eyes—and ears and nose—open. And not let on to Peter what was worrying me.

There were more roses lining the brick walkway and a well-tended lawn. The house was two stories, with dormer windows above and a big bay window to the right of the front door. White wooden shingles and red shutters. Santa Claus was driving his reindeer and sleigh across the black shake roof. As we pulled up, I could see smoke coming out of the chimney.

Cars lined both sides of the two streets bordering the house. I pretended to notice them while I scanned the yards in the neighborhood. I smelled a long-gone skunk, but nothing lupine. No werebeast in hiding.

"It looks like someone's having a party," I said. "Look at all the cars."

Three little kids came screaming out the front door and raced for Peter's legs. "Uncle Peter! Uncle Peter!" The smallest one threw herself into his arms. "Did you bring us presents?!"

Peter said, "That's not a party, Ovsanna. That's us. Just my sisters and brothers. Hey, Sofia, Merry Christmas!" He swung her into the air, and she screamed in delight. "You know I brought you presents! Gobs and gobs of 'em." He freed one arm to pick up one of the little boys. "Merry Christmas, Stefano."

"Who're you?" The second little boy looked up at me with the biggest brown eyes I'd ever seen. He could have modeled for one of those Keane paintings back in the 60s. "Who's she, Uncle Peter? Is she your girlfriend?"

"No, Jeremy, she's my friend. This is Ovsanna."

"That's a funny name. I can't say that name. Did she bring us presents, too?"

"Listen, buddy, I'll bet there are plenty of presents under the tree. And there's a bunch in the trunk of my car. Can you help carry them in?"

Peter put Sofia and Stefano on the ground, and all three children ran for his Jaguar. "Just press the button on the back of the car and you'll see them all." He turned to me with a rueful grin on his face. "Sorry about that. I should have warned you. Imagine an Olive Garden restaurant ad with better food, and you've got my family. Think you can handle it?"

"I don't know. I barely survived the *Night of the Living Dead* Smackdown we just went through. Is it going to be much worse?"

Peter laughed. "Only the noise level. Oh, and maybe my aunt Adelaide."

He was right. As we entered the house, the noise was overwhelming. I damped down my hearing instantly. This was one instance when my heightened senses would only annoy me. Thirty or forty people screamed at one another from across the room. Bobby Helms was singing "Jingle Bell Rock" on the stereo, five children shrieked in a game of hide-and-seek tag, two more wrestled over the back of a sofa, and a baby covered in spaghetti sauce was pounding away on her high chair, with a spoon in one fist and a plastic sippy cup in the other. The decibel level rivaled a rock concert.

Until little Jeremy ran past us with packages in his hands and screamed, "Uncle Peter's here with a lady and she's got a funny name, but she's not his girlfriend and there's lots of presents in his car!" Every adult in the room turned to stare. And as soon as they recognized me, the room went totally quiet.

CHAPTER SIX

I should have thought of it before I walked into my mother's house with a movie star. I was so busy worrying about how to deal with *what* Ovsanna was that I didn't think to tell anyone *who* she was. I hadn't even told my mother I was bringing someone with me. My family's pretty cool, and God knows most of them have been around celebrities at the family catering truck for years. If I'd warned them in advance, they wouldn't have reacted like thirty-five rubes outside Grauman's Chinese. Instead, we were faced with dead silence and a lot of dropped jaws. I think my showing up with *anyone* was as much a conversation stopper as the fact that the woman I'd brought was who she was. But as soon as my mother crossed the room with her arms outstretched and gave Ovsanna a kiss on both cheeks, everyone went back to their normal screaming and the conversations picked up where they'd left off.

My mother launched into her story of meeting Ovsanna's mother when Mom was catering the set food for *The Twilight Zone*. Mom couldn't get over how young Anna Moore had looked at the time, even though it was toward the end of her career, and how much

Ovsanna looked now the way her mom did then. Mom dragged Ovsanna off to meet my older brother, Connor, and two older sisters, all partners in the family business my mother started back in the 1960s: King's Catering—The King of Caterers.

Then Connor introduced her to his wife, and Suzanne and Callie introduced their husbands, and then the cousins and then my younger sister, Quincy, and her partner, Deirdre. My uncle handed her a glass of red, and someone grabbed a picture off the mantel to show her my other sister, Rosalie, who's hiking the Himalayas, and by the time I caught up with her again, my father had her corraled out in his workshop, where he was showing off his handmade chess sets. He's a pretty talented woodworker.

"Peter, these pieces are remarkable. I love this one especially. Your dad did all the famous silent film stars—and look, he's even got my mother as a queen." She had the oddest glint in her eyes, and when I looked down at my father's latest collection of carvings, I saw he'd used Orson Welles as a king. Orson was one of Ovsanna's vampyres, and the last time I'd seen him, just two weeks before, he was a werebull with huge, curling horns—and he *wasn't* a carving.

"Well, my wife was a big fan of your mom's, Ms. Moore. She's the one who suggested this whole set. They sell a whole lot better than the presidents. I don't know if Peter's told you, but Angela has a big collection of movie memorabilia. I used some photos she has of your mom and Mr. Welles to copy the likenesses."

Ovsanna picked up the rook. It was Peter Lorre, another of her Vampyres of Hollywood. If my father only knew what he'd chosen to re-create, he could devise a whole new marketing plan.

"I'd like to buy it, Seth," she said, admiring the expression Dad had captured around the eyes. "Not only because it's my mother, but because some of these actors you've carved were friends of hers. I knew them when I was growing up." She put Peter Lorre down and picked up a pawn. Gloria Swanson. I wondered. Another vampyre? Ovsanna gestured to the whole set. "I'd really love to have this in my home. And you have to call me Ovsanna. Please."

————

Ma had food on the table from the time we walked in the door: anti-pasti, stuffed mushrooms, fried artichoke hearts, marinated mozza-rella, clams oreganata, breadsticks, Parmesan crisps, roasted peppers, caponata, tapenade, aioli, chips and dip for the kids, and a wheel of pro-volone. At seven thirty, she served the first course—farfalle in pesto, linguine in white clam sauce, gnocchi in red sauce, eggplant Parm, manicotti, and vegetarian lasagna for my cousin Camille. Of course, Ovsanna didn't know that was just the first course, and when the tur-key and dressing came out, she looked at me as though *we* were the ones who weren't quite human.

It was all buffet. Everyone was so busy piling up food, no one noticed when Ovsanna put down her plate and excused herself to go to the bathroom. By the time she came back, Aunt Adelaide and my mother were going at it.

"Where's the thirteen fishes, Angela?"

"Nobody eats them all, Addie, I only made seven this time."

"How can you only make seven? You gotta have thirteen! What, you wanna burn in hell?" Adelaide is my ma's older sister. Way older.

"It's a stupid custom, Addie, and it's gonna go the way of purga-tory and fish on Friday. And that last saint they decided wasn't really a saint."

"Madre di Dio!"

My sister Suzanne chimed in. "Oh, Aunt Addie, it doesn't have to be thirteen. It's just got to be an uneven number. Look, Ma's got baccalà, clams in the shell, white clam sauce, scampi, peppers and anchovies, fried oysters, lobster fra diavolo—it's enough already!"

Adelaide's face was getting blotchy. I couldn't tell if it was the wine she was drinking or a stroke. *"Basta!* There were twelve apostles and Jesus, that's thirteen at the Last Supper, there's gotta be thirteen fishes! Let me tell you, Angela, if Ma were alive, God rest her soul, she'd be turning in her grave!" It was the wine.

Ma said, "What the hell does the Last Supper have to do with Jesus's birth? We're celebrating Christmas, not the end of his life!"

"Hey, the paper the other day said it was supposed to be seven fishes for the seven sacraments." This from my cousin Tony, who should have known better than to get involved.

Adelaide started yelling, "Ah, you can use that paper to wipe my ass! What do they know, are they in church on Sunday? No! They're too busy printing lies in the paper!"

Ovsanna put down her plate. "I don't know anything about Christmas in Italy, Aunt Adelaide, but I can barely hear anything in here. Let's go outside. I'd love to hear the story of the fishes."

And it was over as fast as it started. Adelaide followed Ovsanna outside, and I watched them exclaiming over the fruit trees. Ovsanna seemed a little antsy; she kept looking around as though she expected to see someone she knew. She explored the yard while Addie continued ranting about sacraments and sacrilege. I watched them through the kitchen window. Finally Ovsanna put her hands on Addie's shoulders, stared into her eyes, and spoke so softly to her that I couldn't hear what she said. And Addie calmed down, just like that.

My mother shot me a look. Even if Ovsanna weren't a movie star, she'd just passed some kind of test.

"She's a nice girl, Peter," my mom said. "A little old for you, maybe, but an awfully nice girl."

CHAPTER SEVEN

I couldn't believe the dinner Mrs. King served. The last time I'd seen that much food on a table was in 1575, in Kenilworth at the Earl of Leicester's feast for the queen. I was only twenty-five at the time and hadn't had much experience hiding my true nature when it came to feeding, but there were so many revelers that no one noticed the food I didn't eat. Or the footman I did. That feast lasted seventeen days. Looking at Peter's mom's table, I think she had just as much food as they did at the castle.

I couldn't believe myself, either. Normally I would have had a shrew like Peter's aunt Adelaide for lunch. Drained the damn bitch until she was too weak to complain. Instead I was acting like Emily Post, making nice and calming the waters. Well, I did mess with her mind a little when I got her alone outside, but only with the suggestion she back off on the annoyance factor. And when no one was looking, I gave her a mild bite wound on the back of her arm to keep her occupied. She didn't remember a thing, but she spent the rest of the evening itching and scratching. But I didn't do anything else to the old biddy. I wanted Peter's family to like me. Hell, I wanted *him* to like me. I already had a couple of strikes against me, not least of which was involving him in the monster massacre in Palm Springs. I didn't need to make any more problems for him on Christmas Eve.

Peter and I were seated at the kitchen table, chatting with his mom while she wrapped the leftovers. She'd already served enough desserts to feed an entire movie crew. Things I'd never seen, even living in Italy a few hundred years ago: sfogliatelle, cassata, pandoro, pasticiotti. And then the ones I did recognize: cannoli, tiramisu, zeppole, and struffoli. She had gelato for the kids and a bûche de Noël. I guess Peter's side of the family didn't carry much weight when it came to their national dishes. That was understandable; egg whey and blackberry suet pudding don't sound too festive.

Mrs. King had just offered me a double espresso when a beautiful, blond Valkyrie walked into the room and I was saved from refusing. The woman must have been six feet tall, and she had the most remarkable blue eyes. I knew we'd met before, but I couldn't place her.

"Well, Merry Christmas, y'all," she said, leaning down to give Mrs. King a hug. "Ooh, Angela, did you save all of this food for me? Now, ain't you just the best mom in the whole world?" She popped a shrimp into her mouth, tail and all, and kept on talking while she chewed. "Peter, you know how lucky you are to have your mom for a mom? And to have me for a friend?" She turned to me. "He is one lucky son of a gun. Hey, how ya doin', Ms. Moore?" She had a bottle of wine in one hand and a shopping bag of gifts in the other, so she didn't attempt to shake hands, which was fine with me. Physical contact with strangers brings on a bombardment of impressions I can usually do without. "You prob'ly don't remember me, but I wrangled your snakes on *Bride of the Snake God*. I'm SuzieQ, and I live in Peter's guesthouse, and it's sure nice to see you again. You were pretty good in that movie, too."

As soon as I heard her voice, I remembered her. It was four years ago; she'd had a python named Spiro Agnew and another snake named Dick Nixon. We'd hired her and her python for a movie I was starring in. She'd been on the set for a couple of weeks, but most of her work had involved my co-star, Bruce Campbell. She'd done a good job handling the snake. And Bruce, too, for that matter.

"I do remember you, SuzieQ. You're a dancer, too, aren't you?" I remembered Maral mentioning that the cast was going to watch her perform at some Moroccan nightclub. Maral didn't want me to go. She used the excuse that I wouldn't be comfortable having to eat with my fingers, which was a little lame when she knew I wouldn't eat at all. She was just jealous of the striking six-foot blonde.

"Oh, I do just about everything. A little of this and a little of that. Anything short a lyin' on my back with my legs in the air. Gotta pay this man the rent, ya know." She handed Peter the bag of presents. "Here you go, sugar. There's something there for each of the young'uns, and that one on top is for you. Angela, you and Seth get the wine."

We moved into the living room so Peter could give SuzieQ's gifts to the kids. There was a flurry of tearing paper and thank-yous and "Look, Mommy, what I got!" Somebody opened a Jeff Gordon NASCAR Barbie doll, and then rubber snakes appeared and Nerf darts started flying.

I blocked out all the noise and concentrated on the conversation that was taking place across the room. Peter and SuzieQ had moved over to the Christmas tree. I was curious about their relationship. They were obviously close friends. I wondered if it had ever been anything more.

"Sugar," SuzieQ was saying, "what's going on? Why in the name a Jesus have you got Ovsanna Moore standin' in your mama's kitchen? Two weeks ago you were on her ass for bein' a suspect in all those murders."

Peter looked over at me, probably wondering if I could hear them. We hadn't had time to talk about anything personal since he'd learned what I am, but I was sure he'd been reading everything he could get his hands on about vampyres. I wondered if he'd seen *Vampyres for Dummies*. One of the New York Ch'lang Shih clan was the author—his genus unbeknownst to his publisher, of course— and he'd put in just enough misinformation to cloud our discovery for another hundred years. Made me laugh.

"She wasn't a suspect, SuzieQ," Peter whispered. "That was her assistant we were looking at, and besides, neither one of them turned out to be involved. Not really. I just happen to find her attractive. And she was alone for the holiday, so . . ."

"Oh, Peter, you are in way over your head. That woman runs a movie studio, sweetpea. She could eat you alive."

I couldn't keep from smiling. If she only knew. I caught Peter's eye and mouthed, "She's right, you know."

CHAPTER EIGHT

We left the party at midnight. Ovsanna was a big hit with the family, and I think she had a good time, but it may have been a little overwhelming. I saw her eyes start to turn when my nephew ran his tricycle over her foot.

She was quiet on the way home, staring out the window across the houses on Mulholland. It was one of those remarkable evenings in L.A. when the wind had blown the pollution somewhere else and you could see the lights on the mountains all the way across the Valley. If I'd been alone, I'd have been thinking about the people who live out there, separated from one another by acres and acres of scrub. I'll bet they could see stars for miles. I always wonder who they are and what their lives are like. As much as I love the wilderness, I couldn't stand the isolation.

"You're probably not used to that much commotion. Did you have a good time?" I asked.

"I did," she said, and she smiled. She was beautiful when she smiled. She was beautiful all the time, but I realized I hadn't seen her smile often. Maybe it had something to do with hiding her . . .

whatever they were . . . teeth. "It made me feel . . . I don't know what. I'd say homesick, but that's ridiculous. I've never had a home like that to begin with. I guess I experienced the connection you all have to each other—even Aunt Addie—and it was nice. Loud, but nice. Is it like that for every holiday?"

"Pretty much. Except Bastille Day. Aunt Addie's not a big fan of the French."

A pack of photographers stood waiting outside her gate. Seven of them. There'd been more when I'd come to interview her about her partner's murder, thirty or forty, not counting the TV crews. All of them screaming for Ovsanna to come to the door so they could get shots of her to put money in their pockets. But that had died down; she was no longer a suspect, and I couldn't see any reason for them to be there. When they realized I was driving, they stampeded across the road in a herd to get to Ovsanna's side of the car.

"Is it always like this?" I asked her. "It's midnight. How late do they hang around your house?"

"They don't, usually. I don't know what this is all about. And these guys I've never seen before."

I hadn't, either. And I know most of the paparazzi in town. You can't be a cop in Beverly Hills for sixteen years and not know the photographers by name. Half my time is spent smuggling drunken celebrities past their flashbulbs or breaking up fights between them and some star's bodyguard. Or the star himself. Sean Penn calls me Pete. I rolled the window down a few inches. "Haven't you guys got something better to do on Christmas Eve?"

Normally they would have answered back, made some kind of joke, even asked me what I was doing with Ovsanna in the car, was I on duty? As much as I have to police the paparazzi, we've got a pretty good relationship. But these guys, nobody said a word. Nobody yelled, "Ovsanna, over here! Give us a smile!" Nobody yelled anything. They just aimed their cameras at the car, shooting silently through the side window. Ovsanna turned her head toward me, hiding her face from them, and gave me the code to the gate. When I tapped it in, they stopped shooting and stared at us, still without speaking. It bothered me. There was something creepy about it. I wondered where they were from, who sent them. I rolled up the window and waited on the other side until I was sure the gates had closed completely. Maybe I'd get out and talk to them on my way home. Assuming I was leaving.

I had to brake twice on the quarter-mile drive to the house to avoid hitting the geese. Ovsanna has them wandering all over the yard. She says they're as good as any alarm system. They're as loud, that's for sure. And a lot more messy.

Her house was great. Spanish architecture like mine, only on a much bigger scale. Probably ten million dollars bigger. It had a music room, a screening room, a gym, three offices that I knew about, God knew how many bedrooms, a separate guesthouse, a library, and a dining room with a fifteen-foot-long table. I don't even know that many people I'd want to eat with. My sister would have thought she'd died and gone to heaven in the laundry room—a plasma TV, a built-in sewing machine, and spindles holding every color thread in the rainbow. And the art on the walls—original Toulouse-Lautrecs and stuff. What the hell was I doing there? How do you date a woman who spends more on her water bill than you make in a year?

I'm a damn good detective, but I didn't have a clue about what to expect now that we were back at her house. I opened her door and gave her my hand to help her out of the car. Instantly, heat ran up my arm and flooded my chest. It felt like I'd grabbed hold of a live wire and a couple thousand volts were frying my body.

"Jesus!" I said, pulling my hand away. "Did you do that on purpose?" She might as well have Tasered me. I looked to see if my skin was burned.

"What?"

"That heat thing. Shooting out from your hand into my body like a lightning strike."

She'd moved away from me and reached the front door. She put her key in the lock and without looking back said, "I think you'd better come in, Peter. We have a lot to talk about." She opened the door, disarmed the security system, and disappeared into the house, not even waiting to see if I'd follow.

My arm was still tingling. I knew I shouldn't go in. I shouldn't have been there at all; I was already pushing the limit on departmental policy. But I couldn't resist. It had only been two weeks since I'd discovered *True Blood* was a reality series. Everything I'd ever believed about monsters and ghouls had gone right out the window, and I was still trying to get a handle on Ovsanna's lifestyle. Plus, I'd had a great time with her at my parents', and I wanted to talk to her some more. I wanted to find out a lot more about her. I needed to . . . if I was going to decide to see her again.

As long as I didn't get burned.

CHAPTER NINE

It was all I could do to keep my fangs in place and my nails from elongating. I was damned if I was going to ruin another manicure. The last time I'd gotten emotional, I'd left polish all over L.A.

Anger had caused that change, though; this was another emotion entirely.

Lust.

No, not just lust . . . something more complicated. I *liked* this man. He made me laugh. He was strong and fearless, and I didn't intimidate him, even after he found out what I am. I mean, it's hard enough to handle approaching a movie star, but how many men could deal with discovering that an age-old, terrifying myth is actually true? Peter not only rescued the Vampyres of Hollywood—Douglas Fairbanks and Charlie Chaplin among them—he even let me feed on him to save my life. That takes balls.

Figuratively speaking.

I barreled into the house and headed for my downstairs office, not waiting to see if he followed. I knew what was going on, and I had to get myself under control. It's a pattern of mine, although it took me a century or two to recognize it because it happens so infrequently. I'll go years without finding anyone attractive, and then someone comes along—sometimes it's a man, sometimes a woman—with a certain look in the eyes, and I am captivated. It was like that with Rimbaud. You'd think after him I would have learned my lesson. What a mess he turned out to be. But no, when there's a response, when I see the same interest reflected back at me, then a subtle current of sexual arousal sets in. I start sleeping even less than my usual five hours, my skin gets hypersensitive to the touch. I have more trouble keeping my fangs in place, my nails from elongating, and the Thirst comes on me more insistently and too often. It takes a real effort of will not to change.

That's what Peter had felt when he took my hand getting out of the car. I lost control. Not good. I needed either to shut him out completely—walk away and not let him in my life in any way—or to explain to him what was going on with me and let him decide what he wanted the next step to be.

I didn't want to shut him out. I wanted to get closer. I wanted to find out more about him. How his mind worked. Why he didn't run for his life when he discovered what I am. And what it would feel like to kiss him. I'd already tasted his blood; it was spicy and rich. Complex, like the man seemed to be. What would it feel like to have him inside me? That's what I wanted to know.

It would be better for both of us if he walked away.

For the most part, vampyres are solitary creatures. Vampyre couples do exist—I turned Rudy Valentino and we stayed together for several years, and Theda Bara and Charles Brabin have been together since 1921—but they're the exception, not the rule. Mary Pickford and Douglas Fairbanks, both members of my clan, eventually went their separate ways, although I believe Mary still loves him. But vampyres taking human lovers? They tend to be brief affairs, born out of the need to feed off a compliant partner who has some aberration of his own to work out. I have yet to understand humans who have convinced themselves they *need* to drink blood. Psychologists call them hematomaniacs. They've even got vampyre support pages on the Internet, for God's sake, for "sanguinarians" and "vampiric people." And vampyre dating services. If they only knew the reality.

Maral knows.

We've been together for ten years. When I hired her, she was so grateful to get out of the mess her life was in, she would have done anything for me. She was an eighteen-year-old runaway facing a manslaughter charge for killing a man who'd broken into the house where she was staying. He'd attempted to rape her. The cops questioned her claim of self-defense, primarily because she'd managed to decapitate him. They didn't believe a little bit of a thing like her could do that without premeditation. I still wonder about it. Had she been lying in wait for him? At any rate, she didn't have money for a lawyer, and the only job she could get was starring in a porn production "mockumentary" about her story, *The Real Killer Commits the Real Kill!* The producer was a scuzzy weasel who'd just finished knocking off a porno version of my movie *I Scream*. That pissed me off. He'd titled it *I Scream with Pleasure* and used a girl to star in it who bore a slight resemblance to me. At least her face did. Her body looked like Britney Spears on a bad day, and that pissed me off even more. Then, in a real moment of sleaze, he'd given her the screen name Oval Moore. I wanted to kick the shit out of him. When I showed up at his "studio" (a two-bedroom house in the Valley), Maral had just started filming. He stopped the camera long enough to pull a gun on me. She grabbed a fire extinguisher and blasted him. His toupee went flying. I started laughing. She hadn't really saved my life—the gun was a .22, about as effective on me as a mosquito bite—but she'd made the effort, and I was intrigued. I hired her to work for me and hired my lawyer to get her out of the manslaughter charge. She's been committed to me ever since.

A year after we met, I was filming on Slieve More (the Big Mountain) in Ireland. It was our day off, and I'd gone hiking up the mountain alone when the sky turned black and torrential rains started falling. Whether I slipped in the downpour or was pushed, I'll never be certain. The locals believed strongly that banshees lived on Slieve More and that said banshees weren't happy with the movie crew being there—sort of like trying to film in Bolinas, California, where the residents insist on screaming, "Go home!" every time you roll cameras. Whether it was banshees or bad luck, I lost my footing and crashed sixty feet down the side of the mountain, rolling over and over again on scree and razor-sharp shale. I ended up in a river of mud with a broken left arm, two bone fragments sticking out of my calf, a punctured lung, a shattered cheekbone, two cracked ribs, and a broken collarbone. My vampyre physiology attempted to heal itself immediately, but it had been weeks since I'd fed and I didn't have the nutrients I needed to sustain the healing process. My wounds were too extensive. I was dying.

Maral found me before I lost consciousness. I couldn't move my head, but I saw the look in her eyes and knew she was seeing the violent movement beneath my skin as my muscles and bones attempted to fuse back together. It must have been terrifying for her. The blood drained from her face as she watched protruding leg bones angle back towards the top of my tibia, cells reaching for cells to reconnect. "What are you?" she asked in a quavering voice, and eventually I answered with the truth.

"Vampyre. Dying."

She stared at me a moment longer, shaking her head as though to confirm something she might have suspected for a while. And then she sliced her wrist on a jagged rock and she nursed me back to life.

"How did you know what to do?" I asked her later as I healed the wound on her wrist with my saliva. It took only minutes.

"Everyone knows what an injured vampyre needs," she said. This time her voice was stronger. "You see it in the movies all the time."

She's been allowing me to feed on her ever since. Not just allowing—needing. There are times when she begs for it.

The tabloids never tire of questioning our relationship—we're the Oprah and Gayle of the film industry—but only my clan knows the truth.

And now Peter. He knows part of the truth. It was time to tell him the rest.

I wasn't going to tell him everything, though. He didn't need to know I'd been attacked again. There was nothing he could do to help. Not until I knew a lot more about what was going on. Like who was after me, and why.

And even then, I'd take care of it myself.

I heard him enter the house and called out to him to meet me in the library. If Maral had been there, I would have asked her to make him an espresso, but right then dealing with the massive copper machine was more than I wanted to bother with. It was an original; Achille Gaggia had given it to me in Italy soon after he designed it. In 1945. I remember because we were celebrating Mussolini's capture. Achille was so excited that I didn't have the heart to tell him I don't drink coffee.

Peter was standing in front of the bookshelves when I came in. He'd turned on a single amber-shaded floor lamp and the room was bathed in soft gold light and shadows. He had a Gary Disher novel in his hand, the Inspector Challis series. He put it back on the shelf and turned to stare at me. I could see a vein throbbing across his left temple. I heard his blood pulsing through it. He didn't speak, he just stared.

"Would you like some wine or something to drink?" I asked. Tremors of nervousness tightened across my chest. I rarely feel fear, but this was something else. Anxiety. I didn't want him angry with me.

"No. I'd like to know what's going on." He was deadly serious, with not a hint of warmth in his voice. "What's going on with you and what's going on with us. I don't know if you're controlling my mind or what, but I can't stop thinking about you. And I really don't know *what* to think. I don't know how any of this works. It's pissing me off."

"Sit down. Over there." I nodded towards the leather club chair, and I stretched out on the sofa opposite. I wanted to keep the coffee table between us. The closer I was to him, the harder it would be to keep my hands off him. In this light, he looked like a Greek god. If I touched him again, I might not be able to stop.

"Okay, look," I continued, "you know what you saw in Palm Springs. You know I am not of your kind, your race. I *am* vampyre. I am *not* evil incarnate, although I can be a class A bitch when I want to. And I don't go around killing people so I can survive. Give or take a few film critics when I first started acting. But that was when I was Anna Moore, not Ovsanna."

"Anna Moore, your mother? You were your mother?" Peter was struggling to take it all in. I knew I probably shouldn't throw too much at him at one time. But I might not have another chance. Better to get as much out on the table as possible.

"I'm old, Peter. More than four hundred years old. I came to this country at the turn of the century as my 'grandmother,' an actress in silent films, and then when talkies came in I was her daughter, Anna Moore, and when Anna had outlived her career, I let people think she was dying and I showed up as her daughter, Ovsanna, supposedly raised in Europe and here to nurse her mother through her final days."

"You were your mother? Jesus. All this time my mother's been selling Anna Moore memorabilia on eBay. If she only knew." Still not a smile, but his hazel eyes had softened a bit. "She could raise her reserve." With his black hair and high cheekbones, he looked like he should be modeling for Hugo Boss, not fighting crime in Beverly Hills. "What about all the others, those old-time movie stars you introduced me to? And the three that were killed—Jason Eddings and Mai Goulart and Tommy Gordon? What's their story?"

"All members of my clan, all Vampyres of Hollywood. You see, it wasn't until the birth of the cinema that my kind found their true calling. Have you seen us on-screen? Well, you have, you just didn't know we were vampyres. The camera loves us. It's something about our vampyre physiology; we're luminescent on-screen. You can't take your eyes off us. Charlie Chaplin, Theda Bara, Peter Lorre, Mary Pickford, Douglas Fairbanks—so many of my clan became stars as soon as they found the camera. Any vampyre with a shred of talent became a star back in the twenties. And then some, like Pola Negri and Olive Thomas, couldn't make the cut when talkies came in. But that's how I started, or rather, my 'grandmother' started, back in 1915. When the talkies came in, I retired for a while and came back as Anna Moore, and then in the late sixties, right before Anna 'died,' her daughter, who bore a striking resemblance to her—even down to her first name, 'Ovsanna'—arrived from Europe to follow in her footsteps. Some of the others who started with me and became too recognizable to relocate or fade into obscurity simply staged their deaths and went into hiding. I always thought Orson was so clever, waiting until the day Yul Brynner died to dilute the press coverage of his own 'death.'

"And we controlled the industry, so we controlled our mythology," I continued. "All that stuff humans believe about garlic and mirrors and living only in the dark—we made that up. And put it on the screen. As for controlling your mind, I'm not. I can't. My clan doesn't do that. I am Dakhanavar, from the Mt. Ararat region of Armenia. My ancestors weren't the brightest of the clans—remind me to tell you the toe story sometime—but we are guardians by nature and I will fight to protect you, but I will not bend you to my will. If anything, right now, I want you to know the truths about me so that you can make your own decision." I held my breath, just a little bit. He looked so formidable in the dim light.

"What *are* the truths, aside from your ability to change into whatever William Blake–looking creature that was that you became in Palm Springs? What's the story with you and Maral?"

Just like a man, I thought. I'm telling him I'm the überbeast he's only seen in horror films and all he wants to know about is who I'm screwing. "Maral is my family . . . my helpmate . . . and my source of life. I think she's beautiful. She's the only human I've let get close to me in many, many years, and I care for her deeply. She lives with me in this house. Not in my house in Malibu, though. She has her own bedroom and office here. We're lovers when the desire arises, but it's not an exclusive relationship. She knows she can have romances with other people." I didn't tell him she hadn't slept with anyone else in more than a year and the longer we were together, the more emotion she wanted from me. Emotion I wasn't capable of providing. Maral can be a problem sometimes.

"And you?"

"I don't take human lovers very often, Peter. Especially not since I met Maral. Not because of my feelings for her, but because her presence eases my loneliness. It's hard having a long-term relationship with a human. I fall in love with someone and then have to watch him grow old and frail while nothing changes with me. Hard on the loved one as well. Maral is still so young we haven't had to deal with that, but if she continues to stay in my life, we will."

"Can't you turn her into something like you? That's what they do in the movies. Jesus, I let you drink my blood—isn't that supposed to make me a vampyre, too?" He looked down at his left wrist where just two weeks before I'd placed my lips to replenish my strength. There was nothing there, no scar, no wound, no sign of my fangs having been deeply embedded in his flesh.

I laughed. I couldn't help it. The consternation on his face made him look like a teenager. "It doesn't work that way, Peter. That's a myth perpetrated by literature and horror films. In the first place, I would never turn her without her permission. And second, the very act of creation can change the nature of the person. You saw what Rudolph Valentino became—so vicious you had to kill him to save us. He wasn't like that before I turned him. Too often the vampyre I create is not the human I fell in love with. And Maral has her own set of neuroses. Her daddy did a real good job messing her up, and she's got some problems where men are concerned. She's invaluable when it comes to running the studio, but she can go off-kilter emotionally from time to time. Even if she wanted me to turn her, I'm not so sure I would."

"All right. I get that. But what was that thing that happened when you were getting out of the car? That electricity. I thought vampyres were supposed to be cold-blooded. Heat was coming off of you like fire. If I hadn't pulled my hand away, my skin would have fried. That's the reason you didn't shake hands with my family, isn't it?"

"You noticed that, did you?"

"Not at first, because you had packages in your hands. But then when you managed to say hello to everyone and you hadn't put them down, I started watching for it. You did the same thing when it came time to say good-bye."

"Well, I had a different reason then. When I touch someone, if I let them in, I get images from that person's life. Faint and jumbled usually; sometimes I can't make sense of them at all, so they don't do me any good. But other times, they're strong and clear and I find them intrusive. The first time I shook your hand, I saw my special effects artist crucified against the wall, the same way you'd discovered her when you came to talk to me about the Cinema Slayer. I can block the images out, but it's easier most times to avoid physical contact. My touching you, and burning you, was something else."

"So you only burn the people you . . . aw, fuck. This is ridiculous. I'm talking about something I didn't even believe existed up until two weeks ago, and now I'm talking about it like I know what I'm talking about! You know what, I've got to get out of here."

"Peter—"

He was up and out of the chair. "No. Save the explanations for another time. If there is one. I loved the story about the movie stars, believe me. And I'd probably enjoy the toe story about the Armenian vampyre, too, but I can't hear any more right now. It's too much to take in. I had a great time today. I'm glad you came to the house, I'm glad we spent time together, but I don't know how much of this I can handle. Just stay there. I know where the door is."

And he walked out.

So I was right. Imagine his reaction if I'd told him about the were.

CHAPTER TEN

It was two in the morning and I was fighting the Thirst. Peter had left me aroused and frustrated. I wanted to tear into someone. Suck someone dry until I was released. I wished Maral were home.

I could have stopped Peter from leaving. I could have been next to him in less than a heartbeat, and if I had touched him . . . But I didn't. That wouldn't be playing fair, and besides, I didn't want him on those terms. It had to come from him. I knew what I wanted to happen between us, but he hadn't made up his mind. Not yet, anyway. And whatever happened, it had to be his decision.

I went into my office and sat down at my desk. It's a beautiful amber-inlaid piece I smuggled out of the Russian court, right after the October Revolution. Well, it was early July, really, and I did my damnedest to get Nicholas to at least let me help the Empress and their children escape, along with his cook and valet and doctor. But he was a stubborn man for one so young. Never to grow older. I've never thought their martyrdom was worth it.

My computer screen was still open to the views from the security cameras. I studied each split screen for any sign my beastly intruder had returned. The geese were quiet; there was no movement on the screens. Just to be certain, I went out onto the balcony and smelled the air. It was scented with roses and alyssum. And goose shit. But nothing unexpected.

The phone rang in my bedroom. Only four people have my private line—Doug Fairbanks, Orson Welles, my attorney, and Maral. My business partner had it, but he was dead. I knew who was calling. I pulled back the duvet and lay down on the bed before I answered.

"Hello, sweetheart," I said, "how's the bayou?"

"I been callin' you all night, *chère*. Why didn't you pick up?" Subtle accusations colored Maral's voice. I ignored them.

"You've only been in the swamps a day, Maral, and already you sound like you never left. I was out. Having Christmas Eve dinner with Peter King's family, remember?"

"Until after midnight? I just didn't think it'd be this late, is all."

I ignored that, too. Maral can be a bitch sometimes, where the men in my life are concerned. She doesn't trust men in general, and she really hates it if they're paying attention to me. It's one of the few things we've argued about over the years. I changed the subject. "Well, it's even later there. Why are you up at four in the morning?"

"Maw-Maw got me worried about you, is all. She did a reading for me for my Christmas present. She said she figured I been livin' with *les Américains* so long, I need to know what's going on."

Maral's grandmother is in her eighties. She still lives by herself somewhere near Maral's mother in Bayou Go Down. Never learned English. I met her once when we screened *Mojo Working* in New Orleans and Maral brought her family down to see it. We got by just fine with my French and her Cajun. She's a pistol, that's for sure. Raised eleven kids and buried two husbands and still going strong.

"So tell me what she saw." Maw-Maw's been throwing the tarot since she was a little girl. Maral believes she's got the gift of second sight. I'm sure she does. Maral tells story after story of her grandmother knowing things long before they happened. Like the time some neighbor of theirs got struck by lightning. Maw-Maw was home alone, in bed with fever. With no phone or TV, she had no way of hearing the news, but when her twin sisters stopped by to check up on her, she told them that the neighbor had been sizzled.

Or the time last month when she'd told Maral's brother there was a beast in the swamps, and two days later they found one of the Villarubbia boys spit out all over the levee. They still haven't seen the gator, but she knew he was out there.

"What did Maw-Maw see that got you worried about me?" I asked. Maybe she'd seen the were attack. She wouldn't know what to make of it, but she might know I was in danger.

"She saw Peter King. You shouldn't be spending time with him, Ovsanna. There's nothing good gonna come of it. He's a cop and he already knows too much about you."

"Oh, I see. You're not worried about me, Maral. Peter's no danger to me. And he's no danger to you. If that's what you're worried about, you don't need to be." I wasn't going to get into this on the phone. "Now how come your momma wanted you home so badly? What's going on there?"

"She's having trouble with Jamie. She thinks he's doing drugs. I know he's doing steroids, for sure. And smoking pot. I followed him down to the levee and watched him."

"Wait a minute. On Christmas Eve? What was your brother doing down at the levee? Doesn't he know that boy got attacked? Besides, wasn't your whole family there?" Maral's twin aunts, Tante Ruby and Tante Anne, live together on a houseboat in the bayou. They've never married. They wear matching cotton housedresses, sewn at home from the Butterick patterns they've had since the thirties. When they came to the screening in New Orleans, they wore hats to match. "I thought you were all going to midnight mass." I would have loved to see their Christmas attire.

"For sure, everyone was there. All the cousins. And Uncle Erace brought his accordion and Tante Ida played the fiddle. And Jamie was there. But you know how he is in his brain, he's slow. He's like a little kid. And you should see Momma, she's wasting away. I got scared just giving her a hug. And Jamie's gotten so big, Momma

can't control him. He's too big to whup. Well, after dinner, he lied
to her and told her he was going out frogging. She asked him what
kinda fou' does he think she is—she knows damn well it ain't frogging season—and she threatened to pass him a slap, but she couldn't
get him to stay. So I followed him down to the water and saw him
giving money to some guy."

"Did you know him?"

"No. He looked a lot older than Jamie and he wasn't Cajun,
that's for sure. Sounded like backwoods Florida. He was wearing a
wife-beater tee and camo pants—on Christmas Eve. And grungy
jockey shorts. I know because his pants were hanging lower than his
behind."

She pronounced "behind" with the accent on the *be*.

"And was he selling Jamie drugs?"

"For true. He and Jamie were smoking dope, and the guy was
getting ready to pump a needle into Jamie's butt. He had coke nails—
you know, an inch long on his pinkies, for snorting. When they heard
me calling Jamie's name, that *saleau* threw everything in a backpack
and took off. He had to hold his pants up so he could run. Jamie said
that was his podnuh, DeWayne, and he was like a doctor; he was giving Jamie shots to help him get bigger and grow his muscles. Jamie's
been using the money I send to buy the weed and the 'roids. Oh, I
wanted to shake him. When I told him the shots ain't good for him,
they make him crazy and shrink his privates, and make him act mean
to Momma, he started yelling at me to go play and that DeWayne
was his podnuh and he wasn't listening to me. He slammed the screen
door in my face."

"Oh, shit." This wasn't the first time Maral's mom had needed
help with her younger brother. He'd had problems from birth. Maral's
daddy had been knocking her momma around pretty good while
she was pregnant, and right at the end he belted her and she fell and
her water broke. The damn bastard was so shit-faced that he didn't
even help her get up. She crawled to the bedroom and gave birth on
the wooden floor, splinters and all. Jamie came out with the cord
around his neck, blue. The doctors said later if he'd been born in the

clinic, he'd have been fine. Instead he's a little slow. "Is there any-thing I can do to help? Would he listen to me if I talked to him?" Jamie loves my movies, and he's always excited when we talk on the phone, but I didn't think that would hold much water against some redneck juicer from the bayou.

Maral agreed. "No, *chère,* that won't help. And I can't call the police. By the time they got out here that *fils de putain* would be long gone, and they'd just give Jamie grief. No, I'm gonna go out on Monday and track the guy down. See if I can get him to leave Jamie alone. Maybe I can buy him off."

"I don't know about that, sweetheart. What's to stop him from hooking Jamie up again as soon as you leave? Do you want to bring Jamie here?"

"He can't leave my momma, Ovsanna, and she can't be without him. I can take care of it."

"Well, you just be careful. I don't like the thought of you con-fronting some doper. Take one of your uncles with you, or a cousin or someone. God knows you got enough of them down there. And don't take any chances. Even if he took off when he heard you com-ing, that doesn't mean he's not dangerous. If there's anything I can do to help, you let me know."

"You could talk to me . . . make me feel good. What are you wearing? Are you in bed?" I could tell from the change in her voice what she wanted from me.

"Yes, I'm in bed. And you know what I'm wearing—nothing. Just like I always wear when I go to bed. Remember?" I shut off the light and lay back on the pillows with the phone to my ear. I knew what Maral was doing with her hands.

I might as well talk to her. It wouldn't satisfy my Thirst, but it would take my mind off Peter, that's for sure.

CHAPTER ELEVEN

I spent part of Christmas Day in the office and the other part at home, alone. Reveling in having the place all to myself. No staff, no Maral, no werewolves.

But no Peter, either. Not that I expected him to show up, but I found myself looking at the clock occasionally, realizing the phone hadn't rung.

Maral called again in the late afternoon to wish me Merry Christmas. She said Jamie loved the movies I'd sent him. He'd calmed down, and no one mentioned his podnuh. She'd tried to get him to do a reading with Maw-Maw, hoping the dealer would show up in the cards and Maw-Maw could frighten Jamie away from him, but Jamie wouldn't sit for it. He just wanted to play the PSP Maral had given him.

Momma had told her a little more about the guy. He lived in a broken-down RV, fished with stolen hoop nets, and ran some craw-fish traps, but mostly he hung around the swamps, messing with the schoolkids. He'd been hanging around Jamie since last summer. Maral was going looking for him the next day.

I warned her again to be careful and told her how much I loved the gifts she'd given me, especially the diamond-and-black-pearl cocktail ring. I'd wear it on New Year's Eve. My gift to her was a trip to Costa Rica, as soon as I wrapped up the merger I was working on for Anticipation. I was days away from finalizing a partnership with a consortium of Japanese investors, and when the deal was completed, Maral and I were both going to need a vacation.

Monday morning I called my attorney, Ernst Solgar, a bloodsucker in every sense of the word. He's vampyre, Clan Obour, with his tiny feet and hidden *kirpan*. Although he's almost five hundred years older than I am, he acknowledges my position as the chatelaine of this city. In the *Liber Mortis,* the vampyre bible, ownership of a city is clearly defined as the first to "inhabit, occupy or possess a township of greater than nine hundred and ninety-nine souls." That I did, and every vampyre in town pays fealty to me.

Solgar never charges me for his services.

His secretary put me through as soon as she heard my voice. She's a fan. Maral always makes sure she's on the list for screening invites.

"*Eench bes ek,* Chatelaine?" Ernst asked in formal Armenian. It took me a moment to understand him; his accent is atrocious. The Obour are carrion eaters, they don't have fangs. Hence the need to carry a *kirpan*—in his case, a jewel-encrusted dagger. He's got to be able to cut his meat where he finds it. Solgar has a suckerlike opening on the tip of his tongue, and before his rhinoplasty he had only one nostril. Makes it hard to speak the language of our youth.

"I'm not so fine, Obour," I responded, also in Armenian. It's an easy way to ensure our privacy, unless I'm calling from Macy's in Fashion Square, which is the mecca for Armenian salesclerks. Then I use German. "I had a visitor Saturday night—a were—and I doubt it was a social call."

"And the body? You need me to dispose of it?" Ernst never questions my capabilities. There was no doubt in his mind I'd be the victor in any dispute.

"I didn't kill it. He was powerful, Ernst. Incredibly powerful.

A wolf, and an ancient one at that. Without a pack. He attacked me alone, in my backyard, and I want to know why. Is this business?"

"I've heard of nothing, Chatelaine. Nothing." He cleared his throat. I hate it when he clears his throat; it sounds like the vacuum tube they use in a dentist's office. No, I don't have dental work done, but I've heard the sound. There's an oral surgeon in the building next door to my office, and I can hear him through the walls. I swear last week he gave someone nitrous oxide and went down on her in the chair. It sounded like Tiny Tim coming.

"Ovsanna, everyone is shut down for the holidays; there is no one on the phones. You're probably the only executive who is even in her office. And what would it be about? The Japanese deal? There are only four people in town who know what we've structured, and one of them is dead. You and I and Maral certainly aren't talking. I doubt the Japanese are. I can think of no one who benefits from harming you, Chatelaine."

"Will you make some inquiries, please, Ernst. Discreetly. The were's intent wasn't to harm me. He wanted my life."

I spent the rest of Monday in the office, playing host to the three Japanese businessmen who had the power (that is, money) to catapult my burgeoning film studio into the big leagues. I own the lot, which means income from renting to other production companies, and I've been operating in the black for years, quite successful with my own low-budget horror films and made-for-TV movies, but these fellows had approached me eighteen months ago with a truly seductive offer. They wanted 25 percent of my 80 percent of Anticipation so they could develop straight-to-computer, direct-to-cell-phone-and-PDA, low-bandwidth, high-def movies. I wanted the hundred million they had to offer in cash and technological investments so I could continue to maintain creative control and avoid getting swallowed by one of the majors.

By the end of Monday, we all had what we wanted. My business affairs people went back to their office to put the finishing touches on the paperwork, and our PR department issued a press release about the merger. I went home to enjoy the solitude with Maral out of town. I checked the security cameras and made sure the alarm was on. The geese were quiet. Then I took a hot bath, lit a fire in the fireplace in my bedroom, and cuddled up in my huge, overstuffed chair to read the latest Doc Ford novel. I love Randy Wayne White's character as much as I love Lee Child's Jack Reacher. It dawned on me that that's probably why I was attracted to Peter. He's got some of their same qualities. Maybe not as iconoclastic, but definitely as macho.

I thought about Peter, a lot. I hadn't heard from him. Maybe it was too soon. Or maybe that meant he'd made his decision. Maybe not hearing from him was the message he wanted to send.

I would hate that, but I'd understand.

Tuesday afternoon, he called. Just listening to his voice brought on the Thirst, which pissed me off. I'm too old to be acting like a teenager. About four hundred years too old.

"How are you?" I asked. That seemed safe enough after the way we'd said good night. I was seated at my desk, staring out the window at a hooker soliciting a guy in a Bentley.

"Well, I don't have any burn marks, if that's what you mean."

"I'm sorry, Peter. What happened when I touched you was an accident. I never meant to hurt you. I just wasn't concentrating." The Bentley owner must have liked what he heard; he opened the car door and the girl got in.

"On what? What do you have to concentrate on to keep from sending sparks out your body?" He sounded as if he were interrogating a suspect that he didn't believe.

"On not letting my attraction to you get out of hand." I took a deep breath. Might as well get it all out in the open. "That's what happens when I get aroused. I have to concentrate to control myself—to keep my vampyre self in check."

There was silence for a moment. I heard Peter take a breath and hold it before he spoke. "So I guess it's safe to say there's something going on here . . . right? Even with Maral in the picture? And it's not just coming from me?"

"No, it's not." I heard him exhale. I continued, "But what has to come from you is a decision about what happens next. I want you. You're the first man I've wanted in years. But I don't know what there is in this for you. I'm a vampyre, Peter. I'm not very good relationship material. My needs aren't like yours. And I'm not above taking advantage of you to have them met." The Bentley drove away, the girl's head already below the dash. Talk about taking advantage.

He was silent for so long, I thought the call had dropped.

"Peter?" I asked.

He was still on the line. "I'll tell you what," he said, and his voice had lightened considerably, "let me pick you up around seven or so. I saw the announcement about the merger in today's *Variety,* and I think we should go out and celebrate."

It was my turn to be silent. Except for the blood pounding through my heart, which sounded to me like a kettledrum in an echo chamber.

"Are you sure?" I finally asked.

"Yes. I haven't been taken advantage of in a long time. I'd like to see what it feels like."

CHAPTER TWELVE

I hate driving in L.A. Most of my clan does. It's impossible to filter all the input. If I don't keep my senses tempered, I end up listening to the gangbangers in the Escalade ahead of me, talking about their latest drive-by shooting. At least, I think that's what they're saying. The way they butcher the English language just pisses me off more. Then I want to follow them and do a little killing of my own, which will just make me late for whatever appointment I've got. The whole thing is one annoying distraction. I make Maral drive.

But she'd just gotten home from LAX, and it was already six o'clock. I asked Sveta, one of our office receptionists, to drive me home. I sat in the backseat and thought about Peter and smiled. A real date with Detective Peter King, no family members involved. I wondered if he was putting his job in jeopardy. Was he allowed to date some-one he'd met on a case? And what did he have in mind for the evening? He hadn't said what he wanted to do. Not go to dinner, I hope. What the hell was I going to wear?

"It looks like there's something going on at your house, Ovsanna,"

Sveta said from the front seat. "I can't tell what it is from here." She slowed the car.

There are times when my heightened senses of smell and hearing intrude on my existence and I have to damp them down deliberately to concentrate on other things. Not so my vision. Being able to see the minutest details from hundreds of feet away, even in the dark, always comes in handy. I stared up the road at the shapes Sveta couldn't decipher.

It was the paparazzi again. The same seven who had been there Christmas Eve night, plus two more. They were milling around the middle of the road, cameras dangling from their necks. Waiting for me. What the hell was going on? Well, I wasn't going to give them any more photo ops, whatever they wanted them for. The Mercedes had tinted windows. They wouldn't even know I was in the car. I stretched out in the backseat and let Sveta drive through, parting them like Moses at the Red Sea. As the gate closed behind us, I turned to watch them. They were eerily silent, staring at the car.

Maral was waiting outside the front door, anxiety on her face. She'd gone back to her natural hair color the day before she'd left for Louisiana. The red looked gorgeous on her, but it was stringy and unwashed, and there was a peculiar smell coming off her, as if she'd brushed up against something briny. I wondered if the paps had gotten any shots of her. She wouldn't like it if she showed up on *TMZ* under "Celebrity Hair." Not looking like that, at least.

"What's wrong with you? You look like shit," I said. Two days at home with her family in the bayou and she was a mess.

"I have to talk to you. Before you go in the house. I've got someone in there, and I've got to explain." Her voice was brittle with tension. She stepped in front of me to block me from entering. Normally I would have taken her in my arms to calm her down, but the smell wafting off her made me keep my distance. It was someone's body odor, not hers, and it had settled on her like skunk spray. It was foul.

"What the hell is going on, Maral?" I said. "What's that odor? Who's in the house?"

"It's my brother's friend. But he's not in the house, he's in the guesthouse. That's what I have to talk to you about. I had to get him away from Jamie. I had to bring him back with me from my momma's. I know I smell, I sat next to him on the plane. We just got here and I haven't had time to take a shower. But I don't trust him enough to leave him alone anyway, so I was waiting for you to come home."

"All right. All right. Settle down. You'd better tell me what you've got to tell me fast because I have a date and I've got to get ready. I'm leaving here at 7:30."

"A date? With who?"

Like quicksilver, accusation replaced the nervousness in her voice. I didn't have time to deal with it. "Never mind," I said slowly. "Just tell me who the fuck this guy is, and why have you got him in my house?" I drew out every word deliberately.

"He's that dealer, Ovsanna. He was selling drugs to Jamie, and I couldn't get Jamie away from him. Jamie thinks they're best friends. I didn't know what to do. I just want to get rid of him. Jamie told him I work for 'that scary lady in the movies,' and he thinks you're Mary Tyler Moore. He thinks you can introduce him to Ashley Judd. He wants to do a commercial for zit medicine so he can make a lot of money and get his face cleared up. It's absolutely gross, covered in pussy pimples. I told him you'd put him in the movies if he came with me, and he believed me."

"You told him what?"

"He thinks he's going to meet Jack Bauer. Like *24* is real."

"Maral, are you nuts?"

"Well, I tried to pay him to leave Jamie alone, and he said, sure, he'd take my money, and as soon as I left, he'd get the retard to pay him again. That's what he called Jamie—a retard—and I wanted to kill him. I couldn't think of anything else to do. I just wanted to get him here; I thought if I could get him here, maybe you could—"

"What? I could what?" I was getting pissed. "What were you thinking, bringing a drug dealer into my house?! Get him out of here!"

"Don't yell at me, Ovsanna, please." She clenched her hands in front of her as though she were praying. "You offered to help. You said if there was anything you could do . . . well . . . I thought you could—do what you do. Get rid of him somehow. Like you got rid of those beings in Palm Springs."

"Oh, damn it, Maral. You've been around me ten years and you still don't understand how any of this works. I am an actress and the head of a film studio. I am not a hit man. I don't go around baring my fangs whenever someone becomes an inconvenience. And I am not going to kill someone just because you ask me to!"

"But Ovsanna—"

"Now, look, I don't have time for this right now. And I definitely do not want to see this person in my house. It's bad enough I can smell him. Get him out of the guesthouse. Put him in a hotel. Take him to the studio tomorrow morning and find him something to do to keep him busy until we can deal with him. And for God's sake, tell him to take a bath!"

I moved around her and opened the door, but she grabbed my arm before I could enter. "What?" I demanded, shaking loose of her grip.

"You're going out with Peter King, aren't you? You're going out on a date." There was panic in her voice.

I hated seeing her upset. She's like a little girl whose mother leaves her on the first day of school. I put my hands on her shoulders and forced her to look in my eyes. Again, I spoke slowly. "Maral, what I do when we're not together is no business of yours, unless I choose to make it so. Yes, I'm spending the evening with Peter, and when he arrives—after you've had a shower—you're going to greet him like my personal assistant and stop acting like a child. What's gotten into you?"

"It's him, Ovsanna. You shouldn't be seeing him. He's a cop and he knows what you are. You can't trust him."

"That's ridiculous. He helped save our lives two weeks ago. He saw my clan, the Vampyres of Hollywood, and he saw Lilith and Ghul and every one of those Ancients and weres we were battling. He killed some of them, for God's sake. And he hasn't said a word to anyone. Nor will he. I trust him already."

"No, Ovsanna! You give him enough time to think about what he knows and he's going to have to tell someone. He's a cop, and that's got to come first. And he's a man. He'll turn on you if he has to. They all do!" She was pleading with me, yelling in my face. "He can't be trusted!"

I grabbed her face with my hand and dug my fingers into her jaw. She couldn't move her mouth. Her eyes filled with tears. I held her like that.

"Breathe, Maral. Calm down and breathe." She did what I said. Her eyes softened and her face went slack. I released her jaw. Her cheeks were red with my fingerprint. I pushed her hair off her forehead and said as gently as I could, "He's become my friend, Maral. I want you to accept that. If he does something to betray my trust, I'll turn my back on him—instantly. But until then, I want him around. Do you understand?" When she got out of control like this, I had to talk to her like a child.

She didn't answer. Like a child.

It was a scene we'd played out many times before, in one form or another. Maral doesn't have a lot of self-worth. She doesn't know she's valuable simply because she's a good person. She has to rely on her position as my assistant to make her feel important. She needs the adulation and ass kissing that comes with being with me—the reflected glory—to help her believe she's worthwhile. I suppose it's the same mind-set that keeps the wives of all those philandering Republicans standing in the back on the dais while their husbands utter their mea culpas for CNN.

So Maral can share me with my career, but if anything else, anyone else, takes my attention, she sees it as a threat to her place in my life. And without me, she doesn't think she exists. I've spent years trying to reassure her. It's exhausting. More and more these days I just lay down the law.

"And I'd prefer it if you spent the night at the Malibu house. I'd like to have some privacy when Peter and I come back."

CHAPTER THIRTEEN

What the hell was I going to do with Ovsanna on a date? The woman's a movie star—more than that, she's a *vampyre* who's a movie star; it's not like I could just take her anywhere. We couldn't go bowling. She's too strong. She'd probably take out the back of the building with a spare. She's got a screening room in her house; she doesn't need to go to the movies. She'd be mobbed at the Grove or the Promenade. And she doesn't eat. Normally I would have reserved one of the private booths for dinner at La Bohème, but what was she going to do, sit there and watch me devour a steak? That seems rude. Not to mention maybe dangerous.

From my kitchen window, I looked across my yard and saw SuzieQ on the computer in her breakfast nook. She was online, so I IM'ed her a single word: "Help." She was out her door and in my kitchen in a flash. For five years she's been a great friend and neighbor and the perfect tenant. Well, except for the times her snakes get loose. Jesus, there's nothing I hate worse than waking up to a errant python in my bed.

She never bothers to knock. "Hey, sugar, what's up? I got your sweater on. I just love it." She was wearing the turquoise sweater I'd given her for Christmas. "My babies do, too. I swear Ollie North gets off just rubbin' against it." Ollie North is one of SuzieQ's snakes. She's named them all after crooked political figures. I was hoping she'd buy another one and call it Blagojevich.

"Do snakes really get off, SuzieQ?" I stared at the sweater for a second, hoping she was exaggerating. I still hadn't recovered from the night she'd called me over to see one of them giving birth. Twenty-four baby snakes popping out on the closet floor. Gave me nightmares for a week.

She opened my fridge and poured a glass of eggnog while I picked her brain about where to go on a date with Ovsanna. I couldn't tell her about the eating thing, so I just said I wanted to do something other than go to a restaurant.

"Why don't y'all drive to the beach? I love doing that. 'Course, I haven't had a date in so long, I don't even know if the water's still there. I swear, I don't know what's wrong with the men in this town. Look at me! I'm a good-lookin' woman."

"You're an intimidating woman, SuzieQ, and the snakes don't help. You're hot as hell, but you're scary 'cause you're larger than life. A lot of men can't handle that. It's like me asking Ovsanna out. She's a movie star, for Christ's sake. She's got more money than God and almost as much power—in her business, at least. She hangs out with other movie stars." Okay, okay, so some of them have been "dead" for thirty years, but I couldn't tell SuzieQ that. "What's she going to see in me, was my first thought."

"Yeah? And what was your second?"

"You can guess. But right now I'm trying to think of a place to take her. So drink your eggnog and give me some help here. Look through this copy of *City Beat*."

By the time Suzie and I came up with a plan and I had showered and shaved, it was almost seven thirty. I put the top down on the Jag and hoped Ovsanna wouldn't mind a little wind in her hair. "The Jag" sounds more impressive than it is, believe me. It's forty years old and needs a new clutch kit. It was my father's, back in the days when a gallon of gas cost thirty-one cents. He sold it to me just before 9/11. Any day now, my ego is going to lose out to my budget and I'll start using a patrol car for my dates.

This time, there were no photographers at the gate. I was glad about that. The less anyone knew I was seeing Ovsanna socially, the better. My Captain would shit. Ovsanna had been connected to the Cinema Slayer case. As long as he thought the case was still open, he'd be less than happy about my seeing her. That reminded me, I was going to have to come up with some way to provide a perp for the five dead victims. I knew the killer was Lilith, and I knew she was dead, but there was no way I could deliver her to the Captain. I couldn't even tell him about her. I pressed the button on the intercom and checked my teeth in the mirror while I waited for the gates to open.

Once again Ovsanna was waiting for me outside the front door, once again looking fantastic. Come to think of it, the only time I'd ever seen her not looking great was when she turned into that prehistoric monster, with wings coming out of her back. Even then she'd been pretty striking. This time she had on black leather pants and a hunter green sweater. My eyes went to her necklace. Carved gold lying flat against her chest, with a tiger's-eye scarab resting on the spot I'd like to be.

"That's a great necklace," I said, nervous all over again, as though we hadn't already spent an entire evening together. Well, hell, it was impossible to predict what an evening with her might bring.

"Thanks," she said, looking down at the carved beetle. "I've had it for years."

"I'll bet. A gift from the Etruscan who made it?"

"Wow!" she teased. "A police detective who knows what an Estruscan is? I'm impressed."

"Hey, I like studying historical objects. Why do you think I asked you out?"

"Oh boy," she said, laughing, "you're going to pay for that."

I wanted to take her someplace she hadn't seen before. I didn't get the feeling vampyres made a big deal out of Christmas, and it didn't seem very movie star–ish to cruise the streets of the Valley, so I took a chance she'd never been where I wanted to go. I drove out the 101 and exited at Winnetka. That put us in the middle of a long line of cars driving through a neighborhood of decorated houses, each one more elaborate than the next. Candy Cane Lane in Woodland Hills. With light bulb reindeer bouncing over every roof, and red and green garlands roped around the palm trees. One yard had an entire crèche made out of Legos. Another one had a full-size Frosty made of popcorn balls. There was a red-capped SpongeBob fighting for lawn space next to a ten-foot-tall inflatable Santa Claus with an electric air blower up his butt. SpongeBob's blower must have been broken because he couldn't stay upright; his nose kept bouncing on the ground. Made him look festive, though, like he was dancing—or drunk. The requisite Salvation Army solicitor—human, not inflatable; nothing up her butt that I could see—stood on a corner with her cauldron and her bell. Passengers handed her dollar bills. She wasn't doing as well as the homeless guy across the street, though. He was raking it in. The sign he was holding said: "Aging comedy writer. Will work for Disney."

Ovsanna laughed. "Maybe I should get his card," she said. "See if he's got a spec script sitting on a shelf. If there's one thing vampyres are sensitive to, it's ageism."

The traffic slowed as we drove past three wise men and a cardboard camel. Time to find out more about Ovsanna. "So . . . I started to ask you the night of the fire, but I got sidetracked . . . do you celebrate Christmas? I mean . . . not just . . . vampyres in general, but you . . . did you celebrate when you were growing up? How *did* you grow up? How does all that work with . . . your people?"

"Well, I was born a vampyre, not made. Not turned, which is

what I did with Rudolph Valentino. Rudy was in his mid-twenties when I turned him. But I was born vampyre—of a vampyre father and a *strega* mother. Do you know what a *strega* is?"

"Not the way you do," I answered. "As far as my family's concerned, it's an Italian liqueur my mother made us drink if we had a stomachache. You weren't born in a bottle, were you?"

She laughed again. "No," she said, still smiling. "Although *strega* means 'witches' love potion.' Somebody had a good idea for a marketing ploy. No, my mother was a witch—a real witch who could put spells on people and hex them and wreak havoc with their lives if she chose to, which she didn't, very often, at least. Except for my father. That's how she kept him in line. And you've got to know she was really powerful, because he was a vampyre of the Dakhanavar clan, in Armenia. Not easy to control, except by my mother. She'd mix up some powders and potions and set them burning, and when my father inhaled the fragrance, she'd put a spell on him. Then he'd follow her around like a puppy. He roamed the countryside a lot, defending the villages from interlopers, and my mother raised me, most of the time alone, in a village near Mt. Ararat. And of course, by the time I was born, the Armenians were all Christian. In fact, Armenia was the first nation to adopt Christianity as its state religion, back in the fourth century. So the villagers celebrated Christmas—on January sixth, that's the Armenian Christmas—and I used to listen to the music and go to the feasts. I never ate the food, but I had a good time."

"But you don't believe in God, do you? Heaven and hell?" I wanted to stare at her. Her face was so animated when she talked that I couldn't stop watching. I dragged my eyes back to the car in front of us, barely missing the guy's bumper before I braked.

"You know, it's not a concept I spend much time considering, Peter. When you're fairly immortal, you don't worry about an afterlife. You don't need to create an idea of what it might be like after you're dead. And you certainly don't need anyone to pray to—for forgiveness or anything else." She tucked her feet under her on the seat and turned to face me. "Plus, I think most of us are so bored after living eight or nine hundred years that the thought of dying doesn't carry with it any fear. Maybe just relief. When you've seen firsthand what humanity does to itself . . . well, as young as I am in terms of my kind, there are days when I wouldn't mind if it were a little easier for me to get gone."

Chapter Fourteen

I shouldn't have said that to Peter. We were having a good time looking at the Christmas decorations, and I think I dampened the mood of
the evening with my diatribe about humanity. I had the were attack in
the back of my mind, and the fact that I didn't know who he was or
why he'd come after me was pissing me off. Not to mention that I
hadn't done away with him when I had the chance. So I started railing
about the Deluge and the War of the Triple Alliance, the Herero genocide, and, of course, the Armenian genocide. "You know what Hitler
said when he ordered his death-head units out?" I asked Peter. " 'Gas
the Jews; who remembers the Armenians?' " That left Peter sort of
speechless; I don't think he'd ever heard it. Actually, Hitler's exact
words were "Who, after all, speaks today of the annihilation of the
Armenians?" I memorized them at the time. Right after I drained an
SS officer. But I shouldn't have brought it up in the first place; it wasn't
very festive. And certainly not on a second date. I shouldn't have gotten
started. But, you know, it's one thing to read about the horrors man-
kind has perpetuated over the last five hundred years and quite another
to have seen a lot of them with my own (sometimes raging red) eyes.

Anyway, I finally changed the subject. Peter asked about the films we had in production, and I told him one of my favorite agent stories—about the time we offered Matthew MacFadyen a role in *Drown with Love* and heard back from his agent that he hated the script and wasn't interested, but that they had Denis Leary as a client and he'd love to do it. So we started negotiations with Denis, whom I love as well, and that weekend I ran into Matthew at a fund-raiser for blood disease. I told him I was sorry he hadn't liked the project, we thought he'd be great in the role. He didn't have any idea what I was talking about. His agents had never shown him the script or told him about the offer. They figured they could get more money for Denis, so screw their own client Matthew. Needless to say, Matthew's not with them any longer.

That was the same agent who made an appointment with me to discuss a series idea he wanted Anticipation to produce. He handled the writer and Jeff Bridges, who was interested in starring. The writer and I made a date to meet at the agent's office, but when we got there, his secretary said he was tied up on a conference call and it might be a bit of a wait. We waited. A half hour later, she tried to persuade us to reschedule the appointment because she said he was going to be on the phone a while longer. I rarely go to an agent's office to begin with, they come to me, so I was already beginning to steam. I said we were there and we weren't going anywhere, we'd wait. A half hour later, I got a call on my cell phone. It was the agent. He said he was in Aspen, Colorado, at the Comedy Festival and he'd gotten hung up and was really sorry, but he was going to have to reschedule. I told him he'd better look for another studio to "reschedule" with because I wasn't interested in wasting any more of my time. The writer went home, hopefully to change agents, and Maral drove me over to Universal, where I was meeting Ron Myer at the commissary. And guess who walked in? Aspen—my ass.

I regaled Peter with a couple more industry stories, and then the Doobie Brothers came up on his iPod and we took turns trying to hit Michael McDonald's high notes. Peter won.

We sang all the way to our next stop, which was a funky little outdoor restaurant in Glendale, with a four-piece band playing Armenian music and Peter's friend SuzieQ doing a belly dance. I loved it.

I noticed Peter was careful not to get too close to me when he opened the car door, which was good; the smell of him only weakened my control all the more. He was worried about getting burned, and I was worried about doing the burning. If I didn't concentrate, I'd be changing in the middle of the parking lot.

He smelled like fresh rain. Like green apples and comfort. Like "come lay your head on my breast and let me crush you to me"— whatever that smells like. I write horror films, I'm not so good with romantic descriptions.

He looked great, too. In black pants and a black David Bowie concert tour T-shirt with a beautiful dragon graphic and Japanese writing on it. It must have had Lycra in it, because it hugged every muscle on his chest, just the way I would have liked to.

SuzieQ was in the middle of her set, dancing to a guitar, a clarinet, a dumbek, and an oud. The host led us to a round table away from the dance floor. I suspected Peter had requested it because it was one of the more private spots on the patio. Peter ordered meza— a large plate of appetizers SuzieQ could share with us (and no one would notice if I didn't eat)—yalanchi, souboereg, tourshou, keufteh, little squares of lahmajoon, and taramasalata, hummus, and tabouli for scooping onto pita. I felt like I was back in the old country again.

"Did you remember I was from Armenia when you decided to come here?" I asked. Very few people know my real nationality. As far as the public is concerned, Ovsanna Moore is third-generation Hollywood royalty. My "grandmother" came over from Europe in the early 1900s, and until "I" arrived, my "mother" had me going to boarding schools in London and Paris. Certainly no one except Maral and my clan knew my real name—Ovsanna Hovannes Garabedian.

"I wish I could say I did. That would make me pretty thoughtful, wouldn't it?" He used three fingers to pop a stuffed grape leaf in his mouth. "But the truth is, SuzieQ suggested it. She's here every other Tuesday. And she likes having friends in the audience."

She was great fun to watch in her two-piece outfit: a push-up bra that barely covered her nipples and gave her generous breasts plenty of room to bobble; and an ankle-length, low-cut skirt made of a gauzy fabric sheer enough to see through, cut in panels so it opened when she danced. Her legs were long and muscled. I remembered the exotic dancers from my parents' village; they didn't look anything like SuzieQ. They were short, dark-skinned women with plenty of belly fat to roll around. And mustaches. Plenty of mustaches. Armenians thought they were sexy.

SuzieQ didn't have a lot of belly fat, but she could really roll what she had. The women at the tables laughed and poked their husbands in their sides. The husbands laughed and tucked one-dollar bills into the waistband of SuzieQ's skirt. The single men smirked and tucked five-dollar bills on top of the ones. By the time she finished her number, I couldn't see her navel for all the cash. She took a bow and came to sit with us.

The host turned out to be the owner of the restaurant. He arrived at the table with a bottle in his hand. SuzieQ introduced him as Kerop Shamshoian.

"*Ahman asdvatz.* You're the movie star, aren't you? In my restaurant! *Parev!* Welcome, welcome. Have some raki. It's good! We make it ourselves." He pulled three shot glasses out of his pocket and set them on the table.

Raki is Armenian moonshine. If Kerop made it himself, it was probably two-hundred-proof alcohol. I shot Peter a look that said, "Help me out here," and hoped he remembered that drinking anything but blood wasn't high on my list of favorite things to do. Kerop uncorked the bottle and filled the glasses. Peter distracted him with a question about the menu, and while he was raving about his shish kebab, I emptied my shot glass under the table. Then we all said, "*Kenats't,*" and Peter and SuzieQ downed the raki while I pretended to do the same. Even SuzieQ didn't notice my sleight of hand. It helps, being an actress.

CHAPTER FIFTEEN

The raki was having an effect on me. Or else it was Ovsanna. She actually got up and danced with Suzie in the middle of the room, doing one of those chain dances where everyone holds hands and snakes through the tables, stomping and kicking their feet. I scanned the restaurant, worried about photographers or somebody from the job recognizing one of us, but I didn't see anyone I knew. A birthday celebration was taking up one side of the room, and all the attendees were speaking Chinese. I don't think anyone there recognized Ovsanna at all. I could tell from the head nods and whispers at a couple of the other tables that some of the patrons knew who she was. Two teenage boys, twins, came over to ask for her autograph. One of them gave her his baseball cap to sign and the other his skateboard.

She was gracious with both of them. Not like some of the jerks I have to ride herd on when I'm working. It seems to me these celebrities are where they are because of their fans; it doesn't take much for them to be courteous, at least. Of course, I haven't been on the receiving end of the obnoxious asshole fans who think it's their right to demand the stars' attention, either. Maybe hanging out with Ovsanna would change my mind.

God knows I'd changed it more than once already, where she was concerned. Seeing her again, after the way she'd KFC'ed me on Sunday night, didn't seem like the smartest choice I could have made. But I couldn't stop myself. Even there in public, all I wanted to do was grab a handful of her black, curly hair, and pull her across the table and kiss her. I didn't care who was watching, I just wanted to feel her under my lips, explore her mouth with my tongue. Hope I didn't cut myself on any hidden canines.

Instead, when she reached out to pull me on the dance floor, I flinched.

She laughed and dropped SuzieQ's hand. Suzie grabbed the next person, and the line danced on past us. "Ah-ha, afraid you're going to get burned again, huh?"

"Well," I said, "can you blame me? You've never been on the receiving end of whatever that thing is that you do, have you?"

"No, I haven't. But I promise you, Peter, the next time I lay my hands on you, you won't suffer." She had a teasing smile in her eyes.

"And when might that be? This laying on of hands?"

"Oh, I don't know. What did you have in mind for the rest of the night?"

CHAPTER SIXTEEN

I had to give Peter credit: Any other man would have driven right back to my house to take me up on my offer (Casanova pounced on me within hours after we met). I wouldn't have minded, either. Every cell in my body was bouncing around in anticipation.

Instead, Peter said he'd planned one more stop, and he drove us to another street, this time in North Hollywood. It had only one house on it decorated for Christmas, but the decorations were unlike anything I'd ever seen. We parked across the street and walked over to stand on the sidewalk in front of it.

It was a one-story suburban home, painted white, I think. I couldn't tell for sure because every inch of the house was hidden behind the most incredible decorations. Movable miniature sleigh rides and ice-skaters on a rink. Santa's Workshop, where elves pounded hammers and slid down a pole to deliver toys. The Elf Diner with red paper flames flickering in the fireplace. Thousands of lights formed icicles, candy canes, Christmas bells, Santa's sleigh and reindeer on the roof. It must have taken a month to design.

"How did you know about this, Peter? It's exquisite."

"It's my nephew's teacher's home. She and her husband decorate it like this every year. It's been on the news. Pretty amazing, isn't it?"

I nodded, stepping in front of him to look more closely. He wrapped his arms around me. Tentatively at first, I think until he knew it was safe. I leaned back against his chest, my head fitting just under his chin. I could feel his heart pounding against my back, my own heart matching his in its rhythm; I could hear his blood running through his veins. And smell him—God, he smelled good. His hands were warm on top of mine. My body started to tingle, a weakness spreading up from between my legs to my breasts and down my arms. I was melting inside. I turned and looked into his eyes. I saw desire there, and acceptance. I raised up on my tiptoes to meet his mouth—

And a car pulled up next to us. Five screeching kids slammed open the doors of a minivan. They shoved their way around us, pushing us back towards the curb, their parents yelling at them to keep their hands off the decorations.

I almost released my fangs. Goddamn it to hell. I was so aroused that I was on the brink of a change. I had to close my eyes and concentrate to keep the whites from turning red. Those kids didn't know how close they'd come to getting tossed down the block.

Peter started laughing. He grabbed my hand and we ran to the car.

"It could have been worse," he said. "They could have recognized you and asked for your autograph. And then asked why your eyes were so bloodshot."

We got back to the house, and Maral's car was gone. Good. I wanted to get Peter inside and pick up where we'd left off. He'd run his fingers down my arm while we were driving, and my whole body was vibrating.

Until I saw movement at my bedroom window. Shit. Another werebeast? The same one? What the hell was going on?

I grabbed Peter's arm and whispered to him to stop the car. We were halfway up the drive.

"What is it?" he asked.

There wasn't time to tell him much. "Someone's here, Peter. In the house. Someone or some thing." He gave me a look that said, "You're kidding, right?" and then reached across me and took his Glock out of the glove compartment.

I wished I were.

My vision sharpened. There was a thick cloud cover, but I didn't need moonlight to see. I sniffed the air and scanned the grounds. Nothing was out of place. The geese were quiet. That briny odor Maral had brought home with her was still in the air, but nothing else. Whoever—or whatever—it was had been inside for a while. If it was a vampyre, getting in wouldn't have been a problem, but a were would have had to break something. All the front windows, at least, were intact.

We got out of the car quietly. Peter didn't have to tell me to leave my door open. He stepped in front of me, his gun held loosely in his hand, and led the way to the front door. I had to smile at his chivalry. Maybe it was just his cop's nature, but it tickled me to know he thought he could protect a vampyre from danger.

Silently he motioned me to unlock the door and check the alarm. It was off. Something was definitely wrong; Maral always armed the system when she left the house.

We both heard the movement at the same time. Whatever it was was in my upstairs office. Something scraped across the wood floor. Peter took the stairs two at a time, and I was beside him in an instant. My claws were out; I let my fangs unsheathe. If it was the werewolf, Peter's Glock wasn't going to do us much good. I didn't want to tell him that.

"Police!" he yelled. "Come out of the room with your hands in the air."

That wasn't going to do us much good, either, but that was another thing I didn't want to tell him.

More scraping and then the weight of something moving across the room. I put my hand on the knob to tear the door off its hinges.

Maral's voice came from the other side. "Ovsanna?"

"Oh, my God. Maral?"

Peter pulled me away. He had his gun on the door. "It's Peter King, Maral. Will you come out, please? With your hands above your head."

"Maral, are you alone? What are you doing in there?" My body was flooded with adrenaline.

The door handle turned slowly. Maral pulled it open and stepped back into the office with her hands up. She looked terrified.

"Come out, please. Are you alone?" Peter demanded.

She nodded, her eyes wide with fear. "What is it? What's going on?"

Peter pushed past her and cleared my office. He passed through the adjoining doorway into my bedroom, cleared that and my dressing room, and ran down the stairs to check the rest of the house.

I turned on Maral. She didn't know about the incident with the werewolf and I didn't want to frighten her, but boy, was I pissed. And frustrated as hell. My desire for Peter had brought on the Thirst big-time. I wanted to tear somebody apart. What the fuck was she doing still in the house?

It was all I could do to retract my fangs. "Where's your car, and why are you here?" I snapped. "You were supposed to go to the beach house."

"I gave my car to Jamie's friend to go get something to eat. Then he was gonna check into the hotel and drive himself to the studio in the morning. I didn't want him staying with me. And I just thought I should wait until you got home to make sure it was okay if I took the SUV to the beach."

That was a fucking lie. The media call me the Scream Queen because I've starred in so many horror films, but the people who know me well know there's another reason for the name. You don't want to piss me off. Maral knows that better than anyone. She also knows she doesn't have to ask me to use one of the cars. She was pissing me off.

"That's bullshit, Maral," I hissed. "I wanted you out of here and you stuck around on purpose. And now you're lying about it. If something's bothering you—"

Peter walked into the room before I could say any more. Maral was cowering against the wall.

"There's nothing here, Ovsanna. Not in the garage or guest-house. And I'm sorry, I've got to go. The Captain just called, I've got a dead body to look at. Will you be okay?"

"Not as okay as I would have been if you could stay and every-one else would leave . . . but"—I turned to stare daggers at Maral—"*we'll* be fine."

I walked him down the stairs and out to his car. He warned me to put the alarm on when I went back inside and gave me one of his busi-ness cards to give to Maral, so she'd have his number in case of a real threat. I'd made the right decision, not telling him about the were at-tack. I didn't want him worrying about me. He drove away with a wave and nothing more. The mood had definitely been broken.

But my Thirst hadn't. I was so frustrated, if I could have bitten my own arm and satisfied myself on myself, I would have done it. But that doesn't work. At least not for me. It's impossible to concen-trate on sucking while I'm being sucked, if I'm the one doing the sucking.

I stomped back up the stairs and threw Peter's card on the hall-way table. Maral was in her bedroom, sitting on the edge of the bed, staring at the doorway. I was across the room in an instant, pushing her down on the satin coverlet, grabbing both her wrists, and hold-ing them above her head. I straddled her body, kneeling with my legs on either side of her. I didn't want her wrist this time. I was too angry to be seductive. I wanted blood. Right then. I wanted to feel her flesh split open as my fangs pierced her skin and sank into the wetness of her, all the way up to my gums.

She stared at me. Tears welled in her eyes and spilled down the sides of her face. "I'm sorry," she said, and she turned her head to the right, resting her dampened cheek on the sage-colored satin. I doubt if she meant it. After all, she was getting what she wanted.

I jerked her head back and put my mouth on her throat and fed.

CHAPTER SEVENTEEN

I drove over the hill thinking about what I'd just seen and overheard. The image of Ovsanna's fangs, claws, and glowing red eyes burned into my brain. That didn't bode well for romance. Not for me, at least. I know, I know, I'd already seen her shifting into another form completely, but that wasn't when I was imagining her beneath me on a king-size bed. I don't care what all those vampyre novels say, protruding cuspids don't do it for me. Maybe that's a female thing.

Although I didn't mind when she'd used my wrist as a protein shake. I felt her sucking, all the way down to the soles of my feet, and let me tell you, it was a whole new experience. I could definitely get into that.

The Captain had me driving to the Sportsmen's Lodge in Studio City. There was a woman's mutilated body floating in the duck pond. One of the hotel bartenders had called it in.

The mutilation sounded like the Cinema Slayer's MO. He'd left a charnel house behind when he'd eviscerated nine people in an S&M club in Boys Town. I mean, body parts chopped up and strewn everywhere. Studio City isn't Beverly Hills precinct, it's North

Hollywood, but I was lead detective on the Slayer case, and as far as everyone else knew, that case was still open. So my Captain wanted me in on this.

I knew it wasn't the Cinema Slayer. I knew the Cinema Slayer was dead. But I hadn't come up with a plausible explanation I could spoon-feed to the department and the media. Lilith was the Cinema Slayer. Well, Lilith and her boy toy, Ghul. Somehow I couldn't see releasing the news that three movie stars, a studio exec, and a makeup artist had been killed by some sort of vampyre beast, and that beast in turn had been killed by yours truly and another vampyre, who just happened to be a major Hollywood player. That's a stretch, even for the *Enquirer*. So my Captain thinks whatever went down in Palm Springs had to do with some cult getting fried, and his Cinema Slayer is still on the loose.

The parking lot was swarming with photographers, most of whom I knew. I bypassed the valet and left the Jag at the front of the hotel. It was the same scene that had played out nearly three weeks before, with paparazzi and reporters screaming out my name, asking if the Cinema Slayer had killed again. A couple even asked if Ovsanna were involved. The din lessened as I stepped over the crime scene tape and headed toward the pond in the back.

A walkway divided the water into a large area on the left, bounded by the windows of the restaurant, and a smaller pond on the right, with a rocky plateau and a waterfall splashing into a short stream. There was a waist-high wooden rail fence keeping anyone from joining the ducks in the water. Four white swans and a black-and-white one squatted on the plateau, oblivious to the body resting ten feet away.

A small crowd, hotel guests most likely, had gathered behind the crime scene tape in the parking lot at the back of the pond. A couple of officers from the North Hollywood division had their notebooks out, taking names. I badged my way in, climbing over the fence as quietly as I could so as not to spook the swans. The Coroner Investigator hadn't arrived yet, so I couldn't touch anything, but I pulled a pair of evidence gloves out of my pocket, just in case. I knelt down and stared at the corpse.

Or what was left of it.

The victim was a woman, Hispanic probably—from the texture of her hair and what few features were left to study. Her huge breasts popped up over the scooped neckline of the bloodied blue T-shirt she was wearing. The water had washed them clean. She looked like she was serving up two smooth-skinned casabas on a turquoise platter. She had on tight black capri pants and a single turquoise ankle-strap high heel. Its mate was floating against the side of the pond. It was going to take a while to get an ID—her mouth and lower jaw had been torn off, as though some kind of sharp-toothed tool had clamped onto her face and ripped her jawbone out of its socket. Man, it wasn't pretty. Both her arms had been severed, leaving jagged stubs above the elbows, and a huge chunk of her midsection was missing, along with the bottom of her T-shirt. No wonder the Captain thought it was the Cinema Slayer; the viciousness of the attack was right in the same league.

It looked as if she'd been in the water a while, although the water wasn't as bloody as I would have expected. Hard to tell in the dark. There were pole lights along the walkway and low-level up-lights staked into the ground. They didn't throw enough light to search the scene. One of the North Hollywood cops said they'd ordered halogen lamps, but she didn't know when they'd get there. She looked a little queasy. I don't think she minded the wait.

I made do with my flashlight. The walkway was clean; the grounds staff probably rinsed it every day. The sides of the pond were cement—no dirt to hold footprints. What little foliage there was hadn't been disturbed. I didn't see any sign of a struggle. I didn't see anything out of place.

Except for one of the swans. In the decorative lighting she'd looked black and white, but in the high beam of my flashlight, the black turned dark red. She was a white swan with blood on her back. Blood and something else, something about an inch long and a quarter inch wide, resting on her feathers. I didn't want to take the chance she'd swim off and toss whatever it was into the water, so I pulled on my vinyl gloves and moved toward her very slowly. Carefully, I reached out to remove it.

It was the tip of a fingernail. A long, unpolished nail, partially covered in blood. I dropped it into a Baggie and put it in my pocket. I'd hand it over to the evidence techs when they got there.

The swan slipped back into the water, and that's when I saw the prints near her resting place. Two small handprints, like those a child might make in clay for a Mother's Day gift, embedded so deeply into the dirt that it seemed as though someone had taken all his weight on his hands and not his feet. Tiny hands, though. In fact, there were no footprints at all, although it looked as if a big dog had been there recently. Just two palm prints and a fingernail. I wondered if they belonged together.

It was the bartender who had called 911. I walked to the front of the hotel and came in through the lobby. They'd remodeled since the last time I'd been here—the weekend Jenny and I had gotten married and her parents had stayed in one of the rooms. Now there was a bar in the lobby, off to the left, next to a white leather banquette. The banquette curved around most of a freestanding brass fire pit, complete with artificial flames. There was a pool table on the other side and a white-flocked Christmas tree in front of a wall mirror with a full-size plastic marlin hanging on it. I liked the old décor better.

The bartender was a woman.

"I take it you're not Robbie," I said, showing her my badge. "Did he go off work?"

"Nuh-uh. He's working in the Muddy Moose. What's going on? Everybody's got a different story." She was mid-twenties, tall, with short black hair that looked like she'd styled it in a Mixmaster. She probably paid somebody to cut it that way. Ah shit, I thought, I must be getting old. Her name tag said "Joc."

"That's really your name? Jock?"

"No, man. It's Joc—like J-o-s. Short for Jocelyn."

"Oh. I'm sorry. What time did you start work, Joc?"

"Right at seven."

"And have you been here ever since?"

"Left around nine thirty to go to the john, but that's just up those stairs. I wasn't gone long. What should I have been looking for? There's a dead body out there, right?"

"Yep. That's right. Young woman, long black hair. Blue T-shirt, black pants, blue high heels. Maybe a working girl?"

"She didn't come to the bar. Not this one, at least. You know where the Muddy Moose is? On the other side of the pond?"

The Muddy Moose was the sports bar attached to the restaurant on the west side of the property. I found Robbie working behind the bar, his back to a wall full of windows opening on the crime scene. From this angle, the body was hidden. The Coroner Investigator had arrived. I could barely make him out through the window, kneeling by the waterfall.

The Muddy Moose kept up the sportsmen's lodge theme. Dark wood walls, low timber beam ceilings, and rusted iron chandeliers. The bar was tumbled stone boulders with a wood and stone surface. I expected animal heads on the walls. I got vinyl football pennants instead. For sportsmen of all kinds, I guess.

Robbie had a name tag, too. Partially covered in what looked like dried vomit. It was hard to tell in the low lighting, but I thought he seemed a little green. He had two customers at the bar, both drinking beer. An empty shot glass sat behind him by the register. I introduced myself and asked for a ginger ale.

"You found the body?" I asked while he was pouring. He put down the ginger ale and poured an inch of Johnnie Walker into the shot glass. Downed it before he spoke.

"Nah. I was in here, working. One of the guests came running in, telling me to call 911. Fuckin' thing, I had to wait almost three minutes before I talked to a real person. You know how long that is when you've got an emergency? Fuckin' politicians, spending our tax money on everything but what we need. The teachers aren't getting paid, they're bailing out AIG, but cops are getting laid off. What if that girl had still been alive? When were you guys gonna get here to help her if nobody even answers the fuckin' phone?"

"I know. It's a nightmare. Who was the guest, Robbie? Did you get his name?"

"Ah, hell, sure. He's a regular. Lives back east, stays here all the time when he's in town. He's an actor. Tom Atkins. Likes Rolling Rock beer. Or sometimes Sam Adams."

"He's the one who found the body?"

"Yeah. He waited while I called 911, and then we both went back to the pond. I couldn't help it, man, I lost it. That girl looked like she'd been eaten alive."

CHAPTER EIGHTEEN

In my four-hundred-plus years as a vampyre, I've never understood why women scream when they see a mouse. They don't scream when they see a mole, or a gopher, or a hedgehog, or anything else that comes out of a hole. Why a mouse?

It was Wednesday morning early, and I was in my office on Beverly Drive. Sveta and Ilona, my two receptionists, were both screaming in that high-pitched tone they only use when they've seen a rodent. In Beverly Hills, we see a lot of them. I ran down the stairs to the lobby to find Ilona standing on her chair and Sveta scrunched into a corner with a staple gun in her hand, aiming it at the mouse as if it could fire lethal silver slivers or something.

As soon as I reached the floor, the damn thing ran past me and back up the stairs. It wasn't a mouse at all; it was a rat. A nice big fat rat that was waiting for me on the sofa in my office.

I don't have a problem with rats. I've worked with them in a couple of my films. They don't seem to sense I'm not human, the way some species do. The only real problem with them in terms of making movies is that they can't be trained to do anything. When I did *The*

Rat Movie, we had to wipe me down with fish heads to keep them swarming over my body. As long as they thought I was something to eat, they'd stay in the shot.

So I stared at this rat and he stared at me, and the next minute, he was standing on his back paws with his stomach distending. His snout shortened, his tail disappeared, and suddenly Orson Welles plopped down on my sofa, covering his considerable nude girth with my cashmere throw.

"Ovsanna, darling," he said in those same stentorian tones he'd used to sell Paul Masson, "do you think your business partner, the dear deceased Thomas, might have something in his office closet I could wear temporarily? I seem to remember he had great taste in clothes."

I buzzed Maral and asked her to bring Thomas's robe from his bathroom. He always wore it if he had a masseur come to the office after work. Then I locked the door and waited for her knock. She knew Orson was one of my clan, one of the Vampyres of Hollywood, but she didn't need to see him *en dishabille.*

"What the hell are you doing here, Orson?" I asked. "And why did you come in as a rat?"

"It was easier than passing myself off as one of those Orson Welles impersonators you can hire by the hour. My God, have you seen that fellow in front of Grauman's Chinese? I was never that huge, even when I was huge! All those people making a living off my visage, it's absolutely annoying." He rearranged the throw so it reached his chest.

"Well, you do look good. Living in seclusion must agree with you."

"On the contrary, Ovsanna, that's exactly what I want to talk to you about. I'm bored with hiding; bored with reading biographies about myself written in the past tense. Killing Lilith's *dhampirs* and weres was more fun than I've had since the Dean Martin roast. I want to come back to the world. Specifically, I want to come back to the business; it's time I was creative again."

"And what do you want to do? Act again? Direct? Orson, you're too recognizable; how will you explain your appearance?"

"I won't have to if I take over Thomas's job as your head of development. Thomas rarely left the office except to get his ashes hauled at those S and M clubs he loved so much. I've thought it all out. I can start out doing everything on the phone, and then you can introduce me as outside talent you found through a headhunter or something. There isn't an agent in town who's old enough to remember what I sound like, and after all, I'm an actor, my dear. I can create an illusion. I'll lose a little more weight and shave my head. I'd get plugs, but I wouldn't be able to explain why my scalp was healing before they'd even inserted the roots."

Maral knocked on the door. I opened it just enough to take the robe, but when I turned around, Orson had shifted back to his rat form. His tiny little eyes were peeking out from under the afghan. I blocked Maral's view.

"Peter King is on the phone, Ovsanna," Maral said. If her voice had been any colder, I would have needed the afghan myself. "He wants you to meet him at the Coroner's office. Now, if you can."

"The Coroner's office? Can I? Do I have anything scheduled this morning?"

She shook her head.

"Well, find out where it is and tell him we'll be there as soon as we can. And tell the girls downstairs not to worry about the rat, I'm getting rid of it."

I closed the door and turned back to Orson. He still had his tail and his snout, and he was perched on the arm of the sofa. "Honest to God, Orson, I don't know what to do with you. I hadn't even thought about who I want to replace Thomas."

The rat made little biting noises with his teeth. The look he gave me could only be described as cunning.

"Let me sleep on it and let's talk tomorrow," I said. "And for God's sake, if you're going to shift again, bring a suit with you."

CHAPTER NINETEEN

I'd never been to the Coroner's office. Vampyres don't have a lot of relatives who end up dead. And I didn't understand why Peter wanted me there to begin with. He'd told Maral he wanted me to look at a body; I thought bodies went to the morgue.

Maral drove us down the 5, past Chavez Ravine, and onto North Mission in Boyle Heights. We'd barely spoken since I'd bled her, save for my asking her for Thomas's robe and her telling me Peter wanted to see me. I noticed she'd removed my ring from her finger. It was a serpent carved in coral, something I'd had since Victoria was queen. Not only was she not talking to me, she'd stopped wearing the gift I'd given her. Her childish way of letting me know she was pissed.

She looked haggard. She'd gone out last night after I left her bed, probably thinking if she were quiet enough, I wouldn't know. You'd think after all these years she'd remember I can hear everything. I heard the click of the space bar on her computer—she must have been scrolling down Web sites—and then her bare feet on the stairs when she tiptoed outside to smoke a joint. I hate it when she smokes;

she gets paranoid and crazy. Especially this new weed she gets from one of the actors in the kids' movie we just wrapped. Leave it to a seventeen-year-old Disney star to have high-quality cannabis. He probably laces it with something. She thinks if she goes far enough onto the property, I won't smell it. Not only can I smell it, I can hear her striking a match all the way across the yard. Plus, I taste the THC curdling her blood for days afterwards.

After she got stoned, I heard her come in to get her shoes, and then she left again. At least she took Peter's warning seriously—his business card was missing from the table. She must have taken it with her. I should have stopped her from driving, but I knew she needed to put some space between us. I figured she was going to stay at the beach house, and at that hour, with so little traffic, she'd be okay.

Instead, she was home a couple of hours later. She must have really been loaded because she started making tea in the kitchen—some god-awful herbal concoction, from the smell of it—and then she locked herself in her bathroom at four in the morning and took a shower. She was talking to herself. It sounded like she was praying. I stopped listening when I realized that's what it was.

My dear, sweet Maral. She's got her own demons to contend with. And some of them I can't help her with.

The view of the downtown skyline from the freeway was spectacular. The street we ended up on wasn't. It looked like an aging industrial park, bounded by a hospital maintenance building, a parking lot, a reproductive biology lab, and the L.A. County College of Nursing and Allied Health. There were also a thrift shop, a flower shop, and a Jack in the Box. Maral parked at a broken meter in front of a tortilla stand. Instead of flashing "fail," the meter flashed "dead." Somebody in the Department of Transportation had a sense of humor.

The Coroner's building was a turn-of-the-century architectural gem in the midst of all that grayness. Red and taupe brick with a lot of neoclassical stonework and beautiful black cast-iron streetlamps. The floor tiles in front of the huge glass doors spelled out "Los Angeles General Hospital." They looked original. Peter was standing on them, waiting for us. He was wearing the same clothes he'd had on last night, and when I saw the fatigue on his face, I realized he hadn't been to bed yet.

"Thanks for coming. This is the homicide I went out on last night. Body was found at the Sportsmen's Lodge. If I didn't know better, I'd swear it was the Cinema Slayer again. I want you to look at it. I know you get images sometimes when you touch things. I can't believe I'm even asking you this, but I'd like to know what I'm dealing with here. I need all the help I can get."

Inside the lobby, Peter stopped at a glass cubicle and told the receptionist he was there to see Investigator Shin. Maral sat down to wait on a wooden bench across the room, and I drifted over to an opaque glass door labeled "Gift Shop." The sign said they opened at eleven, but I tried the handle and it was unlocked. I couldn't resist. What kinds of gifts could they be selling in the Coroner's office?

Beach towels and welcome mats. With a chalk outline of a dead body on them. And mouse pads reading, "We're dying for your business."

The woman behind the counter said, "Welcome to Skeletons in the Closet." Only in L.A., I thought. The whole place was filled with merchandise aimed at those "of dubious distinctive taste." That's what it said on the catalog: body bags for traveling, "Undertaker" boxer shorts, Department of Coroner lunch boxes, a kitchen cutting board with the dead body outline and the line "We have our work cut out for us" on it. They even had golf balls and club covers with dead bodies on them. My favorite was a hoodie with the drawing of a foot with a toe tag; it reminded me of my Dakhanavar ancestors, who liked to suck feet.

Peter joined me as I was browsing through the Cutting Edge office supplies. Looking past him into the lobby, I saw an elderly woman and her family come out from a side room. They were all crying. The woman fainted into the arms of one of the men, and an attendant rushed over to help.

"What is this place, Peter?" I asked.

"Well, it started out as an adobe infirmary in the late 1800s. It's the last of the four original brick buildings that made up Los Angeles General Hospital, and now it's the administration building for County. And the Coroner's office."

"I thought they kept dead bodies in the morgue."

"They do, if they've died of natural causes and if they're identified. Jane and John Does and homicide cases come here. Welcome to the crypt."

We walked back into the lobby.

An attractive Asian woman came down the stairs. Peter introduced her as a Coroner Investigator and thanked her for helping him out.

"Only for you, Detective King. I'm breaking all kinds of protocol, letting you take someone in there with you. If I didn't owe you big-time, this would never happen," she said under her breath. "Don't let me down." She opened a door and motioned the three of us inside. Peter knew where he was going; she left us to get there on our own.

We walked through a hallway with a large scale set into the floor. An attendant was weighing a body on a gurney. A young girl with a string of bullet holes across her chest. My first thought was that she'd been caught in a drive-by. What a tragedy. At least when my kind kill, we choose our victims deliberately.

I damped down my sense of smell. I was aroused enough just being around Peter; the last thing I needed was the smell of blood. It didn't matter whose. Even old, dried blood—still an aphrodisiac.

Maral never said a word. I don't think she saw the little girl. She stared straight ahead until we reached our destination and then stopped behind me, standing just inside the door.

It was a long, refrigerated room, with metal trays extending out from the left wall, stacked four high with a three-foot space between them, thirty in a row. Filled with dead bodies. Some were covered loosely in sheets, others were wrapped in clear plastic and tied with rope. I was amazed that there could be that many unidentified bodies or homicide victims dead at the same time. I guess with upwards of five hundred gangs in the city of L.A. alone, I shouldn't have been surprised. I wondered if any of my kind were responsible for any of the deaths.

Peter rolled a metal lift over to the sixth row, cranked a handle to bring it level with a tray holding a sheeted body, and pulled the tray out to the middle of the room. He uncovered the body.

I understood immediately why he'd asked me to come. This body had been shredded. Eviscerated. If a human did this, he'd have had to use some kind of serrated knife or cutting tool. It could very well have been done by an animal. Or a beast.

I reached out and touched the woman's forehead, the only part of her face still intact. Sensations flooded my body . . . a drug high, and then terror. And then I couldn't breathe. I was in water. Drowning. Something had sliced into my stomach and was holding me down. Churning the water around me. The water was so bloodied that I couldn't see through it. Something had me by my body and was turning me, rolling me over and over, and making a loud, ratcheting sound—like a mechanical growl. A lion's snarl in a tin bucket or an idling motorboat engine or something. I couldn't place it. I pulled my hand away from the woman's forehead and took a couple of deep breaths to center myself. This woman's last moments had been horrific.

"I think you're going to find she drowned, Peter. Whatever tore her apart pulled her down in the water first, the way alligators do. She wasn't alive when she got shredded. But he must have attacked her from behind because I don't think she saw him before she drowned. At least, I didn't see any other images."

"You think it was human?"

"I couldn't tell. Maybe. Whatever it was, it was strong. I'm sorry, that's not much help."

"Well, it was worth a try. Thanks for making the drive down here. At least I got to see you."

Peter walked us back to Investigator Shin's office. He tapped on her door and opened it long enough to thank her and tell her he'd let her know as soon as he got an ID on the body.

We stepped out into the sunlight, and the yelling started. Reporters raced up the steps to shove mics in our faces. News crews from the local networks had cameras set up. The paparazzi were waiting at the bottom of the stairs.

"Detective King, what's going on with the body you found at the Sportsmen's?"

"Is it another Cinema Slayer case?"

"How come you're here, Ms. Moore? Did the dead woman work for Anticipation? Did you know her? Look over here! Give us a shot!"

"Come on, Ovsanna—smile!"

"Yeah, Ovsanna, what's your connection to the case? Come on! Come on, speak into the microphone!"

"What's your connection to Detective King? Can you tell us that?"

"Is that Zac Posen you're wearing?"

Peter put his arm around me and shielded me with his body as we pushed past the photographers to the car. Maral was behind us. At one point, I turned around and couldn't see her through the wall of paps between us. They were yelling at her, too.

"Miss McKenzie, is your boss helping the police?"

"How come she's here? Is this research for the next film?"

"Was the dead woman a friend? What was she wearing?"

Peter opened the passenger door for me. I slid in and closed it and rolled down the window to say good-bye. Peter leaned in so no one else could hear him.

"I don't know how they knew you were here," he whispered. "Maral wouldn't have told anyone, would she?"

"Not if she wants to keep her job." I looked over at her. She was sitting rigid in the driver's seat, staring straight ahead. Straining to hear what Peter was saying, I think.

The photographers had followed us down to the car. They were still yelling, but now they were jostling for the best angle to shoot Peter and me together. Peter turned on them.

"Take a hike, fellas. I'd hate to have to ruin someone's morning with a trip downtown. That means you, Eddie." He glared at the photographer who was leading the pack. It was Steady Eddie—a bald, three-hundred-pound behemoth wearing lime green suspenders and two Nikons around his neck. I see him outside my house from time to time. He's got a reputation as one of the town's top paparazzi.

"Ah, the illustrious Beverly Hills sleuth, winner of medals for heroism, destroyer of fine photography."

"What's he talking about?" I asked.

"It's nothing," Peter responded. "The last time I saw him, he made the mistake of showing me some fast-frame shots he'd taken of something he shouldn't have. I borrowed his camera to get a closer look and handed it back with a reformatted disk and no forbidden pictures."

Eddie overheard him. "Well, you ought to tell her the whole tale, Detective. Who are you trying to protect? They were shots of your abode, Ms. Moore, with some nice detail work of the code for your gate. Truly creative on my part, I thought."

"Get fucked, Eddie, and get out of here, or fine photography won't be all I destroy."

"In truth, Detective, methinks the time you're spending with the lovely Ms. Moore is not all in the line of duty."

Peter advanced on him, and he scrambled back to the safety of the pack. They were still firing off shots. Peter pulled himself together and came back to me.

I asked him if that meant he'd known my security code all this time. He avoided an answer, which was an answer in itself. Interesting. Maybe Maral was right when she talked about trust.

Instead he asked, "How do you deal with this every day? They're like a pack of wolves waiting to get their teeth into something juicy. I've watched them do it for years, but they seem to be getting more and more vicious. There are no boundaries anymore."

"You get used to it," I said. "Although they're not usually on me like this. I'm not nineteen and in rehab, I'm not starving myself to death, and I haven't got any kids to fight for in a bloody divorce. Unless I have a film coming out, or we've made a deal with some other celebrity, they usually leave me alone. All this attention started with the Cinema Slayer. And for some reason, it got worse after we came back from Palm Springs."

Maral started the car. "We've got to go, Ovsanna." She still hadn't looked at me.

Peter stared at her for a moment. I'm sure he was trying to figure out what was going on. He'd been around the two of us enough to know something wasn't right. Then he shrugged and smiled at me. "Thanks for your help," he said. "The autopsy's scheduled for tomorrow morning, so I should know something more then. We got a print off the woman's Saint Andrew medal; the investigator's running that, too. And a fingernail I found at the scene. If we find a suspect, we may be able to match DNA."

"I wasn't much help. I'm sorry. Sometimes the impressions I get are so clear, but not this time."

"Well, it wasn't a total waste. I got to spend the morning with you. And you got to see the gift shop. Let's see, Christmas Tree Lane and Skeletons in the Closet. Can I show you a good time or what?" He stepped back from the car. "I'll call you later," he mouthed.

Maral peeled into the street before I could even wave good-bye.

I've seen a lot of gruesome deaths in my life. They don't faze me. When you've lived through the Reign of Terror, the Inquisition, and Ivan the Terrible, you get inured to the visuals. Vlad Tepes might have given me pause, but he'd finished impaling by the time I was born.

But the trip to the Coroner's office had obviously upset Maral. She was pale and tight-lipped all the way back to the office.

"I'm sorry you had to see that," I said. "I should have had you wait in the car." We pulled up outside the building and waited for Jesus, the valet. I bought the building because I love the design—a gem of two-story weathered brick and stone in the midst of the gray cement on the rest of South Beverly—but I had to sacrifice underground parking. Jesus parks our cars in a lot down the street.

I scanned the block before I got out of the car. It had been three days since the were had made himself known. Or not known, which was my real problem. I still didn't have any idea who had attacked me, and until I did, the only thing I could do was stay alert.

Once again, there were paparazzi standing on the curb. Just two this time, but that was two more than usual. These two hadn't been at the Coroner's. And they weren't shooting anything, just watching as Maral and I walked up the steps. It must be a slow news day, I thought.

"It wasn't seeing the body that upset me, Ovsanna. It was Peter. It was you and Peter. You're going to sleep with him, aren't you?"

"I might. I just might. Depending upon what he wants to do. But what I do with Peter has nothing to do with you and me. You just remember that." I would have kissed her to reassure her, but the paparazzi hadn't taken their eyes off us. I didn't need that kind of photo on the evening news.

She turned on me just outside the door. "I see the way you look at him. You've never been like that with anyone since we've been together—not Thomas, not Robson, not Al. I know you see other people sometimes, but he's different. He's a cop. It scares me. Whatever you're feeling about him, that scares me."

"Lower your voice and keep your wits about you. This is not a conversation to have in public. In fact, this is not a conversation I'm going to have at all. Peter is a good man, and he's not a danger to us. You are my family, Maral, I'm not going to abandon you, but Peter may be in my life right now and you need to accept it. End of story."

There was a woman sitting on the red velvet sofa when we walked in the lobby. She stood as Maral and I entered. She had short, spiky black hair that looked as if she'd chopped it with a pair of nail scissors. Her eyebrows had been plucked into oblivion and then drawn back in a skinny brown line. She was dressed like a teenager, in a yellow and blue striped tunic and psychedelic paisley print leggings, with gold ballet shoes on her feet. Stick-thin legs that never should have seen a pair of tights. Her makeup base was so thick, I couldn't guess her age. It looked like clay she'd applied with a trowel. She seemed vaguely familiar, but it wasn't until I heard her voice that I realized who she was.

"Ovsanna," she said, reaching out her hands for me. I was so surprised at recognizing her, I pulled back.

My secretary, Sveta, was up and around her desk in an instant. "I'm sorry, Ms. Moore, she wouldn't give me her name. She insisted on waiting for you here without an appointment." She stepped between us like a pit bull preparing for the ring.

"It's all right, Sveta. She's a friend. Would you hold my calls, please?" And with that, I ushered the most powerful female star of her era up the stairs and into my office. Mary Pickford had come to call.

"What the hell have you done to your face, Mary?" I asked, locking the door behind me. "And your hair. You look like shit." I didn't even want to mention the outfit.

"Yes, but I don't look like myself, do I? You don't recognize America's Sweetheart anymore, do you?" She twirled around to give me a full view of the horrendous haircut and then struck her classic pose with her hands clasped under her chin and the left side of her face towards me. She'd always insisted on being photographed from the left so the hump on her nose wouldn't show.

Mary is one of mine—one of the Vampyres of Hollywood. She, too, is full-born, of the Leanan-sídhe clan. She came to me in 1910 when D. W. Griffith brought his Biograph players to Los Angeles. She was only seventeen, but she'd been performing onstage since she was five and had already made more than fifty films when I met her.

"I just saw you three weeks ago, and no, I didn't recognize you at all. What have you done to yourself? And why?"

"I dyed my hair, darling. And got rid of my trademark curls. That broke my heart—remember when I auctioned one off for fifteen thousand dollars to help fight World War One? Now, *that* was a war! Don't get me started. I would have had my nose bobbed, but you know, unless you're Obour, it's impossible to reset our bones; they just heal exactly the way they were. It's damn inconvenient, if you ask me." She walked over to the window and stared up the street towards the shops on Two Rodeo, Beverly Hills' homage to kitsch.

"You have an adorable nose. Why would you even think about such a thing?"

"Because I want to work. Not on the screen, necessarily, I was happy to stop that years ago, but in the business. I'm a brilliant producer, Chatelaine, you know that. I was one of the most powerful women in Hollywood, and you need me." She sat in one of my wing chairs, slipped off her shoes, and tucked her feet under her butt, looking very much like she was making herself at home.

"I need you?"

"Yes. To take over for Thomas, God rest his soul. This never would have happened if you had turned him, Ovsanna, but you didn't, and now he's gone and you need someone in his place. Who better to hire than the woman who co-founded United Artists *and* the Society of Independent Motion Picture Producers? I can help you turn Anticipation around."

"Anticipation isn't facing the wrong way, Mary. Did you read the trades today? We're a day away from signing a major merger. Solgar should have the papers ready tomorrow afternoon." My intercom buzzed.

"Detective King is here to see you," Sveta announced.

"Oh, that's the lovely young man who killed Rudy, isn't it?" Mary asked, jumping up to go to the door. "I never got a chance to thank him properly. Oh, this will be perfect; let's see if he sees through my disguise."

There was a quick tap on the door, and Mary walked over in her bare feet to unlock it. She looked like Kelly Osbourne on a bad day. With pearls.

I couldn't wait to see Peter's face.

Mary opened the door, and Peter stood there, staring.

"You see, Ovsanna, it works! You didn't recognize me, did you, Detective King? I'm Mary. Mary Pickford. We just battled all those beasts together! You were *so* helpful. Oh, I'm delighted. I knew this would work. Ovsanna, darling, you *must* consider my proposal. I am the perfect person for the job."

I couldn't resist. "Mary's auditioning for one of those magazine layouts," I said, smiling. "You know, 'When Bad Clothes Happen to Good People.' With the caption 'Move over, Cyndi Lauper.'"

I got up from my desk and went to the door where they were standing. "Are the paparazzi still outside?"

"There are two out there," Peter replied. "None of the regulars. You still don't know what that's about, do you?"

"I haven't got a clue." I turned to Mary. "It *is* an interesting proposal. I'll tell you what. Put your shoes on and go take a walk. Neiman's is having a sale on furs, if you're not afraid of the PETA people. No, wait . . . that's a terrible idea. If you're going to come back to the business in disguise, you don't want to call attention to yourself. Forget the furs, just take a walk, and let's talk later this afternoon. You'll know immediately if anyone thinks you look like yourself. Although you should be prepared, that hairstyle alone will have people staring at you."

I watched the woman who'd starred in more than two hundred films in the early 1900s walk down the stairs in her Marilyn Manson haircut and psychedelic leggings. The last time I'd seen her, she'd shifted into a bat-faced beastie. This outfit was no less scary.

Peter stared after her. "If my mother were here," he said, "she'd shit a brick."

The proposal Mary made to me wasn't such a bad idea. She'd been brilliant at running United Artists with Douglas and Charlie and D. W. Griffith, breaking the practice of Hollywood studios at the time, which had the studios controlling the theatres and the distributors, putting filmmakers at their mercy. UA producers didn't have to endure much creative interference; Mary and the fellas set up the studio so their producers were able to keep control of their work. That was a major change in the industry. There's never been a woman in Hollywood who's had as much influence as Mary did then. Not Dorothy Arzner, not Sherry Lansing, not Dawn Steele. Mary might really make a difference at Anticipation.

I wasn't sure I could work with her, though. The Leanan-sídhe are essential vampyres. They feed on the sexual essence of their victims, and they're very seductive. Hence Mary's three husbands, I'm sure. If Douglas Fairbanks hadn't been Blautsauger, she might have drained him dry before they ever separated. I don't think she practices her wiles much anymore, but I couldn't have her killing off the actors she was hired to employ. And of course, she'd definitely have to do something about her "disguise." Orson in his rat form would be easier to look at every day than her skinny legs in those psychedelic tights.

Orson, on the other hand, was a brilliant moviemaker. He could create gold with no budget, no studio behind him, barely anything to work with save his own artistry. He's Strigoi Vui, a master of witchcraft. Imagine what he could do with Anticipation if I gave him free rein.

Well, I'd think about all of that later. I still had the werewolf attack to worry about. It was two days since I'd asked Solgar for information, and I hadn't heard anything back from him. I needed to contact the rest of my clan, find out if anyone else had had a run-in with a beast.

But right then, all I could think about was Peter.

It was the first time we'd been alone together since our date the night before. I'd been a mass of nerve endings ever since, all of them set on lust. The blood in the Coroner's office hadn't helped. I wanted to wrap my arms around him, feel him hard against me. I wanted to finish the kiss we'd almost started. To scratch my face against the stubble of his beard and feel the smoothness of the skin on his neck. I wanted to sink my fangs into that neck and feed on the hot fluid in his veins while I fucked his brains out, but that probably wasn't going to happen anytime soon. Not with Maral in her office next door and Sveta and Ilona at their desks downstairs. And not with him trying to solve a homicide, with a chewed-up victim and shit for clues. I tried to get back to business.

"I didn't expect to see you so soon. Something else I can help you with?" I asked. I kept my distance, not sure what his reaction to romance would be while he was on the job.

"Yeah. The hotel just faxed over the reservations sheet from last night, when our Jane Doe was found. We still don't have an ID on her, no one's called in a missing person report, and we didn't get any help from the bystanders last night. No fingers to print . . . hell, you saw her—no hands. But I'm heading back over there later today to ask some more questions. She probably wasn't married—she was wearing a Saint Andrew medal."

"What does that mean?" I asked. "There's a saint for women who want to attract a man?"

"There's a saint for everything. Don't you know that? There's a saint for anesthesiologists, running sores, ice-skating. Hell, there are three saints for difficult marriages; I know because my mother was praying to all three before my divorce. None of them came through. From her point of view, at least. Anyway, Saint Andrew is the patron saint of single women. So I figure our Jane Doe didn't wear a ring. The way she was dressed, she could have been looking for a honey at the bar." He rifled through the papers he was holding in a manila envelope and pulled out a single sheet. "The Sportsmen's Lodge has five rooms being billed to Anticipation Studios. Any idea why?"

"We almost always have someone there. The Sportsmen's is halfway between the studios in Santa Clarita and my office here, and that's where our travel agency books anyone from out of town—directors, designers, anyone who might need to be in both places. If it's an actor, we put him in a hotel in Valencia, closer to the studio, but otherwise, it's the Sportsmen's."

"Would you take a look at these names and tell me who they are?"

He handed me the paper. I hit the intercom and asked Maral to come in. She deals with this kind of stuff, not me. But I did recognize four of the names. I'd just spent days meeting with them. "Mr. Takeyama, Mr. Ito, and Mr. Yoshiri are the execs from Japan representing the consortium involved in the merger. Mr. Ito is the lawyer in the group. And Cody Carpenter, who lives in Tokyo when he isn't working in the States, is the composer I'm using on *Hallowed Night,* the film we wrapped last week. He scored *Vatican Vampyres* for me and *Demons in Distress,* and he did such a great job, I flew him over. This other name I don't recognize." Maral came to the doorway. "Who's DeWayne Carter?" I asked her.

She was wearing her black-frame Buddy Holly glasses. Behind them, her eyes started blinking like she was sending Morse code. Her voice, when she spoke, was an octave higher than usual. "Why? What's he done?"

"Nothing that I know of. What's wrong with you?" She'd been acting strangely ever since she returned from Louisiana. That morning, after Orson left, I'd gone into Thomas's bathroom to return the robe, and I'd smelled something coming from her office, something I couldn't identify. I found a devil pod jammed behind her door—a shiny black seed that looked like a leering, goat-horned devil. She must have brought it back with her from the swamps. It had some viscous liquid all over it, as if it had been dipped in oil. Hoodoo doctors—they called them rootworkers in the South—use devil pods to ward off evil. It's folk magick. Maybe she thought it was going to help take care of the odoriferous drug dealer. Using one stench to fight off another. Sort of like the models at Bloomingdale's perfume counter, spraying Liz Taylor and Céline Dion.

I left it where it was.

"Nothing. Nothing. I was just surprised to hear his name, that's all." The blinking settled down, but she wouldn't make eye contact. "I just got off the phone with him."

"Well, we're paying for a room for him at the Sportsmen's and I don't know who he is. Is he an actor?" I'm supposed to be kept informed if casting wants to fly someone in from New York to audition, but sometimes they're working so close to a deadline that I don't hear until after the fact. In this week between Christmas and New Year's, I had two films in pre-production, but no casting going on. I knew that.

"No . . . no . . . he's that guy . . . that friend of Jamie's, my brother . . . the one I told you about. He checked in last night." More blinking.

Peter butted in. "He's a friend of your brother's and Anticipation is paying his hotel bill? Why? What's his connection to the studio?"

Her eyes were all over the place. She wasn't looking at me, and she wouldn't look at Peter. "Ovsanna said I could hire him, maybe to do some P.A. work or something. I never told her his name. He flew in with me from Louisiana. I want to help get him located out here. Ovsanna knows about it."

"Well, I know a little about it." I knew about the devil pod, at least. I stepped in front of her, forcing her eyes to settle on me. "Obviously, not enough. I didn't know you put his room charge on the studio. Will you call the hotel, please, and give them your credit card. Now." My voice was like ice. This was the third time she'd pissed me off in less than twenty-four hours, and I was definitely losing my patience. She started for her office.

"Wait a minute," Peter said, stopping her midway out the door. "I need to talk to all five of these people. And as of twenty minutes ago, no one was in his room. You have cell phone numbers for them? Possible locations? I need all the information you've got."

Maral directed her response to me. "Cody Carpenter is laying down orchestra tracks at WhiteBreadSound. He should be there all day. DeWayne Carter is out at the studio now. He's getting food set up for the mixing session tonight. I've got the rest of the information on my computer."

She walked out. I closed the door behind her and turned to look at Peter. We were alone. Finally.

CHAPTER TWENTY

There was something going on with Maral and Ovsanna that I couldn't pin down. Maybe Ovsanna was still pissed about last night. God knows it might have ended differently if Maral hadn't been at the house when we got there. Well, we were alone now.

Ovsanna was staring at me. Her eyes were as big as marbles—shooters, not peewees. And black as obsidian. A lot more appealing than when they turn red. I wanted to kiss them closed and run my tongue over her lashes. I wanted to feel her eyelids flutter beneath my lips.

I read about that on the cover of some romance novel SuzieQ left at the house. *When His Kiss Is Wicked.* Sounded worth a try.

What I did instead was put down the folder I'd been carrying and stand there and stare back at her. She was wearing tight jeans tucked into knee-high black suede boots; their heels brought her forehead up to my nose. She barely had any makeup on. She didn't need it. Her lashes were thick and black against her pale skin. She ran her tongue over her lips. I didn't see any fangs.

I stepped toward her and bent down to kiss her.

Maral walked in.

My lips never met their mark. "Well, this isn't going to work, is it?" I said, straightening up and taking the papers Maral handed me. I was smiling.

"What?" asked Maral.

"He wasn't talking to you, Maral, he was talking to me," Ovsanna answered. "And you're right"—she turned to address me— "this doesn't seem to be the time or the place." She wasn't quite smiling. I think Maral was really getting on her nerves. "Would you like to come out to the beach house this evening? I'm driving out right after work to spend the night there."

Maral's eyes flared. "What about the mixing session on *Chupacabra*? Don't you have to be at the studio?"

"They can live without me for one night, Maral. Just have them upload the reels and I'll look at them out at the beach." Her voice had turned cold again. I wasn't so sure I'd want to be around her on a day she wasn't happy.

"I'll see what I can do," I said. "I've got to go back to the office and write up what we've got so far, and then I've got to get over to the Sportsmen's and do some interviewing. How about I call you later when I know what's going on?" I didn't tell her I hadn't slept since yesterday morning and I was worried that once we were alone together, I'd get as far as taking her in my arms and then I'd pass out.

CHAPTER TWENTY-ONE

"King! My office. Now!"

Aw, shit. It wasn't often the Captain stepped into the corridor to yell out someone's name. I flashed a look at Del Delaney, seated at his desk across from mine. He shrugged his shoulders and shook his head. He didn't know what it was, either.

The Captain had gone back to his desk. I walked in his office and closed the door behind me. Whatever it was, I didn't want anyone else to hear.

The Christmas tree he'd had in the corner was gone, and his TV was back in its place. It was on, but he had the sound turned down. The snowflakes his grandkids had cut out were still taped to the wall. The corner of one had come unstuck and was curling down on itself. I wanted to walk over and retape it, but I didn't think the Captain would appreciate that. I sat in the chair facing his desk instead.

"What the hell were you doing with Ovsanna Moore at the Coroner's office?" he barked. He picked up the remote and hit the TiVo button and the sound at the same time. I caught a glimpse of

Judge Judy in his lineup before he clicked on a news report. He must have hit the record button partway through a broadcast because the anchor was in the middle of a sentence. I recognized her as the reporter from that morning who'd yelled the question about Ovsanna's involvement in the case. It was the noon news the Captain was watching when the segment came on. Channel 9.

"And with a possible connection to the Cinema Slayer case," the reporter was saying, "police are investigating the brutal slaying of a young woman that took place in Studio City last night. Film star Ovsanna Moore was seen exiting the Coroner's office this morning with Beverly Hills detective Peter King. Ms. Moore is the head of Anticipation Studios, where several of the Cinema Slayer's victims were employed." The Captain hit the mute button.

"Okay, how much of that is bullshit and what's the truth? What do we know about this body? What does Ovsanna Moore know? You had her down there for some reason. What was it?"

My mind was going a mile a minute. There was no way I could tell the Captain I asked Ovsanna to touch the body to see if she came up with some psychic vision. No way I could tell him Ovsanna felt what the woman felt right before she died. The Captain was a Methodist. He'd take me off the case and send me to the shrink.

"I saw the body last night, Captain. The NHPD was right to call you. There's enough similarity to the way the other bodies were torn apart to make me think this could be the Slayer again, even though a lot of the rest of the scene doesn't match up. Ovsanna Moore knew all the other vics; I asked her to look at what was left of the body, see if she could identify her."

"We still don't have a name?"

I shook my head.

"So . . . did she know her?" he asked.

"There wasn't much left to recognize. No face, no arms, no midsection. But no, she didn't think she knew her."

"What's the evidence at the scene? Anything to give you an angle?"

"Not much. No witnesses. No one heard anything. Well, that's not quite true. One of the guests heard a loud, ratcheting sound that went on long enough to catch his attention. He said it sounded like a truck stripping gears, but he checked the parking lot outside his room and didn't see anything. So that doesn't help. We won't have the autopsy report for a couple of days. Don't know if she was attacked first and then drowned or the other way around. Pulled one print off a necklace she was wearing and found a fingernail—could be the perp's. Take a while to run the DNA, rule it out as being the vic's. Vic didn't have any hands or arms left, so we couldn't check for a match."

"What do you mean, no hands or arms? They weren't lying around somewhere? The perp took them with him? In what? The guy shows up to rip someone's face off and brings his own garbage bags? What was it, a Hefty commercial?"

"We didn't find anything, Boss."

"I don't know, Peter, doesn't sound like the Cinema Slayer to me. That maniac left body parts all over the place."

"I know. Well, they're dragging the pond this afternoon. Maybe we'll find something in the water. I'm on my way over there now. I want to talk to Tom Atkins, the actor who found the body and had the bartender call it in. He's staying there, but he was filming on location last night so I didn't get to him."

"He's not working for Anticipation, is he? That could be another connection."

"I don't think so. They don't have anything in production right now. I'll find out for sure when I talk to him."

"And what about the print?"

"I should have something tomorrow afternoon, the latest. If he's in the system, we'll find him."

"Well, make it fast. I just got the press settled down and now they're screaming about a serial killer all over again. I'm glad this vic wasn't tied in to Anticipation . . . less grist for the mill."

I was glad, too. I wanted to keep my involvement with Ovsanna—whatever it turned out to be—as far out of the limelight as possible.

———

I drove back to the Sportsmen's and tracked down Tom Atkins. He'd checked into the hotel Monday afternoon.

"Ah hell, yeah, I saw some jamoke out by the pool last night, musta been ten o'clock or so. I had an eleven P.M. call time out in Simi Valley—we were doin' a car chase on the 118—and I was waitin' for transpo to pick me up. My room's on the ground floor, opens right onto the pool. He was a creepy little guy with no neck. Major acne. Made my teenage son's face look like a baby's butt in comparison."

"What was he doing?"

"Nothin'. That's why I thought he was creepy. Just standin' there, lookin' around and wipin' his face with a towel. Jeez, I hope he threw it in the trash and not the laundry bin. I'd hate to end up with that in my room, I don't care how many times they washed it."

We were in the Patio Cafe, which is never called the Patio Cafe, at least not by the regulars who hang out there whenever they're in town. Years ago, before I bought my place in Beverly Glen and I was still living at my mother's, I used to stop there in the mornings for coffee and a bear claw. I'd eavesdrop on the actors I recognized— Robert Cummings and Jack Palance, Mike Connors, Pat Buttram, and Monte Hale, and the guy that played Moe Greene in *The Godfather,* Alex Rocco. They just called it the coffee shop. I guess part of it is a patio. There's a semi-enclosed space between the glassed-in restaurant and the first- and second-story hotel rooms. That's where all the paintings are. Big portraits of western TV heroes—Jock Mahoney, Dale Robertson, Sam Elliott, Lash La Rue, Tom Selleck, and Ronald Reagan—all painted on tile and framed as a mural across the walls. Inside the restaurant, they've got western movie posters and a shelf holding Gene Autry's boots, spurs, and Stetson. Tom was seated at a booth underneath Gene's duds. He had two men at the table with him: an overweight, loose-fleshed boozer (from the looks of the veins on his face) and a weaselly little guy in jeans and a T-shirt. The weaselly guy had thinning, Grecian Formula black hair and was missing a couple of teeth. He was seated under a display of Jerry Mahoney, Paul Winchell's ventriloquist dummy. They looked alike. Except the dummy was wearing a suit and he hadn't dyed his hair.

I'd met Tom Atkins years ago on the set of *The Rockford Files,* when my mother's company was doing the catering. I was about sixteen at the time. My mother hoped my hanging around the set would spark an interest in acting, but Tom was playing an LAPD lieutenant and he was so cool, he just firmed up my resolve to follow in my father's footsteps and join the force. I never told my mother that; she would have burned Tom's food.

I'd seen him in a lot of films since. He hadn't changed much. He was wearing khaki pants and a beat-up leather jacket over a black T-shirt with a white caricature of his face on it. He was a handsome man, in good shape. He could still play an Irish cop. Only now, with that great head of white hair, he'd have to be the commander. I didn't bother to tell him we'd met, but I did tell him I liked his work.

"Aw, thanks, kid. Spent a lot of my life pretendin' to do what you're doin' for real. You want a cup of java?"

I shook my head. Jamoke and java in the same conversation, hadn't heard that in a long time.

"What about my work? Did you like it? Jimmy Schmidt, Officer, pleased to meet you." The man on Tom's left stood up and leaned over the table to shake my hand. No question about the veins on his face; he was a drinker. "I was on *Rockford* once, remember, Tommy? Hell, though, I don't think we had any scenes together. I played a drunk in a bar, hitting ol' Jim Garner up for a dime to use the pay phone. It was a good scene. I used it on my reel."

Jimmy Schmidt didn't look familiar. He was big. Six feet, about 280 pounds. He was a snappy dresser: salmon-colored sports coat and madras pants, in the middle of winter. Maybe he was on his way to San Pedro to catch a Carnival cruise.

"You're so fulla shit, Jimmy. That reel musta been forty minutes long, with all the 'good scenes' you keep sayin' you got on there." It was obvious Tommy and Jimmy went back a long way. "He's a co-median, Detective. Does the condo circuit and the cruise lines," Tommy said, chuckling. "Can't act his way out of a paper bag. He's funny, though."

"And this is Ritchie," Tommy continued. "Ritchie Wollensky."

Bad teeth gave me a couple of quick nods. No handshake. "How d'ya do, Officer? How d'ya do? Pleased to meetcha. Yessir, yes, I am. Very pleased to meetcha."

Ritchie was bouncing out of his skin. I was pretty sure if I patted him down, a nicely filled Baggie would fall out, but I wasn't interested in drugs right then. "Are both you fellas staying at the hotel?" I asked.

"No, Officer. Oh, no, no, no." Wollensky shook his head so fast, what little hair he had separated in the middle and fell down over his ears. Made him look like a particularly mangy breed of dog. "No, no. Me and Jimmy here just meet up for coffee a couple days a week. And always when Tommy's in town. Tommy was just tellin' us about last night. No, no. We wasn't here for that. Huh-uh."

"Can't say I'm sorry I missed it, either," said Jimmy. "Doesn't sound like a very pretty sight."

"Aw, jeez, it was a mess," said Tommy. "I think I was the first one to see the body. Looked like something out of one of the movies I did—*Night of the Creeps* or *MBV3D* or somethin'. Jeez, that poor girl."

"What the hell is *MBV3D*?" Ritchie asked. "Sounds like a disease."

"Aw, it's the movie I just did. *My Bloody Valentine 3D*. Had a good time on that film. We shot it in the Burg. Director was a great guy."

"So you called 911?" I asked, trying to get them back on track.

"Oh, hey, yeah . . . I didn't have a cell phone on me. I was just takin' a walk back from the bar to get my stuff and go to the set. I hustled back in there and told Robbie, the bartender. He made the call. Then he went outside with me and tossed his cookies in the bushes."

"Yeah, we found that," I said. "You're not working for Ovsanna Moore, are you? Over at Anticipation Studios?"

"Nah. I'm doin' a TV gig for TNT. Wouldn't mind workin' for Anticipation, though. They do some fun stuff. I loved that last one . . . *Return to Bitch Mountain*. That was a hoot."

The waitress came over to top off the coffee cups. She was a Phyllis Diller look-alike, with Mercurochrome red hair and chartreuse eye shadow. I didn't think her hair color existed in nature. I was sure of it when I looked toward the patio. The waitress there had the exact same color. Maybe it was part of the job description. They probably had it done in the hotel salon.

"You gonna join these guys, mister? Want some coffee?" The plastic name tag above the Sportsmen's Lodge logo on her shirt said "Arlene."

I declined the coffee and showed Arlene my badge. She'd finished work at five the day before and hadn't seen anyone or anything out of the ordinary. I described the victim as best I could, without having a face to go on.

"About five feet six, dark skin, long black hair, maybe Hispanic. Large-breasted woman and not afraid to show them off. High heels, skintight pants. She might have been a pro, but you don't get many at this hotel, I'm told. And she might have been Catholic—she had a Saint Andrew medal around her neck."

"I don't know, Detective," Arlene said. "Unless she came in and ordered something, I wouldn't remember. I got enough on my hands dealing with these jokers."

"Hey, hey, I gotta go." Ritchie Wollensky was up and out of the booth, throwing a ten-dollar bill on the table. "Gotta go, gotta go. Sorry, guys, gotta get out to Santa Anita. Gotta meet some people there. Hey, Officer, great meetin' ya. Great. Hope ya figure out who the gal is. I hope ya do."

With his fingers he swiped both sides of his hair back up to meet in the middle. They stayed. He bounced toward the exit. He was moving fast, but I caught him midstride with my voice. "Mr. Wollensky," I said, "I'd appreciate it if you'd take my card. Anything comes up you can think of that might help us, give me a call. And good luck at the track." I stuffed my card in his T-shirt pocket.

"He always that hyper?" I asked Tom. He was coked up, that's for sure, but it seemed like my description of the dead girl had spooked him.

"Aw, yeah, that's Ritchie. What a jamoke. Always bouncin' on his toes, especially when the horses are running."

Tom and Jimmy Schmidt didn't have anything else to add. I wasn't so sure about Ritchie Wollensky. Maybe I'd track him down and ask a few more questions. I took down Tom's contact information. He was staying at the hotel for another week while he guest-starred as G. W. Bailey's twin brother on *The Closer*. I gave them both my card, repeated the routine with Arlene, and walked out to see how the divers were doing searching the pond.

CHAPTER TWENTY-TWO

By the time I got home from the Sportsmen's, I was going on thirty-six hours without sleep, which is par for the course when I'm working a case. You'd have to be living in a cave to not know the forty-eight-hour adage. Hell, A&E even used it for the title of a series. The chance of solving a murder is cut in half if we don't come up with a lead in the first forty-eight hours.

I'd interviewed everyone I could interview, and for the first time in my career I had information no other cop could possibly possess. Unless Ovsanna had some of her clan on the force, and that didn't seem likely. I was the only cop in town who knew our L.A. perps could be creepy-crawlies . . . shape-shifters, creatures from the black lagoon, *The Thing* in its 1980s version. I'd seen them with my own eyes, and I was a believer. So when I saw the way that girl's body had been torn up, I didn't think forty-eight hours of intensive police work was going to break the case. That's why I'd asked Ovsanna to touch the body. I'm a fast learner. I knew supernatural killers need supernatural help tracking them down. In the meantime, all I could do was talk to everybody I could talk to, wait for the autopsy report, and see if the print the crime techs had pulled off the St. Andrew medal was in the system.

Besides, asking Ovsanna down to the Coroner's had given me more time to spend with her without breaking any rules about fraternizing with someone who's involved in one of my cases. But I didn't know how much longer I could push that envelope. I'd had an acceptable excuse when the Captain asked what we were doing together at the Coroner's. There was no way I could explain the Armenian restaurant.

I needed to get some rest and think about what the next step was with Ovsanna. There really couldn't be one. Not as long as the Cinema Slayer case was still open. I was going to have to pull the plug; I just wasn't sure how. I flashed on the monster she'd become when she was enraged—no, I mean *literally* the monster she'd become—and wondered how she'd react to being told I couldn't see her anymore. Maybe I'd better stock up on Solarcaine.

My problem was I wanted her. Badly. I wanted inside her. Not just inside her body—I didn't know *what* to expect from that—but inside her core. Her being. Whatever she was. I wanted to know her, all five centuries of her.

This could be nothing but trouble. Not just her connection to the case, but what about her connection to Maral McKenzie? It's not enough I'm attracted to a bloodsucking female, she's got to have another female in her life she's sucking?

Damn.

I was so tired that I almost missed the mess under my front gate. Remains of a coyote, maybe, or a bobcat. Just the hair, but a lot of it. How the hell did it end up under the gate? It wasn't just one animal, either. Some of it looked like cat hair, and some was thick and coarse, a coyote or a dog. I unlocked the side door to the garage and pulled a broom off the wall. When I swept the hair into the dustpan, a handful of needles and pins and rusty nails went with it. Where they'd come from I didn't have a clue, but I was too tired to give it much thought.

I went right to the living room and sat on the floor, my back against the couch and my legs crossed. I do a form of self-hypnosis I learned from a writer on *L.A. Undercover,* the cop show that used me as a technical adviser. They weren't too interested in making anything technically correct, especially if it interfered with the plot, so I ended up with a lot of time on my hands, and I used to watch this guy sitting at his laptop, mumbling to himself before he'd zone out for ten minutes. Then he'd be up and bouncing around. We were on the set sometimes for sixteen hours straight, and he was always energetic. At first I thought it was speed, but I finally asked him, and it wasn't; he was hypnotizing himself into relaxing and coming out of it as though he'd had a full night's sleep. So I had him teach me.

I took three deep breaths, then visualized a flight of stairs leading down to a cool basement room. Started counting backward from ten as I saw myself walking down the stairs. Never even made it to number four.

Fifteen minutes later, I woke up, feeling like I'd slept for hours. SuzieQ was sitting at my kitchen counter, staring at me. I hadn't even heard her come in.

"I just think that's the greatest trick in the world, sugar. I tried TM once; I have a friend who went to that Maharishi University— MUM, they call it—in Iowa, and she swears it lowers her blood pressure. But I just can't sit still long enough to ever do it right."

"I think that's the point, SuzieQ. Sitting still *is* doing it right."

"Well, whatever floats your boat, hon. Speakin' a which, how did the rest of the evening go with Ovsanna? Did you spend the night at her house? Ooo, fuckin' a movie star. That is so hot!"

"You don't know the half of it."

I hadn't had breakfast or lunch, and watching Tom Atkins down a burger at the Sportsmen's had my stomach growling. I put a couple of apple chicken sausages in a fry pan and beat half a dozen eggs for omelets for Suzie and me. Suzie likes sun-dried tomatoes and Gruyère; I add avocado to mine. It's a custom we got into after my divorce from Jen. On Sundays, if I'm not working and SuzieQ hasn't had some guy spend the night, I cook breakfast for us. We sit outside and read the paper and eat.

This afternoon, I just needed food and energy. I washed down a couple of ginseng tablets with a can of Guru while Suzie made coffee. We ate at the kitchen counter.

"So, tell me," Suzie said. "Is she as hot as she looks? And what about her friend, that McKenzie gal? What's the story there?" Suzie had worked with both women on a film several years earlier and had warned me about Maral after I'd first interviewed her and Ovsanna. Suzie thought Maral was overly possessive of her boss. Seemed like it was months ago we'd had that conversation, but it had been only three weeks. A lot had happened in the interim.

I couldn't tell her the real story—"Oh hey, Ovsanna's a vampyre and Maral is her food supply"—so I kept it simple. "It's a business relationship. Ovsanna bailed McKenzie out of a legal mess years ago— you know, the one where she killed the guy and claimed self-defense— and Maral's been working for her ever since."

"Well, I told you, when I was doin' *Snake God* I sure got the feelin' they was more than employer/employee. I didn't know she was a killer. I didn't like her very much. She was real protective of Ovsanna; wouldn't let anybody get near her. And look, now you're datin' her. Maybe you better be careful." She got up to pour us both coffee.

"I can take care of myself, SuzieQ, I'm a big boy. What I've got to be careful about is my professional responsibility. I shouldn't be seeing the woman at all." I drink mine black. I watched while Suzie stirred three teaspoons of sugar into hers. "In fact, I think I've got to stop."

"Why?" She looked at me like I was crazy.

"Because she's involved in the Cinema Slayer case. I could lose my job if the Captain finds out." And besides, she's a fucking vampyre. Who I'd like to be fucking. I think. Jesus, I don't know. I didn't know what I was getting myself into. I wished I could tell SuzieQ the whole story. I could have used her advice.

On the other hand, she's a six-foot-tall bisexual Texan who likes kissing snakes—not exactly Dear Abby.

CHAPTER TWENTY-THREE

I love my house in Malibu. I'd love it even more if it were in Massachusetts or Maine, but I'd never get there, so Malibu it is. North of Malibu, actually. On a cliff at the end of a finger of land jutting out into the Pacific. It has stairs cut into the rocks, leading down to a beautiful stretch of beach. It's only ten acres of land, but it's fairly inaccessible and completely private, and that's why I love it.

I bought the land in 1979, two years after I'd seen Jane Fonda and Vanessa Redgrave in *Julia*. I saw the movie once, but the location they used—that house on the east coast of Maine—resonated so deeply with me that I couldn't forget it. At the time, it was completely impractical for me to leave L.A. or I would have attempted to buy that very house. Instead, I found this piece of land on the West Coast that was as isolated as the one in the film, and I held on to it until I could afford to build the house I wanted.

Which I did, six years later. It's a Cape Cod colonial with gray clapboard shutters and white shingles and a red front door. Not very large. I don't entertain there, I withdraw; it's my hideaway. Lots of windows facing the ocean. Lots of comfortable sofas covered in yellow and white Ralph Lauren florals and stripes. Lots of books to read in front of the four fireplaces. Mostly mysteries: John Sandford, Julie Smith, Henning Mankell, Robert Crais, Robert Parker. And my collection of Van Goghs, gifts from Vincent when we left Paris for Arles together.

Once again I was getting ready to see Peter, and this time I was even more nervous than Christmas Eve or last night. It seemed pretty likely he was coming to spend the night. I hadn't made love to anyone besides Maral since I shoved my dead business partner's welt-marked ass out of my bed six years ago. I'd been going through my "wouldn't it be nice to have someone to take care of me" stage, and Thomas seemed to fit the bill. For all of about four minutes. I kicked him out when I realized I wasn't the source of the welts. He made a better business partner than lover, anyway.

I stepped into my closet and stared at the clothes I had there. On the far wall was a window separating the shelves where my sweaters were folded and the hanging rods that held my skirts and pants. I could see through it to the edge of the cliff and the beach far below.

Someone was down there. Someone who didn't belong. Someone with a camera and a telephoto lens.

Shit.

It was probably a fan. Maybe a paparazzo. He was alone, so I didn't think it was anyone I knew from the usual crowd of photographers who cover all the industry events and celebrity sightings. They always travel in packs. Probably a lone wolf who hoped he could get a candid shot of me in a string bikini, with cellulite-dimpled thighs and a stretch-marked belly, locking lips with some young stud on my private beach. That'll be a cold day in hell. Literally. I could live long enough for the fires of hell to burn out and I'd never have cellulite or stretch marks. I barely have a belly.

The young stud part could happen, though. Maybe tonight. Peter might not qualify as young, but compared to me . . .

Anyway, I wasn't going to do anything about the shutterbug right then. I had Peter coming over; I didn't want my security company arriving while he was here. There was no way the guy could get closer to the house without climbing the stairs up the cliff, and the stairs were secured with gates at the bottom and the top, requiring my face scan to unlock them. He'd probably get bored and leave on his own once he realized he couldn't get any shots through my treated windows.

I pulled an Elie Saab sleeveless sheath off a hanger and went back in the bedroom to slip it on. No bra. The neckline was low and the dress had one built in. I don't need a bra, anyway. No cellulite, no stretch marks, no belly fat, no drooping nipples. The advantages of being vampyre.

The phone rang as I was brushing my hair. Very few people have the number at the beach house. I picked it up, expecting Maral.

"Ovsanna, darling, it is I, Pola." Pola Negri, one of my clan. One of the Vampyres of Hollywood.

"Hello, Pola. How did you get this number?" Maral knows better than to give it to anyone without asking my permission. Even members of my clan. This is my private place.

"I called Ernst Solgar. I hope you don't mind, darling. I told him it vas an emergency."

"And is it? Are you all right, Pola? You disappeared so quickly after that night in Palm Springs, I assumed you'd gone back to San Antonio to hide."

"I did. Oh, darling, I so vish I had turned my friend Margaret before she died. These last forty-five years have been so lonely. And then Ronnie Reagan passed and there vas no one to campaign for. And my beloved Rudy—the great Rudolph Valentino—turns out to be the shit heel of all time. I am still reeling from the vay he treated us all in Palm Springs. Your detective friend killed him not a moment too soon. Not a moment too soon, darling. How *dare* Rudy speak to me like that, that Italian Guinea Vop."

"My detective friend is half Italian, Pola. If he hears you talk like that, he just might kill you, too. Now what's the emergency? I don't have much time to talk." Peter would be arriving any minute and I didn't have my makeup on.

"Ovsanna, darling. I'm so bored. I'm going crazy sitting around after all that excitement in Palm Springs. I need someting to do. I need a job. I vas tinking, now that Thomas is dead—"

"Don't be ridiculous. You couldn't do what Thomas was doing. He was practically running the studio, for Christ's sake."

"No, no, darling. Not Thomas's job. I vant to act again. I couldn't ask vhile Thomas vas around, but now, you could put me in one of your movies. I can change my name. Let my eyebrows grow in. I don't tink anyone vould recognize me. The ones who might—Tallulah and Gloria and that pig Milton Berle—are all dead. Except for our clan, and they von't say anyting. Oh please, Ovsanna. I'm so bored. I need a job."

"Pola, have you been to the movies lately? Have you seen any good roles for women your age? Unless you're Dame Judy or Helen Mirren, the only place you might find something interesting is cable television."

"Vat do you mean, my age? I am ageless, darling. And you do interesting tings all the time. Surely you can find someting for me. Maybe a remake of *The Graduate* with Adam Lambert."

Oh, my God. Anne Bancroft must be turning in her grave. I told Pola I'd see what I could do and got her off the phone. I didn't tell her her accent hadn't improved at all in the last eighty years and that was the reason her film career came to an end to begin with. Or that the reason I do interesting things is that I write them myself. She'd be begging me to write a film for her.

A half hour later, Peter arrived. I had fires burning in two fireplaces, candles lit all over the house. I didn't know what kind of music he liked besides the Doobies, so I went with Nina Simone to start. She seemed right for the fog that had settled outside. God, it had been so long since I'd shared music with someone. Maral had been working for me for a year before we became lovers, and ours was never a romance to begin with. We liked some of the same music—Peter Gabriel, 3 Doors Down, Phil Collins, and of course the Nevilles, the Radiators, and BeauSoleil—but I'd never gotten excited about introducing her to any of the artists I loved or the operas and symphonies whose premieres I had attended. I'd never told her I was sitting with Diaghilev for the first performance of *Le Sacre du Printemps,* when the riot broke out. She didn't even know who he was. I wondered if Peter knew Tyrone Wells or Eva Cassidy. Valerie Carter. Judy Henske. Marshall Chapman. I couldn't wait to find out.

CHAPTER TWENTY-FOUR

It took me more than an hour to drive up the coast and find the dirt road that led off PCH to Ovsanna's driveway. I pressed the button on the intercom and waved at the camera. The fog was pretty thick, but there were high-intensity lights cutting through the blackness; with the top down on the Jag, I must have been easily recognizable. The gate opened. I drove another quarter of a mile to a second gate. Repeated the procedure. Finally parked in front of a magnificent Cape Cod house that looked like something out of a movie. Like the Kennedys' compound in Hyannis Port.

Ovsanna was waiting outside the front door. She's done that every time I've gone to her house. I like it. She was barefoot, with her arms exposed. I don't think vampyres notice the weather very much; she never seems to be bothered by the cold. Except for her hair. The moisture in the air had frizzed it into a mass of black ringlets.

I grabbed a handful of them and brought her face up to meet my lips. I kissed her, hard at first because I couldn't wait any longer, because I'd been thinking about it for the hour it had taken me to get there and all the hours before, my lips grinding against hers and feeling the shock of her response. And then softer and gentler, exploring just her lips, not her mouth; not sure what I'd find there when I ran my tongue over her teeth, not quite ready for anything nonhuman.

She pulled away and looked up at me. Her eyes were huge. Liquid black. She was smiling. "Pardon the pun," she said, "but . . . would you like to come inside?"

Chapter Twenty-Five

Peter looked so sexy that it was all I could do to keep from throwing him down on the porch and fucking him right then and there. He had on jeans, a leather jacket, black Johnny Ramone Vans, and a Rolling Stones T-shirt. The jeans fit. The T-shirt fit even better. I didn't give a shit about the Vans.

Without my heels, my head just grazed his chin. He made me feel small and feminine, and I liked that. That's not the way I see myself, so it's fun for a change. I was smiling when I led the way into the living room.

But when I turned around to resume our embrace, he walked past me towards the back windows.

"There's someone out there," he said, pressing his face against the glass. "I just saw movement down on the beach." I saw him reach his hand around to touch the small of his back and realized that's where he had his gun.

"It's just a fan, I think. Or a photographer with nothing better to do on a slow news night. He can't see in. The windows are tinted for privacy. And he can't get any closer than the beach, so you can relax.

If he gets really annoying, I'll turn into a pelican and go down and poke out his eyes." It was a new experience: teasing about my true nature. I was having fun. Maral's the only other human who knows what I am, and her sense of humor ends with using "Werewolves of London" for her ring tone.

Peter wasn't smiling, though. He declined my offer of wine or something to drink and perched on the edge of the sofa, waiting for me to sit opposite. "I can't relax, Ovsanna," he said, "not until I can explain why I came out here, and why I'm not staying."

I felt the blood begin to pound in my body. My skin started to flush. "I thought the reason you came out here *was* to stay. What was that kiss you just gave me?" Anger flashed through me. I was aroused, wanting desperately to change. I tried to stay calm long enough to let him talk.

"Look, Ovsanna, you *know* I'm attracted to you. Every minute we've been together since Christmas has been leading up to this. It was all I could think about, driving up here. I want to make love to you. I have the feeling if I do, I'll never want to stop. And that would be great, if I didn't have a job to do. But I do." He stood up and walked back to the window. "I mean, I've already done it, but no one knows that except you and me and your . . . fucking vampyres! No one else knows the Cinema Slayer is dead. So I can't close the case. And you were involved in the case. Hell, Maral was even a suspect for a while. So as long as the case is open, I can't sleep with you! I can't even see you without a good excuse for the Captain. Do you understand that?" He turned back and looked at me with such pleading in his eyes that I couldn't let my anger overwhelm me.

But I couldn't keep it under control, either. My fangs unsheathed and my eyes turned red. I was royally pissed. I'd been imagining this night for days now, and this was not what I'd imagined. My vision sharpened, but the color leached out of everything. Peter's face was defined in shades of black and gray. I looked past him out the window at the photographer on the beach, and my frustration and rage found an immediate target for release. Fuck Peter King and his ex-

planations. Fuck his attack of conscience and his integrity. I wanted
to tear something apart. I wanted blood.

In an instant I was in the sand, screaming at the poor bastard
with the camera. He stared at me with his mouth hanging open,
stunned at my sudden appearance from nowhere. "What the fuck
are you doing out here?" I screamed. "You're trespassing, you son of
a bitch!" Talk about misplaced anger. I tore the strap from around
his neck and hurled his camera into the water. It was heavy, but I
tossed it like a pebble.

I turned back, expecting to see him cowering. My fangs hadn't
dropped yet, but even in the dark, he'd seen my red eyes. And my
voice, when I'm angry, can level a baseball stadium. They don't call
me the Scream Queen for nothing.

He wasn't cowering. He had something around his neck, some
sort of fur band, and he was rubbing it, muttering to himself. His human scent dissipated, replaced by something lupine and feral, and I
knew in an instant what was happening. That band was a talisman; he
was using black magic. His clothes ripped apart as his body changed
shape, his shirt and jacket shredding at the seams. His haunches tore
through his jeans as if they were tissue paper. The smell of wolf was
eye-watering.

The paparazzo was a fucking boxenwolf. He'd used the talisman
around his neck to shape-shift, and he was coming at me. What was
it with me and wolves these days? First the monster were at the
house in Bel Air and now this prick bastard. You'd think I was in
heat or something.

The boxenwolf was big. Not as big as the werewolf from Saturday
night, but big enough to give me trouble. Bigger than a Grey and a
lot more vicious. He circled me, snarling and snapping. I extended
my claws and dropped my fangs. Wolves are very expressive; you
can see their emotions in their eyes. This one wasn't surprised I was
a vampyre.

He backed away from me and started howling. I moved in on
him, slashing at his throat. The fur talisman protected his neck. I

came away with clumps of mangy brown hair under my nails but no flesh. He backed away again, his hind legs in the tide. I didn't understand why he was retreating—until fangs clamped around my bare leg and something powerful struck me from behind. I went down in the surf, and the rest of his pack attacked.

There were five of them. All wearing fur-pelt talismans around their necks. All boxenwolves. Powerful. Ferocious. I shoved myself up from the waves, used one hand to throw one of them—a gray-coated female—farther into the ocean, and sank my teeth into the snout of the male who had me by the leg. I shook him loose; he came away with a chunk of my calf in his mouth. The smell of my blood and his blood together worked on me like a shot of meth. I crushed his muzzle between my teeth.

The gray female was fighting the undertow twenty feet from shore. That left my buddy the photographer and his three pack mates. We had a moment's standoff while the four of them circled me and I held down the fifth in the sand. The pain in his snout left him barely struggling. He was yipping instead.

And then again they attacked.

CHAPTER TWENTY-SIX

Ovsanna had barely heard my explanation and she was out the door. At least, I think she was out the door. She disappeared. One second I was telling her I couldn't see her until I had some way to close the Cinema Slayer case, and the next she wasn't there.

I called out for her. The house was silent; she wasn't anywhere near me. The front door was locked from the inside, but I opened it and scanned the driveway. Nothing. My Jag was parked in front of the door. I popped the trunk, grabbed my jacket and my flashlight, and walked over to the south side of the house, letting my eyes adjust to the dark. Whatever moonlight there might have been was obliterated by fog; I couldn't see past the cliff face. I could hear something, though. Ovsanna's voice cut through the blackness. She was screaming.

I pulled my gun and made my way to the back of the house. I still couldn't see the beach; the fog was impenetrable, a moving wall of gray moisture. Ovsanna had lights set low to the ground along a stone path in the grass, leading out to the edge of the cliff. I followed them. The face of the cliff on either side of the house was sheer granite, almost straight down. Huge boulders jutted out in the center. With the flashlight, I could barely make out the footholds they had carved in them—a stairway down to the sand.

It was blocked by a decorative iron gate with some kind of keyless lock. The lock held the whole thing shut with a foot-long steel bar. I couldn't shoot it off. The decorative parts were razor-sharp fleurs-de-lys across the top edge, some designer's version of barbed wire. I looked around for something to stand on.

Ovsanna had stopped screaming. Instead, I heard coyotes. There must have been a pack of them, howling and yipping. I'd seen Ovsanna in action; I wasn't too worried about her ability to handle a few coyotes. But I didn't like hearing her scream, even if she was just pissed at me. And on second thought, what if the one thing vampyre powers didn't work against was coyotes?

I hauled a patio table over to the gate, stacked a ladder on top of that, and scaled the fleur-de-lys spikes, putting just a few gouges in my legs. At least I was up-to-date on my tetanus. I used my flashlight to follow the stairs down the rocks.

Goddamn it, wouldn't you know there'd be another gate at the bottom of the stairs. This one was just as tall, maybe sixteen feet. Same keyless lock. Same spikes.

I climbed back up the stairs to a point where I thought I'd cleared the top of the gate. The fog was so thick, I couldn't be sure. I went up a couple more feet. Studied the face of the cliff in my light and then shoved it in my jeans, still on and facing up. Using the spaces in between the boulders for handholds, and feeling for places I could wedge my feet, I climbed onto the cliff, my body hanging vertically, and moved south, toward the sound of the coyotes. When I was sure I was past the side of the gate, I loosed one hand and foot and swung out so I was facing the ocean with my back to the rocks, grabbing on to the far boulders. Then I prayed for soft sand below me and let go.

I landed on my hands and knees. Nothing broke but the flashlight. The lid came off and the batteries rolled toward the water. The fog wasn't quite as thick on the ground, but I didn't bother trying to find them. Those howls I was hearing weren't coyotes. Fifty feet away from me, Ovsanna was on the ground in the surf, surrounded by what looked like a pack of wolves.

I pulled out my Glock and fired into the darkness.

Chapter Twenty-seven

Even over the growls and howling, I could hear someone coming, and then I smelled Peter—his scent and his blood. It was flooded with endorphins and adrenaline. He's worried about me, I thought as I kicked the wolf closest to me in the ribs and heard bones crack. I didn't want to call out to Peter because I didn't want the boxenwolves to know he was there.

The wolf I'd kicked retreated behind the mangy brown one that had been a paparazzo minutes earlier. I understood now why he'd been on the beach: to get me out of the house and lure me down where his buddies could tear me apart. He lunged at me, teeth bared in a rabid snarl. I let loose the muzzle of the gray male and rolled to the left, just as a gun fired. The brown boxenwolf crashed onto the sand, all two hundred pounds of him, right on the spot where I'd just been. He was bleeding from his shoulder; Peter had hit him from the back, behind his right foreleg.

I used my claws to hamstring him, then threw myself on his back and tried to sink my teeth into his neck. The talisman was thick and wide, like one of those collars African tribeswomen wear to elongate their necks. I shredded it with my teeth and tore the thing off with my hands, spitting out flesh and fur. I had a momentary image of a blond woman in a fur coat, playing video games.

Peter fired two more shots. Either he trusted himself as a marksman or he wasn't worried the bullets would harm me. He aimed past me at the three remaining beasts. They'd turned tail as soon as the brown one went down. They were racing down the beach. Faster than a speeding bullet, I guess, because Peter's shots missed. The Grey with the crushed muzzle was gone, too. I didn't see the female in the ocean. I don't think she could have survived that undertow.

The brown boxenwolf was still alive, but he wasn't going anywhere. Except back to his original shape. Peter got to my side just in time to see the wolf's body shift back to its human form: pale-skinned, tall, and narrow-chested, with a round beer belly protruding over his skinny legs and little penis. No wonder he needed magic.

Peter covered him with his jacket, bent down, and shone his flashlight on his face. "What's your name?" he asked, but the man was beyond speaking. Blood frothed out of his mouth and washed away in the surf. I sheathed my fangs, retracted my claws, and helped Peter pull his dead body onto dry sand.

Chapter Twenty-Eight

I holstered my gun and kept the flashlight on the body. "What the hell just happened?" I asked. "I was shooting at a wolf and there's a dead man on the ground."

"He's the photographer we saw from the house. He was a boxen-wolf, Peter. He was using magic to transform into a werewolf."

"Magic? What kind of magic turns someone into an animal? I thought he was one of you. What the hell, Ovsanna? Are there more weirdos around than just vampyres and those things in Palm Springs? How much more of this supernatural shit am I supposed to buy? Goddamn it to hell!"

"I don't know if I'd call it supernatural. It's magic. He was using a talisman and a mantra. I saw him mumbling to himself before he changed. That wolf pelt was the talisman." She motioned to a shred-ded strip of drenched fur lying next to the dead body. I picked it up and studied it. Looked like roadkill to me.

"And what about those other guys? I counted three wolves around you and one on the ground. Did they start out as humans, too?"

"Yes, I think so. There was another one in the water. I threw her out there, and I don't think she made it back. They all had fur collars around their necks—pelt belts, I guess you could call them. Talismans. They were all boxenwolves, Peter. Five men and a woman using magic to shift. Running in a pack, just like regular wolves."

"Who do you think they are? And why were they after you? Are they all paparazzi? Have you sued some tabloid lately?"

"The last time I had a problem with a tabloid was when the *Enquirer* printed I was using Botox to get rid of my wrinkles. Pissed me off. I can't watch these actresses who distort their faces with that stuff. They can't move their muscles and they expect to emote? They're even using it on their children! And what's the message they're giving society—you're only valuable if you've got an unlined mask for a face? I wouldn't use it even if I needed it. I sued the damn magazine for a retraction."

"Well, somebody's out to get you. And this guy was a photographer, so that's where I start." I searched the area for a wallet or some kind of ID, but if he'd been carrying anything before he changed, the tides had taken it. There was no sign of anything that had just happened, except for his body. And that gave me an idea.

"Ovsanna, I'm going to go back to my car to get my gym bag out of the trunk. I've got a pair of sweats and a warm-up jacket that should fit this guy. Then we're going to talk about what just happened. How you called me because you'd found a threatening note from the Cinema Slayer in your mailbox out on the highway, and how you'd taken a walk while you were waiting for me to arrive, and I'd gotten here just in time to see someone attacking you on the beach. Thank God you'd left the gates open." I could see Ovsanna's mind working as she understood what I was planning. She shook her head in surprise.

"I thought I was the horror writer," she said. "Are you sure this is what we should do?"

"Look, this guy tried to kill you. We don't know who he is, but we know he was running around as a werewolf. No one's going to believe that. Just like no one will ever believe the Cinema Slayer was a Baby Jane look-alike who was born before Christ and has a bunch of werecreature kids running around. I can't produce her body, even if I wanted to try to convince someone. And without a body, I can't close the case. Well . . . here's a body. A human body. He was after you, just like Lilith was, and I can't think of one good reason why he won't work as the Slayer in her place."

I pulled out my cell phone to call the Coroner. "We've just got to get our stories straight."

CHAPTER TWENTY-NINE

Peter and I went over the details of our version of the attack. The waves had washed away the pack's paw prints and the photographer's clothes, so there was no crime scene to explain. A chunk of my leg was either in the ocean or some wolf's stomach. It didn't matter; my body was already healing. In an hour, there wouldn't be any sign I'd been attacked. Peter stripped down in the dark and put his briefs on the dead body for verisimilitude. I don't think he realized what a heightened sense of vision I have when I choose to use it. I chose, all right. I'm glad I did.

Peter's warm-up jacket was way too big on the guy. We soaked it in the water, along with the sweats. By the time the Coroner cut them off, they'd still be wet and clinging. We could easily explain Peter's DNA—he'd carried the body out of the waves. Peter held the jacket in the sand and fired a bullet through it to match the spot on the body where his bullet had entered. The water was a blessing. They wouldn't expect to find much blood; most of it would have been washed away. Along with the threatening note I would say I'd received. I'd had it in my hand when the man had attacked me.

I "remembered" what it said, though, almost verbatim: "I've killed your friends and your partner. You're next. Aren't you sorry you never hired me to take your head shots?" And it was signed "C.S."

If that didn't convince Peter's Captain he'd killed the Cinema Slayer, I didn't know what would.

The only thing we had trouble explaining was how I'd managed to sever the man's hamstring. It took a while, but I finally found a broken abalone shell with a sharp edge. I sliced it deep along the cuts my claws had made on his leg.

We were going to have to find out who the photographer was, to make sure there was nothing about him that wouldn't fit with our story. Peter had to go back to his office to write up the report. He didn't want me to stay at the beach alone, and I didn't argue. I sort of liked having him think he was the boss.

We'd just been through our second battle with beasties and he didn't seem to be running for cover. I decided it was safe to tell him about the earlier attack.

He didn't run for cover, but he sure got pissed. "You fought off one of these things an hour before I picked you up and you never told me?! Why not?"

"Well, it wasn't exactly one of *these* things. These things are box-enwolves. The thing that attacked me Saturday night was a true were."

"It was a *werewolf,* Ovsanna, a fucking preternatural monster that was trying to kill you! I don't care what *breed* it was! You should have told me!"

"Well, I didn't know how you'd react. And there wasn't anything you could do about it, the thing took off. I haven't seen any sign of him since."

"Yeah? Maybe I have. There was animal hair all over my walkway this afternoon. I thought it was a dog or a coyote, but it could have been one of these freaks. If I'd known you were being tracked, I would have paid more attention. Jesus, Ovsanna, you've got to keep me in the loop. I'm on your side here. I told you on the phone—take advantage of me. This may not be what I had in mind when I said it, but it's what I do. I want to keep you safe."

Isn't that sweet? In 450 years, no one's ever said that to me. Of course, they've never had to. I wasn't about to disabuse Peter of the thought. It was fun having a knight in shining armor. Just like I said—Doc Ford and Jack Reacher, only in real life.

Chapter Thirty

I changed into dry clothes, left Peter waiting for the Coroner's van, and drove back to Bel Air. The fog never let up until I got inland, and by the time I got home, it was almost one o'clock.

Maral was awake and waiting. She looked luscious in her long-sleeved nightshirt, but I was too distracted by the boxenwolves' attack to do more than notice. Besides, she was loaded, which didn't help my mood any.

Driving home, I'd gone over and over the story Peter and I had concocted to see if it was believable. The surprising part to me was that it was Peter's idea to begin with. I didn't think there was anything too morally wrong with it, but it was definitely outside the law. I knew it went against his nature, but really, what was the alternative? Blaming the murder on werewolves and vampyres was a stretch, even in a town that buys Anne Heche as Jesus's half-sister Celestia.

"It's late, Maral, why aren't you asleep?"

"I had a nightmare. You and Peter were at the beach, and you were eating real food. He kept feeding you lemon Stilton and you were rubbing your face in a crystal bowl of rice pudding. It was all over you. When I tried to pull you away to offer you my wrist, you laughed at me and poured Kool-Aid on my head. Then you handed me a box of Band-Aids. And then Peter grabbed my MacBook Air and he was scheduling appointments for you in my calendar. I tried to get it away from him, but he threw it at me, and it was so thin it sliced through my neck and cut my jugular. Blood poured out all over the screen. I woke up crying."

"Jesus. And then you smoked a joint?"

"Well, I had to do something, Ovsanna, and you weren't here. What happened? Why did you come home? Didn't lover boy show up?"

"Maral, I know you're upset, but you're acting your age and it's not attractive. Yes, Detective King showed up. Just in time to stop a pack of werewolves from tearing me to pieces."

"Werewolves? Why? Who were they?" She started backing up, her voice rising. "Were they those creatures we fought in Palm Springs?"

"I don't know, sweetheart. I don't know." I followed her, putting my hands on her to try to calm her down. A vision came, of her at a grave site. She had something red in her hand, a flannel cloth or bag or something. I was too distracted to ask her about it. "They weren't werecreatures. Not like Lilith's kindred. Although the one that attacked me on Christmas Eve was. But these tonight were boxenwolves—humans, using magic to shape-shift."

"A werewolf attacked you on Christmas Eve? Where?"

"It was here. He came onto the property and the geese went nuts. I got rid of him."

"Oh God, Ovsanna, why didn't you tell me?" Her voice was shrill.

"I didn't want to frighten you. You didn't need to know. There was nothing you could have done."

"But you told him, didn't you? Didn't you? You think *he* can do something for you and I can't? Did you tell the mighty detective and he came out and saved you? Is that what this is all about?" She was shaking now and yelling at me.

I slapped her. Not hard. Just enough to stop her escalating hysteria. She's uncontrollable when she smokes. I slapped her and she started to cry.

I took her in my arms. "I'm sorry," I said, "but you need to calm down. That's the dope talking." I pulled away and wiped the tears from her face. "Now look, I want you to go upstairs and go to bed. I don't want to talk about this when you're stoned."

"Come with me, Ovsanna. Please, come and sleep with me. I'm frightened. I don't want to lose you."

"You're not going to lose me, Maral, you've got to believe me. And you know I can't sleep in your bed. I'll be right next door and you'll be safe. Just go to sleep. Peter and I are going out tomorrow morning to track down these wolves, and I need you in the office, taking care of business, while we do." I kissed her on the forehead. "Good night, Maral."

CHAPTER THIRTY-ONE

She didn't go to bed. I could hear her from my room, mumbling to herself. She struck a match and I smelled something foul, like burning motor oil. And then she started that same praying again. In the ten years we've been together, I'd never heard her pray before last night. This sounded like an incantation. Maybe more hoodoo she'd picked up when she was home.

I never sleep with Maral, even after we've made love. She's used to that. I explained early on that I can't always control my transformations. There's a constant danger that I might awaken in the middle of a change and need to feed. I've known too many vampyres who've awakened to find they'd drained their lover dead in their sleep.

She finished chanting and ran a bath. Whatever it was continued to burn; probably a candle. It was three o'clock before I heard her get in bed.

Two and a half hours later, she was up again. This time she was trying to be quiet. Whatever she was doing, she didn't want me to know.

I slipped out of bed just as quietly and waited while she dressed and let herself out the kitchen door. From my window, I watched her unlock the Lexus hybrid. She was wearing black sweats and black running shoes, and she obviously didn't want me to know she was leaving the house. She put the car in gear and coasted down the driveway before she started the engine.

I had a feeling she was going to the Sportsmen's Lodge. She was hell-bent on getting rid of her brother's friend, and I hadn't been any help. What she thought she could do on her own I had no idea, but I couldn't let her get into trouble. I was going to have to follow her.

I used a transformation I hadn't used in years. It wasn't easy. The older I get, the less I enjoy shape-shifting. It takes a real toll on my body. When I was younger, in the 1700s and 1800s, I loved using wings to get around Paris or Prague. I'd shift to a hawk or a falcon, anything but a bat. In those days, I thought bats were so clichéd. Theda Bara, one of my Vampyres of Hollywood, is Azeman, and they shift into bats every night. I couldn't do it. Not then and not now. Especially not now, when every time I come back to my "human" form, something is slightly out of whack. Like fur hanging from my ears. Waxing is a real pain in the ass.

The original form of Clan Dakhanavar is the *dragul,* the dragon. That's what I'd chosen in Palm Springs to go up against Lilith in her serpent outfit. God, she was hideous. A yellow-veined body with a scabrous scalp and a black forked tongue. It's a good thing she didn't survive. Once changed into a serpent, a vampyre can never change back. She would have hated giving up her Baby Jane makeup for good.

I couldn't follow Maral as a dragon. Even in L.A. that's asking a lot. And I didn't know for sure where she was going; I didn't feel like chasing the car as a dog.

I transformed into mist. It's not quite as dramatic as smoke, but I wouldn't be noticeable in the early morning cold. It was harder evaporating than it should have been, though. I'm really out of practice.

Maral turned left on Sunset, but instead of continuing to Coldwater and over the hill to the Sportsmen's, she made a right on Hilgard and drove past UCLA into Westwood Village. Then she went left on Glendon and crossed Wilshire and made a left behind the high-rise office building and up the driveway to the Avco Cinema parking lot. She turned right at the top of the drive and drove through the open iron gates into the Pierce Brothers Westwood Village Memorial Park and Mortuary. If I hadn't been mist, my jaw would have dropped.

Last night, holding her to calm her down, I'd had a vision of her at a grave site. Now, here she was again. Why?

The two of us had been here together before. I have friends buried here. Dean Martin, John Boles, Fanny Brice. Cassavetes and Capote and James Wong Howe. Swifty Lazar. Eva Gabor and Eve Arden. Maral came with me when Rodney Dangerfield died. It was the first time she'd seen a headstone with a joke on it. Rodney's reads, "There Goes the Neighborhood."

I've always loved Billy Wilder's: "I'm a writer, but then nobody's perfect."

The last time we were here was for a service for Merv Griffin. I miss him. He always made me laugh. Doing his talk show was great fun because he just loved to gossip, especially during the commercials. His gravestone reads, "I will not be right back after this message."

There was a single light on in the office. Maral parked down the lane from it, closer to Marvin Davis's mausoleum. An old pickup truck with Montana license plates followed her in. It parked on the opposite side of the cemetery, closer to the Farsi-engraved headstones. Three men got out, dressed in plaid flannel shirts, jeans, and lug boots. Two down parkas and an orange hunter's vest. Gardeners, maybe.

Whatever she was there for, Maral didn't want to be noticed. She had opened her car door and was starting to get out when she saw the three men. Immediately she slid back down in her seat and quietly pulled the door shut. She sat staring at them, watching their every move.

They weren't gardeners. All three of them took their Peet's coffee containers and their Maps to the Stars and spread out to read the markers on the graves. It was six thirty in the morning and these guys were fans. I'll bet they drove all the way from Montana just to see Marilyn's final resting place.

One of them went to the Sanctuary of Remembrance, and sure enough, the other two carried a potted poinsettia over to Marilyn Monroe. They took turns taking pictures of each other kissing her crypt.

Maral waited until they joined their buddy in the Sanctuary of Tenderness on the other side of the park. The sky was dark with rain clouds, and I wasn't helping visibility much. That seemed to be what she wanted. She stole silently over to the enclosed garden where Carroll O'Connor and Jack Lemmon were interred. She had a gardener's trowel in one hand. She looked up at the windows of the highrise—probably to make sure no one was watching—waited until the men in the sanctuary had their backs to her, and then reached inside her sweatshirt and withdrew a black candle stub from her bra. It gave off the same rank odor I'd smelled coming from Maral's bedroom earlier. Motor oil. And it looked like it had been rolled in red pepper flakes.

Quickly she dug in the space behind the stone that read, "Jack Lemmon in . . ." She deposited the remains of the candle in the hole and patted it over with the trowel. She was moving her lips as she dug. When I could have heard her clearly, back at the house, I hadn't wanted to intrude. Now that I needed to hear her, I couldn't. Mist is good for getting into places without being seen, but it's not so good for eavesdropping.

I hung in the air while she got back in the car and then followed her through Westwood until I was sure she was heading back to the house. She was using hoodoo, all right. That red bag I'd seen when I'd held her could have been a mojo bag. She must have been to a cemetery before. I didn't know enough about it to know exactly what she was trying to accomplish, but between the devil pod and the middle-of-the-night baths and the reeking candles, I wondered if her maw-maw hadn't told her some spell to get rid of DeWayne Carter, the guy she'd brought back from the swamps. Fine with me.

CHAPTER THIRTY-TWO

I waited until seven A.M. to call the Captain. I must have caught him in the shower; I could hear water splashing in the background. Telling the story over the phone was a little easier than doing it in person.

"It's all over, Chief. You can call the media."

"Hold on a minute." The water stopped. "What are you talking about? The Cinema Slayer? You got him?"

"Yep. The Cinema Slayer took a run at Ovsanna Moore last night. He didn't make it. He's through running."

"You've got him booked?"

"Nope. Not booked. Dead."

"Dead? Jesus! What happened? You're sure it's him?"

"Sure as I can be at this point. He left a note in her mailbox announcing she was his target all along. Then he bragged about it when he grabbed her." Ovsanna had insisted the two of us act out the story we were devising. That was making it easier to fabricate what I knew she'd be saying, too.

"What happened? Give me details."

"She called me as soon as she found the note. She was out at her beach house in Malibu. I got there in time to stop him."

"You shot him?"

"I shot him, yeah. Hell, yeah, I shot him. I didn't have any choice. It was a righteous killing, Captain. There won't be any trouble, believe me."

"Are you all right? You need to talk to somebody?"

"I'm fine. I'm just glad it's over. Hey, this town can get back to normal—whatever that is. And maybe the media will lighten up. I left my gun and my report on your desk. I'll use my backup until the investigation's over. He didn't have ID, but Ovsanna thinks she recognized him—he was a paparazzo—so until the prints come back I'm going to do some digging. I'll be around when Internal Affairs wants to talk."

I was still slightly pissed that Ovsanna hadn't trusted me enough to tell me she'd been attacked, even though it was before we'd spent any time together. Okay, so she didn't know me that well to know if I'd stick around, but I'm a cop, for Christ's sake. First and foremost, she should have known I'd protect her. I wondered if she'd told Maral.

I went out to check the trash cans, but they were empty, tossed on their sides like they always were after pickup. No animal hair left from under the gate. Too bad. I wanted to take a look at it again, show it to Ovsanna. Maybe it wasn't coyote at all. Maybe it was wolf. Werewolf. If those fucking things had come anywhere near my house . . . .

I needed to get an ID on the dead photographer. That much of what I'd told the Captain was the truth.

Ovsanna had gone online to some entertainment Web site and had printed a list of celebrity events happening that morning. I picked her up at her office and we drove down Wilshire to a fashion designer's showroom/warehouse. Dennis Hopper was scheduled to appear; his artwork was being displayed along with pieces by Tony Curtis and Peter Falk. There were bound to be paparazzi there.

I parked in a lot on a side street and gave the attendant an extra five to keep an eye on the Jag. It wasn't the greatest neighborhood. Once we got closer to the showroom, Ovsanna and I split up. She headed for the front entrance, where they actually had a red carpet and TV crew waiting at ten in the morning, and I badged myself into a side door of the warehouse. I made my way to the front of the showroom and watched her through the window. She was wearing a red dress that looked like it was made out of wide strips of Ace bandage. It hugged every curve of her body, and believe me, that was a lot of hugging. "Yes," I heard her tell the on-camera reporter, she'd worked with all three men at some time during her career, and she loved their artistry, on camera and on canvas. She waved at the photographers and came inside. None of the paps were the freelancers I was looking for; they must have been hired by the event planner to cover the show.

The showroom was pretty large. All along one wall there were mannequins posed like hookers, with their butts sticking out and tits exposed, wearing what I guessed were the designer's clothes. They looked as though they'd been through a shredder. My mother could have designed something better, and she doesn't sew. Live models, in the same shreds but without the flashing tits, stood like statues around the room. Occasionally they changed poses. That didn't do anything to make the clothes more attractive. Who wears this stuff? I wondered. Waiters walked through the crowd, offering mimosas. Maybe that would help.

Each wall had one piece of art displayed. All Tony Curtis. All very colorful and fun. Peter Falk's charcoal nudes lined a large hallway leading to doors that opened onto a loading dock. Dennis Hopper's work hung on the exterior walls of the loading dock, which was where most of the activity was taking place. That's where the bar and the DJ were. There were 150 people milling around, listening to hip-hop, eating miniature quiches and smoked salmon, and trying not to trip over a huge pile of garbage that had been left in the center of the dock. I'm serious. Right next to the bar was a heap of trash—a busted sofa, broken TV, empty paint cans, children's toys, a cable box. Some maintenance man hadn't done his job.

I scanned the crowd for paparazzi, saw a couple of flashes going off by the entrance to the dock. Dennis Hopper had just walked in. He didn't stop for photographs, though, just pushed his way through the crowd to the pile of garbage, right where Ovsanna and I were standing. He had a baseball bat in his hand. He smashed it down on the paint cans. Flakes of dried paint scattered into the air. Then he hit the trashed TV and started crushing the large glass pieces of the monitor. By that time, the paparazzi were on him, pressing in front of me to block my view. I watched the bat swing over their heads while he continued to demolish whatever else was in the pile. For a full ten minutes. Then he walked through the crowd into the show-room, still carrying the bat. He never said a word.

The paparazzi stayed behind, photographing the remaining rubble. I looked at Ovsanna, who was grinning back at me. "It's art," she said. "I'm not sure Leonardo would agree, but Dalí probably would." She tapped one of the photographers on the shoulder, and he turned around to face us. It was Johansson, one of the regulars. Pronounced with a *Y.*

"Hey, Ms. Moore, Detective King, can I have a shot?" He lifted his Canon and I shoved it down again.

"Forget it, Yo. I'm working here. Take a look at this picture, tell me if you know the guy. I think he's one of yours." I showed him a Polaroid the crime techs had shot on the beach.

"I guess he's not gonna be shooting at the Oscars anymore, is he? Ooh yah, that's Smooch."

"Smooch who?"

"Just Smooch. I don't know his last name. He runs with Steady Eddie, though, and that pack. I think they're over at the Celebrity Centre, waiting for Tom to make an appearance."

I wondered if he'd used the word *pack* on purpose or if it was just his figure of speech. "Tom?"

"Ooh yah, at the Church of Scientology. He's supposed to be meeting Kirstie Alley over there, give her some support while she films another fat commercial. I'm heading over there as soon as Dennis comes out and finishes demolishing the sofa."

It didn't make sense to expose Ovsanna to the scene at the Celebrity Centre, so I went west to Beverly Hills and dropped her off at her office, then headed east again to Franklin Avenue and the Manor Hotel, the replica of a seventeenth-century French castle that serves "the desperate few who are often the most neglected," according to the Scientology literature. They're talking about the celebrities.

It's a beautiful building, built in 1929 by Thomas Ince's widow. Tom being the guy who owned his own movie studio in the twenties and was rumored to have been killed by William Randolph Hearst while celebrating his birthday on Hearst's yacht. Now that I thought about it, Charlie Chaplin was on the yacht that day. I'll bet Ovsanna was, too. I'd have to remember to ask her; she probably knows the real story.

The building was originally called the Chateau Elysée, and everybody who was anybody in the thirties and forties stayed there: Gable, Gershwin, Bogart, Cary Grant, Errol Flynn. It's seven stories high, has a couple of restaurants, a theatre, a gym, a screening room, and a garden room that seats four hundred people. I went to a wedding there once. Freaked me out a bit, but nobody tried to convert me.

There were a few people standing on the front steps whose job that might be, but when they saw my badge, they ignored me. Johansson had beaten me to the location. He was talking to half a dozen photographers who were lined up behind a thick velvet rope on the sidewalk leading up to the building. Another thirty or so jostled for position behind a similar rope on the opposite side. Steady Eddie was in the smaller group. He had his back to me. He turned when Johansson pointed. His nose was covered in bandages.

"Eddie. Oh, Eddie," I said, "don't tell me it was you? Last night on the beach?"

He backed away from me a few steps, his hands going to his

nose. His mustache was gone; the doctors must have had to shave it off when they worked on him. I could see now why he'd worn it. His upper lip looked like a baboon's ass.

"What do you know?" he asked, alarm showing in his eyes. "Did I do something wrong?" It was hard to understand him with his nose closed up, but he didn't sound defensive, he sounded frightened. I grabbed one of his yellow suspenders and pulled him toward a side alley. He trotted along beside me until we were out of sight.

"Okay, what's going on, Eddie? What happened to your nose?"

"I don't know. I really don't know. I woke up this morning and it was broken, and my face was ripped open. Someone must have attacked me last night, but I blacked out. I don't remember."

"Someone must have attacked *you*? How about you attacked someone, Eddie? Huh? Someone famous? You don't remember that?"

He backed away from me again, his hands up in protest. "I don't know what you're talking about. I can't even find my camera. Did someone take pictures? Have you got my camera?"

"I don't need pictures, Eddie, I was there. Last night, on the beach in Malibu. You attacked Ovsanna Moore. You and your buddies. Does that jog your memory?"

"Oh no. Oh no. Ovsanna Moore? Oh no, I don't remember that. Oh, please, I'm telling you the truth. Are you sure it was me?" Sweat appeared on his bald scalp and trickled down his nose.

"It was you all right, Eddie. You had your collar on. I know what you are, Eddie, you can drop the charade."

"I . . . I . . . You know about my collar? You know about that?" His face had gone pale. He slumped down the wall and sat on the ground, staring up at me. "It's not a charade. You've got to believe me, I don't remember anything from last night. What did I do to her? Did I hurt her?" Blood started leaking through his bandages. I didn't want him to stroke before I found out what I needed to know.

"Calm down, Eddie, you're gonna have a heart attack. Yeah, I know about the collar. I guess I don't know how it works exactly, because I figured you'd know what I was talking about, but you really don't, do you?"

"I don't. I swear I don't. I don't remember being on any beach. I don't remember seeing Ms. Moore."

"What the fuck, Eddie? Why do you use it if you don't remember what happens when you do?"

"I remember how it feels, that's all. It feels great, Detective King. Suddenly I'm powerful and fast and strong. I can feel my muscles. And I'm free! I can do anything. Run and hunt—it's all instinct. No money worries, no fighting for the sleaziest shot of Lindsay or Jesse James and the Nazi girl. It's a fantastic high. Except I didn't remember about Ms. Moore. Is she all right? Did I hurt her?"

"You were tracking her, Eddie. You and a pack of your buddies. The only reason she's okay is because I got there and ran you off. But one of the other guys with a collar wasn't quite so lucky. You recognize him?"

I flashed the snapshot in front of him and watched his eyes roll back in his head. Luckily he was sitting down. I slapped his face a couple of times, which couldn't have felt good with the broken nose, and finally got him to focus. Yes, he said, he knew him; his name was Cyril Sinclair, and he was one of the regular paparazzi working the L.A. scene. Everyone called him Smooch. Eddie didn't know Smooch well, but he had his address on a business card in the camera case Eddie'd left in his car. I helped him up and we walked around the corner to where he was parked. Tom and Kirstie must have left already, because the crowd had dispersed. It didn't matter. I didn't need to talk to the other photographers. Without any wounds to help me identify them, I wouldn't know who else might have been on the beach. Eddie didn't remember them being there. And if their talismans worked like Eddie's, they wouldn't remember, either.

Chapter Thirty-three

Peter dropped me off and I went straight into Thomas's office. I needed something the cops could identify as belonging to Thomas: his business card or a sheet of letterhead or something. Something to further incriminate Smooch as the Cinema Slayer. Thomas's robe was monogrammed, but Maral had brought it to my office the day before, and she's not a good liar; I didn't want to risk the cops questioning her about it.

I found the perfect item in Thomas's bathroom drawer, hidden under a dog collar and some silk scarves. Leave it to Thomas to keep his sex toys close at hand. I'm surprised he even bothered to hide it.

It was a sterling silver cock ring with the initials *TDW* carved on it. Thomas DeWitte.

Absolutely perfect.

I found something else in his wastebasket in the closed cabinet under his sink. Something I didn't understand. The room had been cleaned since he was killed and no one should have been using it, especially not opening cabinet drawers to dispose of anything. It looked like part of the figure of a man. It was the broken half of a burnt, greenish yellow candle. The word *and* was cut into the wax, but it was almost obliterated by pinpricks. Whatever word had preceded it was on the missing half, and the candle had been burned down past the word that followed. It looked like more of Maral's hoodoo workings, but why was she leaving anything in Thomas's room?

I walked out of his office and into mine. Tyrone Power was sitting there. If I'd been human, my heart would have stopped. I palmed the cock ring out of his sight and stared at him. He looked just as gorgeous as he had before he staged his death on the set of *Solomon and Sheba* in Madrid in 1958. I never understood why he felt he had to "die" after I turned him or why he didn't wait to have me turn him until after he'd finished that film. He was enjoying working with Gina Lollobrigida and George Sanders. He could have insisted King Vidor get all his scenes in the can first and save the crowd scenes for last so they wouldn't have had to replace him, but he didn't. He begged me to do it in the middle of the shoot. Yul Brynner looked good in the role, but come on, he wasn't Ty Power—even with hair. King said later, "With Power, it would have been a marvelous picture. Without him, it turned out to be an unimportant, nothing sort of film." All Ty's ever said about it is that after doing *Nightmare Alley* and *The Eddie Duchin Story* and *Witness for the Prosecution,* he got on the set of *Solomon and Sheba* and couldn't face another costume epic.

It would be fun to screen the film for Peter sometime, to see if he could find Ty in the long shots they'd managed to keep.

He was wearing a black cashmere sweater and black slacks. His lashes were so thick that he might have been wearing black mascara, but I knew that wasn't the case. Tyrone Power was a man's man, and contrary to what you'd expect, he wasn't terribly vain. He wasn't wearing his hair slicked back with the left side part any longer, either. It was tousled and a little curly, just as thick as it had been the last time I'd seen him. He looked good.

"Chatelaine," he said, rising from the chair to kiss me on both cheeks. "You look stunning." He was right; I'd gone all out that morning, knowing the press was going to be at that art performance. The red Hervé Léger was worth the thirty-four hundred dollars I'd paid for it, even if it felt like I was wearing a full-body girdle.

"As do you, Ty. How did you get in here? You didn't just walk in, did you? The girls downstairs would have recognized you."

"They did. Indeed they did. One of them—Ilona, is it?—thought I was my son, and the other thought I was that good-looking actor on *Lost*. Nestor Carbonell. I hate to admit it, but there are times when a fan is so sure I'm Nestor, I've signed his name on torn pieces of paper. Took me months to get the spelling right."

"Well, at least they're not fainting because they think they've seen your ghost. What are you doing here, Ty?" I hadn't seen him for years. Not since he came to ask permission to turn Roddy McDowall. "You have someone you want to turn? Let me guess—Sophia Loren."

"No. Not at all. Why on earth would you expect me to turn Sophia?"

"Well, you talked about her nonstop in the sixties and seventies. And she's always said you were her ideal man. . . ." I stopped and stared at him, waiting for some juicy bit of gossip.

"Her acting, Ovsanna. I talked about her acting. She's a brilliant actress. For years I thought she was one of us. She's as mesmerizing on-screen as you are, or Theda. And she managed to overcome the stigma of her beauty and be recognized for her talent, something I spent my entire career trying to achieve. But no, I'm not interested in turning her. She's had a remarkable life; we should leave it at that. Not all of us revel in being what we are, like you do."

"Are you sorry I turned you, Tyrone?" I'd never heard him talk like this before. It's been difficult for some of my clan to give up their celebrity, even though they might not have achieved stardom at all had they not been turned at an early age. Still, having to live in the shadows after you've blossomed in the spotlight is a big adjustment.

"No, Chatelaine. I'm not sorry. I miss interacting with my children and I wish I could know my grandchildren, but I'm not sorry. When your father dies in your arms at a young age and then someone offers you the opportunity to live forever . . . no, I'm not sorry."

"Well, you didn't just drop by for a chat about old times. Why are you here, Ty? What can I help you with? Would you like to sit?" I motioned to the sofa and moved to my desk and sat down. Ty stayed standing.

"No, thank you, Ovsanna. I'm here because I want to talk to you about Thomas's job. I'd like you to consider me for the position."

That came as a complete surprise. Ty had been living in Baja for many years; he owns a matador school there. I remembered he said his students were always amazed at how quickly he healed if a bull got too close. "Thomas's job? You want to work for me in development? Why?"

"Because I think I'd be good at it. Remember, I produced several of the movies I starred in, even though I didn't take a credit. And it would give me the opportunity to help actors I think deserve to be seen. And truthfully, it might be a way for me to spend time with my children. If I can find a project Romina or Ty Jr. is right for, I could cast them."

"Oh, that's taking a huge risk, Ty. It's one thing for my receptionists or people on the street to mistake you for someone else, but your own children? They've spent their lives surrounded by pictures of you, watching your films. You've barely aged in the last fifty years. Believe me, you still look like their father. There's no way you could make it work. I think you need to wait many more years before you come back to Hollywood again. Either that or find some way to completely disguise yourself."

"Like this?" he said, anger creeping into his voice. And before I could respond, he'd pulled off his sweater and shifted into a panther.

Wouldn't you know he'd become a beautiful, black-haired creature.

But . . . he looked ridiculous with his pants halfway down his haunches and his paws standing in his huaraches. I kicked him in the ribs and held his muzzle closed with both hands while I commanded him to stop screwing around and get himself under control. Actors are children, I don't care how many hundreds of years old they are. Myself included—sometimes.

He shifted back, apologized, and adjusted his clothing. I didn't mind seeing him without the sweater.

"I'm sorry, Ty," I said, handing it to him. "It's not going to work. Once again, you're a victim of that gorgeous face."

CHAPTER THIRTY-FOUR

It didn't take me long to get the warrant for Smooch's home address. The Captain knew a judge who owed him a favor.

Cyril "Smooch" Sinclair had a loft in Koreatown. The top floor of a four-story building. One big open space, about sixty by one hundred feet. The manager of the building ran the flower shop on the ground floor. He used his spare key to let me in.

It was a great space for a photographer. The ceiling had to have been eighteen feet high at least, and there were floor-to-ceiling windows on the north and south walls to let in plenty of natural light. One of those big rolls of white backdrop paper hung from a rod in front of the east wall, with black, red, and blue rolls stacked on the floor behind it. Someone had created an interior room by using cedar planks to wall off a ten-by-ten-foot space in the southwest corner. The cedar gave off a great smell. A naked red lightbulb jutted out from a fixture attached to the door. Smooch had his own darkroom.

The rest of the space had minimal, modern furniture. A queen-size mattress on a frame, no box springs, no headboard, covered in a white duvet with a wide black stripe across the center. Black shams on the pillows. A freestanding claw-foot tub—I thought that was sort of sexy—a black vanity under the sink, and a tall white Pottery Barn cupboard next to it. One of those rolling clothes racks held Smooch's wardrobe, and behind it, a black-and-red shoji screen blocked the toilet from view. A black leather and chrome sofa, a small flat-screen TV on a glass coffee table in front of it. The kitchen took up the northeast corner. Smooch must have liked to cook; he had some pretty fancy gear on the counters—copper pots, a wok, an indoor grill. The table was only big enough for two.

Photography equipment was scattered all over the place, but the only other furniture was one long, freestanding bookshelf made out of the same cedar as the darkroom. It took me a minute to realize Smooch had all his books alphabetized and categorized: biography, history, photography, and . . . wolves.

Lots of books about wolves. The guy definitely had a fetish. *I Danced with a Werewolf; Werewolves Wear Heels; What You Always Wanted to Know About Werewolves and Couldn't Find Anyone to Ask.* Maybe I should borrow that one. *The Complete Unabridged and Unadulterated Encyclopedic Compendium of Werewolves.* That could come in handy, too. *The Werewolves' Wine Companion. Confessions of a Recovering Were-wolf. Werewolves on the Wagon.* Cyril Sinclair had more than a fetish; he had a problem. He even had books about Hitler's werewolves, the guerrilla force Himmler organized to assassinate German collabora-tors. And the Wolfenstein video games. Those he kept in the history section.

I could see already how he was going to make my story for the Captain believable. Recovering alcoholic, addicted to gaming, de-cides he's a werewolf and attacks Ovsanna in a delirious rage.

There were photos of wolves on the walls. And photos of him with a woman. His girlfriend, from the looks of the poses. She had on jeans and a fur coat. Looked like rabbit. They were cuddling in the woods.

The phone rang. It was an old handheld with an answering machine in the base and no caller ID. I heard Cyril's recorded voice telling the caller to leave a number if he wanted his call returned, and then a woman's voice came over the loudspeaker. "Hey, sweetie, did you have a good time last night? I'll bet you did." Her voice was rough and gravelly. If this was the woman in the pictures, she sure didn't sound like she looked. The woman in the pictures was a good-looking blond, all-American cheerleader type, twenty years past her prime. The woman on the phone sounded like Kathleen Turner with a sinus infection. "Did you do what I told you? Maybe you don't remember. Well . . . I haven't seen anything in the papers yet, so . . . I want to see you, find out what happened. Meet me at the lair at nine thirty. Call me back if you can't."

Shit. It would have been so easy if she'd just left her number on the machine. Now I was going to have to spend time getting another warrant to dump his phone. If this chick wanted to meet him at their lair, it sounds like she's another one who's using magic to change into one of those—what had Ovsanna called them?—boxenwolves? Fuck me a duck.

And how in hell do I find their lair?

I called Del at the office to get him started working on an AMA dump of Smooch's phone. I needed the list of all incoming calls. Hopefully, Ms. All-American Wolf Girl had called him from her cell. Once I had her number, I ought to be able to track her. Then I called Ovsanna to tell her what I'd found at the boxenwolf's loft. She told me she'd found something in Thomas DeWitte's office I could use to tie him to Smooch. A sterling silver cock ring. The evidence techs will love it.

"I've got to go back to Steady Eddie," I said, "find out if he knows where this lair is that this woman is talking about. He may not remember tracking you, but maybe he remembers where his pack hangs out."

"Wait a minute. What were her exact words? Did she say I'll meet you at The Lair?"

"Yeah. Nine thirty. I suppose they wait until dark to do their changing."

"I know The Lair, Peter. It's not a wolves' den, it's a bar. Down on Rowena in Silver Lake. It's where the paparazzi hang out. She was telling Smooch to meet her at the bar."

"You're amazing. And you don't even drink."

"Well, not anything they serve by the glass at The Lair. Would you like me to show you where it is tonight? If this woman shows up and I can get close enough to her, I can at least tell you if she's human or not."

"You can? How?"

"Oh, Peter . . . don't you know you all smell alike?"

CHAPTER THIRTY-FIVE

I'd said to myself it was fine that Maral was fooling around with spells to get rid of DeWayne Carter. I hadn't given him any thought, and she obviously wanted him gone. But discovering that tortured candle in Thomas's bathroom started me wondering exactly what she was doing and if she was putting herself in danger. Hoodoo isn't something to be toyed with. It's not a religion like voodoo, but it's a pretty powerful African-American folk practice that's been around since the early nineteenth century. Very popular in Louisiana. Folks there consult a "two-headed doctor" or "conjure" as often as they go to a clinic, especially if they need help with something penicillin won't treat, like falling in love or winning at cards. Rootworkers do big business around the floating casinos.

I learned about hoodoo when I was writing the script for *Mojo Working*. I rented an apartment in the Pontalba on Jackson Square and lived in the French Quarter for a month, soaking up the culture, meeting the local practitioners. One rootworker would mention another in a neighboring parish, and by the time I had the story fleshed out, I'd been through most of south Louisiana. That was before I met Maral, but it gave me a pretty good idea what Bayou Go Down must be like.

And a pretty good idea of what hoodoo can do.

I didn't want Maral bringing any evil on herself because she didn't understand which spells to use or how to use them. I needed to find out more about what exactly she was doing.

I called Mother Soriya.

Mother Soriya had been my technical adviser on *Mojo Working*. Her Web site says she's available twenty-four hours a day for spiritual advisement. "Divination and Hoodoo Roots." All I needed was a little information. She said she could see me right away.

Her real name is Sally Daniels. She was raised in South Carolina, the daughter of a Southern Baptist father and a Catholic mother. Sally's mother, Emma, believed more in rootworkers than she did the church, and when she finally got fed up with the church folk calling her daughter a bastard (Emma hadn't married in a Catholic service), she left and started on a spiritual quest, taking Sally with her as she tried one religion after another. Sally ended up in Haight-Ashbury in the early sixties, a little older than everyone else but happy to be dropping acid and passing out flowers. When she came out of her hippie phase, she was Mother Soriya, a *serviteur* of the loa, practicing voudon gnosticism. She knows herbs and rootwork, the tarot, and African diasporic religions. And computers. Her Web site is SoriyaSpells.com. You can buy just about everything you need there to wreak havoc on your ex-lover, without ever leaving your desk.

"Hello, dearie," she said, unlatching the screen door to let me in. "I've been expecting you."

"You have?" She had on a short silk lavender kimono with an orange obi. A lime green beret perched precariously on her gray hair. She was barefoot, her ancient toes gnarled over each other like a tree trunk pushing out of the ground. Black mascara smudged under her eyes. She didn't look as though she'd been expecting anyone.

"Oh yes, my dear. The cards never lie. How are you? Before I forget, I loved your last movie. That fantasy sex scene was to die for. Although I thought the actor was a little stiff. I mean, he needed to be stiff, but still, he was a little stiff playing stiff. You really should have used Nick Stahl."

Everybody's a critic. Soriya's seventy-five years old if she's a day, and all she ever talks about is sex.

She went on. "He should have had a Texas toothpick with him on the set. That would have done the trick."

"A Texas toothpick?"

"A coon dong. You know . . . a raccoon penis bone. Does wonders in the romance department."

I'm wrong. She talks about hoodoo and sex. Well, that's what I came to find out about, the hoodoo, at least.

She motioned me into her living room, and I stepped onto the set of a bad sixties drug movie. Every inch of wall space was covered with framed mandalas. Oils, acrylics, and watercolors. Swirling circles of color. A couple were printed on fabric; one was a batik. Seeing so many of them together that way was like getting bonked on the head in a Tweety Bird cartoon, with pinwheels spinning around.

There wasn't an inch of living space, either. Furniture everywhere. Or if not furniture, then boxes and papers and books and plants. I counted three sofas, a daybed, a wicker chaise, and two overstuffed club chairs. She even had beanbags on the floor. Every lamp shade in the room had things hanging from it—necklaces, scarves, a handbag, a dream catcher, a pair of well-worn pink ballet slippers. One Victorian shade was strung with Christmas ornaments. And not a fire extinguisher in sight.

Along three walls of the room, about waist high, was a makeshift worktable. Plywood sheets resting on cinder blocks. That's where Soriya had two computers, a printer, and a fax machine. Next to them was a dented sterling tea caddy on a tarnished tray, jars of dried herbs, and a ten-pound bag of kitty litter. Nestled inside the cinder blocks were stacks of brightly labeled boxes that I recognized from my research: John the Conquerer Root, Hot Foot Powder, Black Cat Sachet, Fear Not to Walk Over Evil Powder, Uncrossing Bath Crystals, Goofer Dust.

I know what goofer dust is. We'd used it to torture one of the characters in *Mojo Working.* The heroine sprinkles goofer dust across the path where she knows one of the killers has to walk. He steps in it, his legs swell up, turn greenish black, start splitting apart, and finally explode. Special effects had a great time with the gag. Real goofer dust is made up of powdered sulphur, graveyard dirt, salt, ground snake's head or lizard or scorpion, red and black pepper, mullein or sage, powdered snails, and anvil droppings. The word comes from *kufwa,* the Kikongo word for "to die." I don't remember what the prop department used, colored sand most likely, but I always loved the heroine's line "He got goofered good." It became a catchphrase for the whole shoot.

"I need your help, Soriya," I said, moving a cactus off the wicker chaise so I could sit down. The other sofas were scattered with drying sticks and herbs. As soon as I sat down, a mangy gray cat landed in my lap. He didn't recognize my scent. Animals never know what to make of my kind. He scrambled to the other end of the chaise, hissed at me, and jumped down.

"Oh, Conrad," Soriya said, "don't be rude."

"I'm worried about a friend of mine," I said, ignoring the cat, who was now staring at me from the corner. "I think she's fooling around with magick, and I'm not so sure she knows what she's doing."

"Oh, of course, I'll bet I saw her in the cards. Is she young? Red-haired?"

"Yes. What did you see?"

"Not much more than that. Not about her, at least. Except that she's important to you. But you, Ovsanna, you've got some danger around you. I pulled three of the major arcana: Death, the Moon, and the Tower. Transformations taking place around you. Nasty, nasty things. A lot of darkness. Maybe I should do an angel healing on you, send you home with some protection."

"I can take care of myself, Soriya. Thank you for offering."

"Are you sure? I did one for Bill when the House was trying to oust him."

I smiled. "I own the studio, Soriya, I don't think I'm in danger of losing my job."

"Of course. Excuse me a minute, I've got something cooking on the stove."

I didn't have a lot of time; I needed to get back to the office. I followed her into the kitchen. No mandalas in this room, but a silk-screen I recognized from the conjure shops in New Orleans. JFK, Martin Luther King, and Bobby Kennedy in black and white on a yellow background.

The kitchen was as crammed as the living room, only instead of papers and books and boxes, there were empty bottles and jars and margarine tubs. It smelled foul. The stench was coming from what-ever was cooking in the spaghetti pot. The fetid smell of a dead rat decaying in the wall.

"Sorry about the smell, dear, I'm boiling cat bones."

"To eat?" I knew there was a reason I trusted this woman.

"No, no. Well, not really. They're for a client I have coming this evening. She'll have to try each of them under her tongue until we find the one that makes her essence disappear. Then, I'll use that one for the reconciliation spell she wants. I boil them till the meat falls off, then I add a little of this and a little of that. White seeds and wil-low wood. It's like chewing on rabbit bones, I suppose. Some of the clients have a hard time—Bobby Brown did a lot of gagging and spitting—but, believe me, they're clean. I strain them real good. And I don't kill the cat. I never do. I just wait until they die peace-fully and then I freeze the carcasses. It works just as well as boiling them alive and you don't have to listen to the screeching. This one here was Conrad's aunt. I've had her in the freezer for months." She scooped a pile of bones out of the cauldron with a strainer and held them over the sink to drain.

"Soriya, my friend had a devil pod hidden in her room. She's been burning candles that smell like motor oil and taking baths in the middle of the night. I can hear her chanting. And this morning, she buried something in a cemetery—part of a burned candle in the shape of a man. I don't think it was the first time she's gone to a graveyard to do something."

"Can you hear the words she's saying?"

"No. When she first started, I thought she was praying. I didn't want to pry. I think she's trying to get rid of someone she hired to work for us. She wants him gone, but she's afraid to fire him because she doesn't know what he'll do. She's worried he'll retaliate by hurting her brother. He already got him into drugs."

"Has she worked with magick before?"

"No. Not that I know of, and I know her very well. But her grandmother has the gift of sight; she may have learned something from her. And I just noticed she's got one of the Harry Middleton Hyatt books in her office. I've never known her to do anything like this before. I can't believe she knows what she's doing."

"Those books are expensive, Ovsanna. Hundreds of dollars for the later volumes and several thousand for the earlier ones. She may not know what she's doing, but she's serious about it."

"Well, what's it for? Why is she burying a broken candle in a cemetery?"

"I'm not going to be able to tell you for certain, my dear. We use candles in so many spells. Divorce candles, offertory candles, figural candles. Tail-up black cat candles. She could be trying to get laid or trying to lose weight. Burying the candle in the cemetery, though, she could definitely be trying to send someone away. And the devil pod, well, that tells me she at least knows there's a danger in what she's doing. The devil pod will repel any evil directed back at her by the person she's tricking. The same with the baths. If she's doing an enemy trick, she could be cleansing herself for protection against retribution." She laid out the cat bones on a linen napkin to dry. "What you're going to have to do, Ovsanna, if you don't want to ask her directly—and I don't recommend that; if she's hoodooing someone, she's not going to want you to know—is to look for her mojo hand and then call me and tell me what's in it. I wouldn't do this for anyone else, but I can feel you're worried about her and I didn't like what I saw in the cards. There's danger around you both, and she could be bringing it on with her spells. Especially if she doesn't know what she's doing."

"And if you know what's in her mojo bag, you'll be able to tell what spells she's using?"

"That's right, my dear. And then maybe we can help her out. There are lots of ways to get rid of someone you don't want around anymore."

CHAPTER THIRTY-SIX

I'd told Ovsanna I'd meet her in Silver Lake around eight thirty, in time to stakeout The Lair before Smooch's honey got there. That left me all afternoon to work on the identity of the dead girl. I reached Tom Atkins on his cell phone, hoping he was at the Sportsmen's shooting the shit with Ritchie Wollensky. He wasn't. He was in his trailer on the set, about to film a scene. He was pretty sure Ritchie was spending the day at Santa Anita again. He told me where to look for him.

My mother took me to Santa Anita when I was seven years old. She had two girlfriends with kids my age, and the three moms loved to gamble, so they took us with them and taught us how to bet. I won twenty dollars on a trifecta and decided the track was better than Disneyland.

It's a beautiful track, built in 1934, and it's still got its original art deco façade. They shut it down in 1942 so the government could use it as an internment camp for Japanese-Americans—not our shining hour—and then in the sixties renovated the grandstand so that now it seats twenty-six thousand people. I think all of them were at the betting booth when I got there.

I scanned the crowd for fifteen minutes before I found Ritchie. He was standing in a betting line, a handful of twenties clenched in his fist, nuzzling the breasts of the tall drink of water standing next to him. He didn't seem that surprised to see me.

"Hey, Officer, hey, how ya doin'? You gonna bet? Let me help ya. I can help ya, I'm tellin' ya. I'm real good at this. I been doin' it for years. Ain't I, honey?" He looked up at the woman who was draped over him like a serape.

Her name was Nancy, he said, and she was his little gal pal. Except nothing about her was little. She had the biggest feet I've ever seen on a woman, and arms like a gorilla. Straight hair, more gray than brown, cut like Mary Martin's in *Peter Pan*. And a glass eye. At least, I think it was glass; it was hard to see through her blue-framed bifocals. But her left eye was slightly larger than her right and it didn't track, so I figured it was glass. She had an eighteen-ounce plastic beer cup in her hand, almost empty. From the way she was hanging on to Ritchie, it must have been her third or fourth.

"Tommy said you was lookin' for me." Ritchie hadn't taken a breath since I got there. "Ya like the horses, huh? Well, I'm the man to help ya. Who do ya like in the fourth? Ah man, you ain't even got a program. Nancy, honey, show him what you got."

"I'm not here to bet, Ritchie. I'm here to ask you some questions."

Nancy peeled herself off his shoulder and pointed her finger in his face. She was having a little trouble staying upright. "Not for nothing, babycakes, I told you. Didn't I tell you? You gotta tell this detective here what you know." She turned to me. "He knows who that gal is, Detective. He just don't want to get in trouble 'cause a how he knows her. Not for nothing, but I told him, he's gotta do the right thing. You gotta do the right thing, Ritchie. You want me to keep sleepin' with you, you gotta."

Ritchie looked like he was going to puke. "Aw man, Nancy. Can't you keep your mouth shut? Look, Detective . . . I . . . I . . ."

We'd gotten to the front of the line while Ritchie was bouncing around. The teller was giving him a dirty look. "I gotta make my bet, you guys, you know? I know what I'm doin' here and you're gettin' me all distracted. Just give me a minute, will ya?"

"I'll tell you what, Ritchie," I said, handing him a twenty, "you put this where you think it'll do the most good and then you start talking to me. Otherwise, I'm going to have to take you back to Beverly Hills and you're going to miss the rest of the action. You don't want that, do you?"

Ritchie made his bet and we moved over to watch the race. His horse was a California stallion named Saved by Julie, and I'll be damned if he didn't come in by two lengths. What a beauty. Ritchie walked back from the teller with four hundred dollars and tried to give me my share. I took twenty from him, bought us all sausage and peppers—knowing I'd regret it later—and coaxed the story out of him.

"So what's the deal, Ritchie?" I said, wiping red sauce off my chin. "You knew the dead girl, right?"

"Hey, look, man, I didn't do nothin' wrong. I mean, I didn't do nothin' havin' to do with her bein' dead, you know what I mean? I mean, I might *know* somethin' about her, you know, but I don't know nothin' about her gettin' dead or anything. I mean, man, I wasn't anywhere around. You can ask Nancy. I don't remember where I was, but I wasn't around, I know that."

"Ritchie, it's cool. Calm down. I just want to know who the girl is. If I'm going to figure out who killed her, I need to know who she was. I need a name."

"Oh, her name. Well, I didn't know her *real* name, you know. I mean, I really didn't know her too good at all. And she coulda been usin' a fake name."

"Why would she do that?"

"Well, you know how it is with these ladies. I mean, I don't think she had a green card or anything. She wasn't doin' anything where they'd be lookin' her up on E-Verify, you know, to see if they should hire her."

"What was she doing, Ritchie? Where was she from, and what was her name? At least, what was the name she gave you? That's all I need to know."

"For Christ's sake, Ritchie," said Nancy, "tell the detective who she is." She turned to me. "Not for nothin', Detective, but he's scared to death he's gonna get in trouble." And back to Ritchie: "Babycakes, you can be a hero. I know you can. Just tell him what you know. He bought you sausage and peppers, he ain't gonna arrest you."

"She's right, Ritchie. I'm not interested in anything but the girl."

"Okay, man, okay. Well, I think she was from Colombia. You know . . . the country, not the school. She said that once. And the name she told me was Graciella de la Garza. Like her nickname was Gracie, you know? Man, she was a good-lookin' woman."

"And how did you meet her? What did she do for a living?"

Ritchie looked at Nancy. She elbowed him in the ribs.

"All right! All right! She was dealin'," he said.

"Drugs?"

"Yeah."

"How'd you hook up with her? Do you know where she lived?"

"Nah. She had a cell phone. I called her a couple of times and she'd meet me here at the track. Shit, man, it's a shame what happened to her. She had some really high-quality stuff."

CHAPTER THIRTY-SEVEN

Del Delaney was sitting at my desk, dipping jalapeño-flavored pita chips into a quart-size container of cucumber-dill hummus. He does that whenever he doesn't want to get his own desk dirty.

"Where the hell are you getting this stuff, Del? Yesterday it was ramen and Tapatío." I had to lean across him to fire up my computer.

"I made a trip to Costco. Besides, you don't know what I ate yesterday. You haven't been around this place long enough to fart. I hope you're making some headway on this Sportsmen's Lodge thing, buddy; the divers came up with bupkes."

"Hey, I'm keeping the Sarge in the loop. Now, if you'll move your 'gourmet to go' and let me get to my computer, I just might be able to tell you about our vic. And clean up the crumbs, would you?"

Del brushed crushed pita chips into his hand and dropped them on the floor. He moved back to his own desk. I typed in "Graciella de la Garza" and hit the jackpot. She was in the system, photo and everything.

Ritchie was right: She'd been a beautiful woman. Even in the booking shot you could see it. Almond-shaped black eyes, wide-set over high cheekbones. A straight nose and full lips. How the hell had this woman gotten into dealing? She could have been a model. Instead, she had a sheet dating back six years.

Del looked at her last known and corraled Jake Long to go with him to check out the address. I went in to update the Captain.

I don't like to lie. Ever. Unless I'm on the job, and then I don't give a rat's ass. If lying to a perp gets me a confession, I'll make up a story faster than Stephen King. "Oh, you didn't know your girlfriend is screwing your partner and they're both ready to talk if you don't beat 'em to it?" or "You're a lot better off talking to me than the feds." Whatever works. But lying to the Captain, even if I'm just changing the names of the players a bit (because there's no way I want to tell him these Syfy network wet dreams really do exist), makes it hard to live with myself. My stomach was playing havoc with the sausage and peppers.

The Captain was taking the last of his Christmas decorations off the wall, carefully pressing his grandkids' snowflakes into a manila envelope.

"You got the warrant?" he asked as he filed the snowflakes under "X" in his filing cabinet. For Xmas. I'll bet you anything he doesn't remember where they are when he wants them next year.

"I got the warrant and I searched the guy's place. He's the Slayer, no question about it. He kept a souvenir from the Thomas DeWitte killing. A sterling silver cock ring with DeWitte's initials on it."

"Ah man, I don't even want to hear that. Who are these people; how were they raised?" The Captain is a staunch churchgoer. Made my fabrication all the more difficult. The sausages were roiling.

"Well, this guy was a real nutcase. Obsessed with werewolves. From the looks of what he was reading, maybe he thought he was one. Remember, he tore all the bodies apart like an animal. I wish Ms. Moore hadn't lost the note he put in her mailbox, but she remembers it, almost word for word. Pays to be an actress, I guess. Unless you don't hire the right photographer."

"He killed all those people because he was pissed at her for not using him to shoot her eight-by-ten glossies? I don't know, Peter . . . it's this town. Everyone loses touch with reality. My daughter just spent six hundred and twenty-five bucks on a pair of shoes. A pair of shoes, for Christ's sake! That's about eight inches of leather. I tell you, I'm counting the days till I can retire and move to Vermont."

"Right. Where Ted Bundy came from."

"Okay, okay. What about the Sportsmen's Lodge? Can you tie this guy to that, too? That poor woman looked like she was eviscerated by the same kind of animal."

"I don't think so, Captain. I've got an ID on the girl. And I've got her cell phone number. She was dealing. Del and Jake are on their way to her house now, and I'm waiting for the lab report on the print we found on her necklace. But there's nothing to connect her to Ovsanna Moore, and Moore says she doesn't know her."

"Unless Moore was buying from her. That's about a hundred percent possibility. Moore's a movie star; you want to convince me she's an angel?"

No, I wanted to convince him she's a vampyre, but I wasn't going to try anytime soon. "I've checked her out pretty thoroughly, Captain. I don't see it. I'm going to put together a timeline on the Slayer, this Cyril Sinclair, see if I can find out where he was Tuesday night when the girl was killed. These paparazzi show up in packs; if there was something going on that night, they'll be able to alibi him. But I think we've got two separate killers here. And one of them is dead."

I left the Captain reading my report, preparing his announcement for the media. I felt shitty about lying to him, but I was convinced it was the best way to handle the whole thing.

I just needed digestive enzymes to do it.

CHAPTER THIRTY-EIGHT

My employees know me. They know I rarely close my office door, but when I do, you'd better knock and wait for me to say "Come in" before you open it. You don't want to deal with the consequences.

Which is why when Maral pushed open the door and took three more steps into my office before she stopped and stood in front of my desk, I knew something was terribly wrong. She was shaking. She stared at me, her mouth working but no words coming out, and then her face scrunched up in tears. I was finishing a conference call with my soon-to-be partners, and I hung up as graciously as I could, which was probably not so gracious by Japanese standards.

"What is it? What's happened?" I moved to embrace her and let the images come. She'd been attacked by something. "Something came after you?" I felt her fear in my body. Is this what happens when she messes around with magick?

I could barely understand her through the tears. "I'm sorry, Ovsanna. I held myself together until I got here, but . . . but . . ."

"It's all right, sweetheart. You're safe. Just tell me what happened.

You were attacked, weren't you?" I guided her to the sofa and sat next to her.

"It was a wolf, Ovsanna, a werewolf. It had to be. It wasn't any fucking dog. I was alone in the parking lot at the mall, and then it was there, trying to kill me. It's the same thing that attacked you, it's got to be!"

Okay, not some hoodoo retribution. Werewolves, I can handle. "Slow down, sweetheart, and start from the beginning. Tell me everything. What were you doing at the mall? It's the middle of the day, I thought you were at the studio dealing with your brother's friend."

Her tears began to subside. "No. I talked to him on the phone. He said he was selling corn dogs at the production meeting and I went nuts. He was supposed to be picking up a deli platter—bagels and lox—not corn dogs. Who do you know in California who eats corn dogs? After I read him out, he tells me corn dogs are big fat doobies dusted in cocaine. That pus-faced redneck was dealing drugs to the crew! I hung up on him. We've got to do something about him, Ovsanna. We've got to."

"Aren't you doing something already?"

"What? What are you talking about?"

"I know about the hoodoo, Maral." She cowered back into the corner of the sofa, looking like a guilty child afraid of getting smacked. I softened my voice. I didn't think she'd done anything wrong, I just didn't want her getting hurt. "I found your devil pod and the candle in Thomas's office." I wasn't about to tell her I'd followed her to the cemetery. "I don't think you should be fooling around with that stuff to get rid of him, but we can talk about that later. What happened at the mall? Why were you there?"

"I wanted to surprise you. Because you've been mad at me and I feel like I'm losing you and I just wanted to do something to make it right again. So I bought an outfit I thought you'd like, a black satin bustier trimmed in red leather and a pair of black lace crotchless panties. I was going to be wearing them when you came home tonight."

"Oh, Maral." She just doesn't get it. "And you're sure it was a werewolf?"

"Yes! It was huge! A huge wolf, with a thick collar around its neck like it belonged to someone. It leapt on my back and smashed me down, and then landed on the roof of the car. When it turned around to slash at me, I fell backward and hit my head against one of those cement pillars. I ended up on the ground where it couldn't reach me; there wasn't enough room to jump. I got my pepper spray out of my purse and shot him in the face, and then I passed out." She dropped to the edge of the chair. "When I came to, there was a security guard there prattling about my blood pressure and how my dog must not have been very well trained or he wouldn't have run away. He was worried about what the poor thing was going to do for food. That thing would have torn me apart, Ovsanna! It's the same thing that attacked you at the house. It's got to be!"

"No, Maral. The wolf that attacked me at the house was a werebeast. Like Lilith's minions in Palm Springs. If this thing had a collar around its neck, it wasn't a were. It was a boxenwolf. Like the pack in Malibu. It doesn't *belong* to someone, it *is* someone. A human . . . well, he's probably a paparazzo, if that qualifies as human—a human who's using a talisman to shape-shift into wolf form. That collar is the talisman. Did you see anyone with a scarf wrapped around his neck? Anyone following you in the mall? Anyone taking pictures?" I rose from the couch and walked to the corner window. From there, I could see east and west on Wilshire and north on Rodeo Drive. A group of tourists were using their cell phones to snap pictures in front of Tiffany's, but no one else had a camera. Or a collar.

"Oh God, yes. There was a young guy who came up the escalator right after I did. I noticed him because he bumped into me with his long-lens camera. Then when I stopped at the map display, I saw his reflection in the glass and he was taking pictures of me. I freaked. He saw me looking at him and blew me a kiss. I didn't know what to do. He disappeared before I could yell at him. And he had a bandanna around his neck, just like the wolf." She started for the door. "We've got to lock the door, Ovsanna. And warn the girls downstairs!"

I stepped in front of her. "Calm down, Maral. Are you forgetting what I am? I can take care of you."

"Can you?" Her voice got louder and more desperate. "Maybe you're the reason I'm in danger! Aren't you the one they want? They attacked you on the beach. And one of those werebeasts attacked you at the house. Maybe they're after me just to get at you, for the same reason they killed Thomas, and Eva Casale."

"Lilith killed Thomas and Eva. She sent Ghul after them. And Lilith is dead. Ghul is dead. So Lilith and Ghul aren't after either one of us. Peter and I will find out who these boxenwolves are and we'll deal with them, one way or another. I promise you, I'll protect you."

"Peter and you!? So now it's all Peter and you? There's just one problem with that promise." She was yelling, out of control. "You've gotta be around to protect me! And you're not, are you? You haven't been around since the great Detective King showed up—"

CHAPTER THIRTY-NINE

I heard Maral spit out my name just as I opened the door to Ovsanna's office. There was something oily spilled all over the door handle. I grabbed a Kleenex from the coffee table to wipe my hand. Both women stared at me in stunned silence, and then Maral turned her back on me and flopped down on the sofa. The look she gave me could have cut meat.

"Did I interrupt something?" I asked.

Maral didn't answer. Ovsanna said, "Maral was stalked at the mall by a guy with a camera and a collar around his neck."

"I wasn't stalked, Ovsanna!" Maral screamed. "I was attacked! A huge fucking wolf came at me, and I'd be dead right now if I didn't have that pepper spray! I thought you were out tracking these things down. You and the great detective!"

"She was stalked in the mall," Ovsanna said deliberately, "and attacked in the parking lot. It's got to be one of the pack that came at me on the beach."

I stepped farther into the room. "Well, we've got one photographer who doesn't remember anything, one who's already dead, and a girlfriend who just might be a boxenwolf herself. I think we'll know a lot more tonight. In the meantime, Maral, I don't want you by yourself unless you're at the house with the alarm on. You've got my card, right? With my cell phone on it."

She wouldn't look at me. "I . . . I lost it."

"Well, all right, here, take another one. And give these to the girls downstairs, just in case. But you should be safe inside the house. They can't walk through walls or anything, can they, Ovsanna? They're just like . . . real wolves, right?"

"They're bigger," she said. "And more powerful. But yes, they're just like real wolves, with human intelligence. The magic stops with their shape-shifting. And if you can get their collars away from them, that's the end of the magic. All the more reason for me to go with you to that club tonight. Maral will be safe here in the office as long as I'm around, and I'll ask Jesus to follow her home at the end of the day." She addressed Maral as if she were talking to a child: "Once you get in the house, you arm the system and stay there. No, these things can't walk through walls."

"Oh? And will you be coming home *eventually*—to take care of me? What . . . will it be you and Detective King? After you've tracked them down like you did so well this morning?"

Man, I hate sarcasm. If my mother had been there, she'd have bopped her. Ovsanna's lips curled back and I thought for sure something vampyre-y was going to take place, which I really didn't want to deal with right then. So I waved the folder I was carrying in front of them and pulled out the photo the crime lab had left on my desk.

"This is a low-level drug dealer named Vernon Cage," I said as neutrally as possible, to lower the tension between the two women— uh, between the vampyre and the woman. "He's done time in Florida, Georgia, and Louisiana: aggravated assault, armed robbery, possession with intent. His fingerprint was on the necklace Graciella de la Garza was wearing when she was torn apart. Turns out she was probably dealing, too. You recognize him?" I asked Ovsanna. "There's a good chance he's our killer at the Sportsmen's."

"No. I've never seen him before." She shoved the photo at

Maral, whose eyes widened when she saw it. From her reaction I expected her to say she knew him, but she stared at it for a few seconds and then shook her head.

I pressed her. "I'm on my way to the hotel to see if he rings a bell with anyone. I've got his prints at the scene and an inch-long fingernail I'm looking to match up when I find him. You sure he doesn't look familiar, Maral? You seemed to react when you saw him."

"He's just ugly, that's all, with all those zits on his face. I've gotta get back to work, where I'll be *safe*—at least until tonight." She walked into her office and slammed the door.

I looked at Ovsanna. "I don't blame her for being frightened. It was a fucking werewolf, Ovsanna. It doesn't matter what kind."

"It has nothing to do with fear," Ovsanna replied. "She's pissed because you and I are . . ."

"Are what?" I took the photo from her and slipped it back into the folder, set it down. "I haven't even told you about my conversation with the Captain. He bought it. I think it's safe to say the Cinema Slayer has been caught. So you're not part of my job anymore."

Ovsanna stepped closer to me, with her hands at her sides and her face raised up to mine. "So what are we, then, Detective King?" I couldn't swear to it, but she seemed to be offering her lips in a challenge.

I met it. With my hands at my sides and my face bent to hers, I kissed her as deeply as I could. No electricity burn this time. Her lips were cool and pliant, and as she returned my kiss, I felt them warm just slightly. I felt them drawing me in, and I sucked on them as though I were the one lusting for blood and not her. Her breath was sweet. I don't know what I expected, but when you're dealing with vampyres . . . well . . . I read those books. Her breath could have been rancid. I wouldn't have cared.

"I think what we are," I said when we finally ended the kiss, "is getting to know each other."

It was hard to leave Ovsanna, hard to leave those lips and that mouth, especially when she shoved me up against the wall and pressed every inch of herself against me. No fangs, no claws, nothing to worry about. But it was almost five o'clock and I had to track down this Vernon Cage, and I couldn't do that if we were tearing each other's clothes off in her office. I told her I'd call her around eight and drove over the hill to the Sportsmen's.

Traffic was at a standstill on Coldwater. I used the time to check in with my mother. She answered on the seventh ring.

"I'm sorry, honey, I was up on the roof helping your father take down the reindeer. Have you eaten? I've got eggplant Parm on the stove."

"Yeah, Ma. I had lunch at the track."

"Not the sausage and peppers, I hope. That stuff will kill you. Did you win?" My mom loves the horses. And the casinos. If she's not cooking, cleaning, taking care of the grandkids, or selling her movie memorabilia on eBay, she's at Hollywood Park, gambling with the celebrities she used to cook for. Hanging out with Jack Klugman and Telly Savalas, when he was alive. She's good at it, too, although I've always wondered about her system. She keeps an eye on the horses until the last second and whichever one pees last before the window closes, that's the one she bets. "They're lighter," she says, "so they're faster." I'll tell you this: She never loses. Between her business and her winnings, she cleared over a half mil last year. Bought herself a red Corvette.

"Naw, I was talking to a witness on a case."

"MSNBC.com had a headline saying the Cinema Slayer is dead, but they didn't give any details. What happened? Were you involved?"

"Yeah, Ma, I think you could say that." My mother's been married to a cop for nearly fifty years; she knows not to ask too many questions.

"Well, I'm glad you caught him and I'm glad you're safe. Now, what's happening with Ovsanna Moore? Are you spending New Year's Eve with her?"

"I don't know, Ma. I haven't even thought about it."

"They had a picture of the two of you on CNN last night. On that *Show Biz Tonight* show—the one where they spend twenty minutes out of the hour announcing what's coming up next. Makes me crazy. I waited through two commercials 'cause they said her name, and then it was just a shot of you outside the Coroner's office. I don't think anyone knows you're dating."

"*I* don't know we're dating, Ma. And I sure don't want the family talking about it to anyone. All I did was invite her to Christmas Eve dinner." Here come the sausage and peppers again.

"Well, you be careful. I heard Kathy Griffith interviewing the paparazzi on *Larry King Live* and you'd be amazed at what some of them do to get a shot. Did you know some of those celebrities— well, the ones with no talent who only have careers because they're in the magazines—did you know they get paid to show up at those places? Then they tell the photographers they're going to be there, and they get a kickback from the photographers who sell their pictures. I don't know, Peter, it's not like it was before *People* magazine came along."

"Right. When all you had was *Photoplay* and *Confidential*. Ma, you were the first in line at the newsstand."

"Well . . . it's still not the same. I saw a Bible the other day with pictures of Angelina Jolie and Bill Gates in it."

"A Bible? Did you buy it?"

"Hell, no. They left out Charlton Heston."

There was a wedding taking place in the gazebo at the Sportsmen's; the parking lot was jammed. I parked on the side and entered the hotel through the coffee shop. Lots of people taking advantage of the early-bird specials. Arlene was behind the counter, making a fresh pot of coffee. She'd replaced the chartreuse eye shadow with hot pink. It was eye-catching, that's for sure. I ordered a chocolate milkshake to fight the lunch mistake and pulled out the photo of Vernon Cage.

"That's not a face you forget in a hurry," she said as she dumped the old grounds into the trash beneath the counter, "even though I woulda liked to. Gave me the creepy-crawlies with that skin of his. And what's with his neck?"

"What do you mean?"

"Well, you can't tell from the picture, but he doesn't really have one. His head just sits on his shoulders. Not very Christian of me, but, man, he was weird. I made Raoul bus his tables; didn't want to get near him."

"So he's been in more than once?"

"Yeah, I think he's staying here."

I tried to pay for the shake, but she wouldn't give me a bill. I left five dollars on the counter and took the glass and the straw with me to the reception desk in the lobby. The place was lively with wedding guests. Lots of powder blue tuxes.

The kid behind the desk recognized Vernon Cage right away.

"Yes, sir, that's Mr. Carter. Staying in room 105. I checked him in myself Tuesday night. Anticipation Studios arranged for his room." He turned the computer so I could read the registration information.

So Vernon Cage was DeWayne Carter. And DeWayne Carter was the guy Maral McKenzie had brought back from Louisiana to "help him get located out here." Which meant Maral had lied to me when she saw the picture of Vernon Cage. I knew it.

DeWayne Carter, aka Vernon Cage, was working for Ovsanna at Anticipation Studios in Santa Clarita. And he'd just become my prime suspect in the murder of Graciella de la Garza.

And what part, I wondered, was Maral McKenzie playing in all of this?

CHAPTER FORTY

The same security guard who'd been on the gate the first time I'd gone to the studio—the day I'd found the body of one of Ovsanna's special effects artists impaled on the wall of the makeup hut—was on duty again. He was older than dirt, but his memory was good; he recognized me and even called me by name.

"How you doing, Detective King? Ever get that exhaust pipe fixed?"

"That was my Christmas present to myself, Officer Gant. Not much gets by you, does it?" I reached across the seat and pulled Vernon Cage's picture out of the folder.

"That's what they pay me for, sir. In fact, if you're looking for Ms. Moore, she wasn't on the lot today, and you just missed Ms. McKenzie. Pretty much everyone's gone for the night."

"Maral McKenzie was here? You're sure?"

"Yes, sir, came in about an hour ago, looking for her car."

"What was she driving?"

"She had Ms. Moore's Lexus sedan, the hybrid. She drives that out here during rush hour because it's got the HOV stickers on it.

Ms. Moore's a good friend of the Governator, and Arnold got them for her, even after the state stopped giving them out. Ms. McKenzie was looking for the fella that's been driving her car the last couple of days. The Beemer."

I showed him the picture. "Is this him?"

"Yep. He took off the same time as Ms. McKenzie, maybe thirty minutes ago. Burning rubber, he was. I hate to see people treat a nice car like that. He's just asking for a head-on."

"You have a master list of all the cars with parking permits for the lot? I need the license number for that Beemer. And for the one Ms. McKenzie's driving, too."

I tried reaching Maral on her cell phone while Officer Gant pulled the information I needed off a computer in the guard shack. She didn't answer. I called Ovsanna at the office. I didn't tell her Maral had been at the studio, maybe to warn her friend I was looking for him, but I did tell her that Vernon Cage and DeWayne Carter were one and the same and that Maral had lied to me when she'd said she didn't recognize him in the photo.

"I don't know why she'd lie to you. She can't be trying to protect him. I think she's been using hoodoo on him, to get rid of him."

"Oh man, don't tell me that stuff is real, too. What else do you know that I don't? Are you buddies with Santa Claus?"

Ovsanna didn't have any other ideas about what was going on, and as far as she knew, Maral had gone home to hide out from future werewolf attacks. She hadn't seen her since she'd slammed her office door.

I put out a citywide on Maral McKenzie's BMW, the one DeWayne Carter was driving, and called the manager at the Sportsmen's Lodge to ask him to alert me if Carter showed up there. It was eight o'clock; I needed to get back on the road and down to Silver Lake to stake out the bar where Smooch's girlfriend expected to meet him.

You could live in L.A. all your life and not realize there's an actual lake in Silver Lake. I didn't. I'd been on the force almost a year before I saw the water from the window of a witness's hillside apartment. It's a man-made reservoir, built in 1906 and divided into two sections. The lower section was named after Herman Silver, a member of L.A.'s first Board of Water Commissioners, but the upper section still retains the original name of the neighborhood, Ivanhoe. Seems the Scotsman who founded it was a big fan of Sir Walter Scott's novel. The streets are named after his characters.

It's a pretty interesting area. Sort of East Greenwich Village with day care meets the barrio and bohemia. Big alternative music scene, lots of same-sex marriages, and plenty of tats, but a real family neighborhood, too. Every other block has a preschool on it.

I called Ovsanna on her cell to see what she was driving. My old Jag is too recognizable to the paparazzi, and if The Lair was their hangout, I didn't want to take the chance someone would see me. She had her Lexus SUV. I figured we could sit in that behind her tinted windows and wait for Smooch's girlfriend to arrive.

I changed my mind when I saw the layout. The bar was on Rowena Street (yep, a character in *Ivanhoe*) with a Japanese-Peruvian restaurant on one side and an acupuncture clinic on the other. There was only one entrance in the front, and the door in the back opened onto a six-foot-wide walkway that wrapped around both sides of the building and fed back onto Rowena. Anyone using either exit would be seen from the street. A yoga studio stood next to the restaurant, and an emergency veterinary hospital bounded the clinic. Between the foot traffic and the valet for the restaurant, I wasn't going to be able to park on that side of the street and maintain my surveillance.

Across the street, however, was Armando's Automotive Repair, "Specializing in Imports." I saw a 1980 diesel Mercedes, a mid-90s Toyota Avalon, a beat-up Honda Civic, a Volvo station wagon, an honest-to-God Studebaker, and a Chevy Impala—imported from TJ, was my guess. They were parked haphazardly in an open lot next to Armando's closed-up, lime green garage. My '67 Jag fit right in. The only lights in the place were attached to the street side of the garage; the lot was dark. As long as I had the top up and we stayed low in the seats, we wouldn't be seen.

Chapter Forty-one

Peter called me twice as I was driving to Silver Lake, once to ask which car I had and once to tell me to park on Herkimer Street across from the schoolyard. I know the area pretty well, although it's changed a lot since the sixties when I used to visit there with Anaïs Nin and her husband, Rupert Pole. Rupert's half brother was Eric Lloyd Wright, Frank's grandson, and he designed a really wonderful arts and crafts house for Anaïs, all redwood and glass and stone. She and Rupert had masquerade parties there, sometimes once a week. I spent a lot of nights sitting in a costume on the terrace, watching the lights beyond the garden and listening to Rupert play the viola.

Peter was waiting with the engine running when I got there. I parked the car and slid into the Jag, and he actually leaned across the seat to give me a kiss. Nothing passionate, just a greeting, really, but it was nice. Obviously we'd moved past his initial fear that he'd get fried. He drove to Rowena, made a right, and parked halfway down the street in the outdoor lot of an auto repair shop, facing The Lair. It was five after nine.

"Good evening," I said. "What are we doing?"

"What we're doing is sitting here until the woman in the pictures in Cyril Sinclair's loft shows up, assuming she's the same woman who left the message on his answering machine to meet him here. His sweetie with the gravelly voice. Have you been in there? Do you know what it's like?"

"It's just one big room with a square bar taking up most of the center space. Decorated like a riverbank, with a mural of boulders on one wall and trees on the other. The bar's made out of rough-hewn logs and there's a long stone shelf, like a table, running the length of the back. Tree stumps for bar stools. They stayed true to the theme. They serve some of the drinks in tin cups and some in canteens. Not much light."

"Well, that doesn't matter. Neither one of us could go inside without being recognized."

"I could, you know." I looked at him with a straight face.

"Are you kidding? You're Ovsanna Moore. They'd know you in a second. Especially if any of them are photographers. This chick's boyfriend and his buddies tried to kill you last night, remember? And from the message she left him, I think she's the one who put him up to it. Maybe she'll be wearing one of those collars."

"You're forgetting what I am, Peter. With a little effort I could get into shape and fly down that exhaust vent on the side of the building. Microchiroptera can fit through a quarter-inch screen."

"Microchiroptera?"

"Bats. Microbats, to be specific. If I turned into a megabat, I'd be able to see better, but I might not be able to get in through a small space." And I'd have to get waxed afterwards. Now I was smiling.

"Jesus, no bats! Watching you change into a dragon was bad enough. At least they're not real. I've been envisioning you naked in my bed, I don't want to see you turn into a bat. Besides, you don't even know what this woman looks like."

"Well, that's true. You'd have to describe her to me." I shifted in my seat so I could face him while he kept his eyes on the bar across the street. We were scrunched down so we wouldn't be visible, and it wasn't extremely comfortable. So much for the luxurious Jaguar. "Now, let's get back to this envisioning me naked in your bed. Is that part of the getting to know each other you were talking about?"

He laughed and kissed my hand and motioned me to look across the street. "That's her," he said. An attractive blonde had just parked her car and was walking towards The Lair. I could see her clearly in the neon lights of the Japanese restaurant. It was the woman I'd had the image of when I tore the talisman off the boxenwolf at the beach, the one playing video games. She looked like an older Anna Torv, probably in her late thirties, with an athlete's body, long legs in boot-cut jeans, with camel color high-heeled boots and a cropped black velvet bubble jacket over a gauzy white tuxedo-front shirt. No collar. Unless she had a talisman in her Kooba bag, she wasn't a boxenwolf. I said to Peter, "You should use me on stakeouts all the time. I've got great eyesight and I could probably tell you where this woman buys her clothes."

She'd told Cyril nine thirty, but she was early. She stopped in front of the entrance to the bar and scanned the street, searching for him, most likely. She opened the door, stepped inside, and disap-peared out of sight for a full minute, then returned to the front side-walk. After ten minutes of waiting outside, she walked back into the bar. It was nine twenty-five.

"What do we do now?" I asked.

"We wait. Sooner or later she's going to decide he's not coming. She may even realize she hasn't spoken to him since she asked him to do whatever it is she mentioned on the answering machine—attacking you is my guess—and maybe she'll go to his house to check on him. I hope not. I hope she goes to her house instead. I need as much infor-mation about these people as I can get. We'll follow her, wherever she goes."

We sat and stared at the bar. It was all I could do to keep my hands off him. I wanted to straddle him right then and there. I wouldn't have minded the gearshift bruising my leg or the steering wheel pressed into my back, as long as we could have picked up where we'd left off in my office.

But we were tracking a pack of werewolves, and I needed to be-have.

CHAPTER FORTY-TWO

Once the woman walked back into the bar, I figured we had at least a half an hour before she gave up waiting. The only thing that kept me from jumping Ovsanna's bones right there in my sweet old Jaguar was the thought that I was dealing with something that might not be human. I don't mean Ovsanna, I meant the paparazzo werewolf's girlfriend. Maybe she didn't have a collar on and maybe she wasn't one of those boxenwolves Ovsanna described, but I sure as shit believed she was behind the attack, and that had to make her something supernatural. I was finding out there was a lot more to choose from in the monster category than I'd ever seen at the drive-in. For all I knew, a duck could walk out of that place and it might be her. I kept my eyes on the door and asked Ovsanna to tell me the toe story.

"The toe story?"

"Yeah. The Armenian vampyre toe story. Something about your ancestors?"

"Oh. *That* toe story. You've got a good memory. Well, my clan was known for being very territorial. They guarded the three hundred and sixty-six valleys in the mountains of Ultmish Altotem near Mt. Ararat, and whenever a stranger appeared, they waited until night-time when he was asleep and then sucked the blood from his toes until he died. One night, two men came into the area, and because they'd heard about the toe-sucking Dakhanavar, they slept alongside each other, head to toe, with each man's toes tucked under his friend's head. The Dakhanavar thought he'd found a fat, two-headed monster with four arms and no feet. He got so upset, he left the valley."

I started laughing. I was a Beverly Hills cop parked in a car on a stakeout with a movie star vampyre whose great-great-great-great-great-great-grandfather ate people's toes for a living. If you put it in a screenplay, no one would believe it.

There was activity across the street. A couple came out of The Lair and walked next door to the vet hospital. I could see them through the glass. He talked to someone behind the counter. She sat on a bench with her head in her hands. It looked like it was going to be a long night for them.

"How did you know about this place?" I asked. "It's pretty far off the beaten track for you."

"Did you notice the Gelson's on Hyperion?" She was talking about an upscale grocery store, one of a small, local chain.

"Don't tell me. You own it?" This woman was worth more than I'd ever make in my life. What the hell was I thinking?

"No. I used to work there." She was grinning.

"You worked in a grocery store? What did you do, cut the ribbon at the grand opening?"

"No, silly. In the thirties, Walt Disney had his studio there. Right there, on the corner of Griffith Park and Hyperion. My 'grandmother' worked for Walt in the animation department when she stopped making films. Talkies had come in, and truthfully, I was a little worried about my ability to make the transition, so I retired from acting for a few years. When I started again, it was as Anna Moore, my 'mother.' But before that I worked in Silver Lake, sometimes at Mixville on Glendale Boulevard."

"I thought Mixville was the name of that bar down the street on Rowena. I passed it when I was scouting the neighborhood."

"Right. It's named after the studio that Tom Mix built so he could shoot his westerns. He had a whole western frontier town there, with an Indian village on the back lot. You should see me in *Cupid's Round-up*."

It was a lot to take in. I thought I'd come to terms with her being a vampyre, but the image of her making silent westerns in the twenties was definitely disconcerting. I pulled my eyes away from the street long enough to study her face for a few seconds. Hardly a line on it. And none of that blowfish ballooning of the cheeks that comes with Botox. She was a natural beauty. Well . . . if you buy vampyres as part of nature. I was beginning to.

I leaned across the gearbox and kissed her. This time her lips didn't need warming.

"Shit," she said, and pulled away.

Ovsanna had heard the woman coming out of the club. I couldn't hear anything but Chad Kroeger singing "Into the Night" from a metallic blue F-150 that was driving by, but she heard Smooch's girlfriend saying good night to someone inside the bar and asking him to tell Smooch to call her if he showed up.

"She sounds pissed," Ovsanna said, "not worried."

"Well, he's a paparazzo, right? She's probably used to him stalking celebrities at all hours. I mean, once they make a sighting, they don't let up. Buckle your seat belt."

The woman was parked half a block up the street, in a red Camaro. It wouldn't be hard to follow her. I let three cars fall in between us and stayed back another two car lengths. She made a right onto West Silver Lake and then another right and a left and headed up into the hills. One of the cars stayed behind her, which was good for me. We went another half mile and a garage door opened. As I drove past, she was pulling in. The door closed behind her.

I made a U-turn and parked across the street.

The houses bordering the reservoir were pretty jammed together, but this one up in the hills was on a good-size lot. It was separated from the neighbors and partially hidden from the street by eight-foot-tall oleander bushes. I could barely see the second story above them. From what I could see from the street, the house only took up a third of the lot; the rest must have been landscaping. I wondered if she knew she was living surrounded by a lethal plant.

"I've got to do this myself," I said to Ovsanna, who immediately started to protest. I overrode her. "We don't know how this woman is involved, or how involved she is, but if she sees you and she's got anything to hide, that'll be the end of getting it out of her."

"What if she's a were, Peter? You're going to need me."

"You've got great hearing, right? If she's got one of those collars laying around and she makes a move for it, I'll let you know. If I can't stop her before she turns into something nasty, you can come in and save the day. But if I remember correctly, it was my Glock that took her friend down. Without me, you could have been so much sludge on the beach. So I think I can handle it."

I was getting pissed off. What? She didn't trust me? I'm the man, for God's sake. And a cop. And half Italian to boot. I ought to be able to protect my woman. At least as well as she can protect herself. Even if she isn't only a woman. Even if she's a vampyre.

And when did I start thinking of her as "mine"?

The oleanders had a wrought-iron gate dividing them. It was locked, but I could see through the bars. The house was a 1950s flat-top with lots of glass, probably designed by Neutra or Schindler or one of those modernists who built so much of the area. It was on a slope up from the street. The landscaping around it was mostly ice plant. There was a name on the intercom mounted on the gate: Sauvage. I rang the bell.

"Yes?" There was no mistaking the voice, even with one syllable. This was the woman on Cyril Sinclair's answering machine.

"Beverly Hills Police, Ms. Sauvage. I'd like to come up and talk to you."

She didn't respond. I turned to look at Ovsanna, who'd put the top down on the Jag and was sitting in the driver's seat in the dark. I knew she could see me a lot better than I could see her. She nodded to let me know she'd heard the voice. A full minute passed and then the locking mechanism clicked open. I waved at Ovsanna and walked up the stairs.

I had to knock at the door. Another minute went by before she opened it. I looked at her neck, first thing. No collar. She'd taken off her jacket, and she had one of those long barbecue flame lighters in her hand. A faint stench wafted off her, like she'd stepped in dog shit. There were lit candles on the coffee table—one of those kidney-shaped fifties things—and a fire in the fireplace. The rest of the room was fairly dark.

She had company. They must have been waiting in the house before she arrived, although I hadn't noticed any cars parked outside. There were women dressed in fifties outfits, standing together in small groups. They all had on gloves and pearls, and one was wearing one of those pillbox hats. One was stretched out by herself on an S-shaped lounger, in a poodle skirt and angora sweater. What the hell—some sort of costume party? I nodded to them, waiting for someone to speak, but no one made a sound.

"These are my ladies, Officer. I'm Madelaine Sauvage. Who are you and why are you here?"

I pulled out my badge. The women still hadn't moved. In the dim light, it was hard to see the expressions on their faces. What did she mean, her ladies? Call girls? She wouldn't admit it, would she—a Heidi Fleiss with a fifties fetish?

"I'd like to ask you a few questions, ma'am. In private?" I stepped farther into the room, and as I did, she moved a dimmer switch on the wall to my left. The swag lamp hanging above us lightened just a bit.

"Oh, you don't have to worry about the ladies, Detective, they can't hear you. They're all dead."

My hand went to my shoulder holster.

"Actually, they've never been alive. They're mannequins," she said. "I collect them. They're my dearest companions."

She may not have been wearing a wolf collar, but she was definitely loony tunes.

"Would you like to meet them?" she asked.

She sniffed the air for a moment, as though she were smelling something for the first time. Jesus, I thought, there's no way she couldn't have noticed that odor before this. She stepped farther outside and sniffed again, her head turned toward my car. Then she came back in the house, closed the door behind me, and motioned toward the first group of figures. "These are Susan, Candy, and Kimberley. They've been with me the longest."

Now that she'd raised the lights and I was closer to them, I could see their molded forms and plastic faces. Each one had a different style wig and different makeup. The one by the fireplace looked like Mamie Eisenhower; the one on the lounger could have been Annette Funicello.

"That's Janelle and Eve over there, Emilie is by the stairs, and Ivy is reclining in the lounger. I love the way her poodle skirt takes up the whole seat. Don't you?" As she spoke, she walked over to the figure by the stairs and adjusted the martini shaker in its hand.

I didn't know which was weirder—Ovsanna and the werewolves or this chick with her baby boomer dummies.

"Ms. Sauvage—," I started.

"It's Savage, Detective. I pronounce it Savage, even with the *u*. I like what it implies. Don't you?" She sat on the square-backed purple sofa and patted the seat next to her. I'll be damned; she was coming on to me. Didn't say much for her romance with Smooch.

"Have you lived here long, Ms. Sauvage?" I pulled out my notebook and stayed standing.

"Years and years. Since the fifties."

She didn't look that old. Either she was lying or she had a great plastic surgeon. Or Ovsanna was right about her being a were.

"And you're a friend of Cyril Sinclair, is that correct?"

"Yes. Cyril gave me Kimberley. She was my very first companion. He'd used her in a photo shoot and he didn't want to throw her away. She's beautiful, don't you think?" She got up and approached the mannequin in the middle of the threesome, straightening the Peter Pan collar and pulling up one of the gloves. She adjusted the head so it was staring straight at me. "She used to work at Saks, but the salesgirls there were so jealous, she left. Cyril was lucky to find her."

No contest. Much weirder than Ovsanna and the werewolves.

"Why do you ask about Cyril? Is he in some sort of trouble?" There was curiosity in her voice, but no concern. Maybe she wasn't his girlfriend after all.

"Do you know where he was last night?"

She kept her back to me, fussing with the dummies. "Probably out chasing movie stars. That's what he does for a living, you know."

"And you, Ms. Sauvage? What do you do for a living?"

"Oh, a little of this and a little of that. I was an executive assistant for Mick Erzatz when he was running WorldWide Talent. That's how I met Cyril. The agency hired him to shoot some of their celebrities' publicity stills."

Mick Erzatz was a little creep of a guy who'd been one of the most powerful theatrical agents in Hollywood. He wasn't anymore.

"Mick Erzatz hasn't been at WorldWide since that scandal in the late nineties. What have you been doing since?"

"I told you, Detective, a little of this and a little of that. I'm an events planner. I put people together, organize entertainment, things like that. I still work for Mick on occasion. I've been helping him get the performers for his New Year's Eve party." She took a hat off one of the dummies, pulled down a veil that had been tucked inside the crown, and put it back on the mannequin so the veil covered her eyes. "Eve is very shy. She doesn't like it when people look at her."

"Did you have anything you were organizing last night? Anything that Cyril Sinclair might have been a part of?"

"No."

"So last night you weren't with him?"

"Well, I didn't say that. I had a drink with him at The Lair early in the evening, and then I came home to rearrange the ladies. I just found that pencil skirt Susan is wearing at an antique shop yesterday and I couldn't wait to see it on her. I think it's perfect for her, don't you? She's the only one of the girls who can really pull it off." Finally, she turned to face me. I couldn't read anything in her expression. "Why are you asking about Smooch?"

"We found a body on the beach last night. I'm sorry to have to tell you, but we think it's Cyril Sinclair."

Her eyes widened for a split second, but then she smiled. "Oh, that's not possible, Detective. I would know if something had happened to Smooch. We're very simpatico. You must have the wrong information."

I've never had to do a next-of-kin notification—I work in Beverly Hills, after all, not East L.A. Our murder rate is 0.00 times the national average. And Madelaine Sauvage, pronounced Savage, wasn't Cyril Sinclair's next of kin. But even so, her reaction was totally wacky. I'd just told her her boyfriend was dead and she'd blithely denied the possibility. Of course, she also talked to full-size Barbies. I didn't know if she was truly nuts or if she knew something I didn't.

It took me a moment to come up with an answer.

"I hope that's true, Ms. Sauvage. Anything's possible. We were just working off a Polaroid. I'll tell you what, would you mind coming down to the Coroner's office to see if you recognize the person we found?"

"Now?"

I nodded.

"All right. Just give me a minute to change."

CHAPTER FORTY-THREE

I couldn't stay in the car any longer. As soon as the woman had opened her door, I smelled the same scent I'd smelled in my backyard when the werecreature attacked me. Pungent and feral. Either he was close by or I'd been wrong when I said that stench couldn't be female. Either way, Peter was in more danger than he knew. That werewolf on my property hadn't been a boxenwolf. There'd be no collar lying around to warn him.

Peter had left the gate ajar. I stepped inside and stood hidden in the darkness against the oleander. The front door was open. I could see Peter standing inside the entrance. The rest of the living room was visible through the windows that ran the length of the house. It was dark inside. Not a problem for my kind.

The woman had company. A living room full of women.

I let my senses sharpen and concentrated on listening to them. Smooch's girlfriend said, "They're all dead," and immediately I was by the front door, my fangs dropped, my claws in place. She closed it, but not before I got a much stronger whiff of that shitty odor. She had to be a were, there was no doubt in my mind. Maybe the other women, too; the only human I smelled in that room was Peter. I moved next to the window so I could watch them all. If she started to shift, he wouldn't stand a chance.

She seemed to be making a pass at him. She motioned for him to sit beside her, and when he didn't, she began fondling the other women in the room. They weren't responding, either. I looked more closely at them. No wonder they didn't smell human—they weren't real. She was using dummies as decorations. Like the life-size fashion dolls we'd used in France in the 1700s. Only these were dressed like Doris Day and Debbie Reynolds.

CHAPTER FORTY-FOUR

Ms. savage Sauvage wanted a minute to change. I walked over to the window and tried to see Ovsanna in the car, through the bushes. No luck. The street was completely screened from the house. The gate was opened wider than I'd left it, though. Ovsanna must be eavesdropping close by. She just didn't trust me to take care of myself, did she?

The stench in the room grew stronger, making my eyes water. I turned around to search for the source, and there was Sauvage. She was changing, all right. Right in front of me. And fast. The buttons on her tuxedo shirt popped off. Her nipples retracted and her bra hooks pulled open as her breasts flattened into a massive lupine chest. Her boots were already on the floor—trust a woman to take care of her shoes—and she was ripping out of her jeans. But instead of a bikini wax, I was staring at the hairy haunches of another werewolf. A big mother of a werewolf—not one of those boxenwolves we'd seen on the beach; this thing was huge—misshapen and grotesque, like the werebeasts I'd seen fighting Ovsanna and her vampyres in Palm Springs. Madelaine Sauvage's aging cheerleader face morphed into

the nastiest snout I'd ever seen on an animal, with pitted yellow canines dripping green slime. She had bulbous, twisted, hairy nostrils.
I didn't know whether to shoot or puke.

She didn't give me a choice. She was on me before I could get
to my gun. Her teeth tore through my leather shoulder harness, and
my backup piece, the .32 S&W, went flying across the room, shatter-
ing the front window. Huge shards of glass blew back at us, but
Madelaine—or whoever she was—took most of it on her right side,
the side crushing me to the ground. I kept my eyes open long enough
to see Ovsanna push through the dangling fragments of glass, and
then I squeezed them shut, wrenched my head to the left, and came
back with all the power I had to head-butt the damn werewolf woman
on the side of its skull.

CHAPTER FORTY-FIVE

I was through the window and into the room before the glass stopped falling. Peter was partially pinned under the werebeast, his leather jacket spiked with glass slivers and his gun gone. He was smashing into her with his head and bleeding from cuts on his face and neck.

Peter's head butt sent the beast scrabbling away from both of us, but it left Peter dazed on the floor. He rolled on his stomach and used the coffee table to support himself as he tried to stand. I launched myself over him as the creature charged at me, raking my claws across her belly in midair. The coffee table flipped when she landed. Lit candles went rolling across the floor. One of them landed at the feet of a mannequin, and her crinoline caught fire.

I'd torn open the beast's stomach when I sliced her. I'd also gotten an image from the contact. I saw Lilith on her back, her legs spread, birthing this thing. I didn't have time to think about it. She came at me again, gnashing and growling, and when she lunged, Peter kicked her in midair from the side. I grabbed the coffee table by its leg and swung it at her as she charged him, smashing her canines back into her throat. She staggered. I leapt on her back, my fangs tearing at her neck until I found her jugular and felt her boiling blood streaming down my throat. She continued to struggle, but I could feel the life pumping out of her. God, she tasted good. I'd just fed on Maral two nights before, but Maral's blood always had a faint aftertaste of cannabis; this were was sweeter, more familiar. I held on, sucking and swallowing, until she was dead.

Lying atop her, I was flooded with images. Split-second images that jumped like a movie preview. She was the paparazzo's lover, all right. I saw him shift to a boxenwolf, the collar around his neck. Madelaine Sauvage was still in human form, standing half bent over, and he was mounting her from behind, his swollen wolf cock disappearing between her legs. Then I saw my battle with Lilith in Palm Springs, me in my dragon form and Lilith morphed into a serpent.

Then Lilith was a woman again: Baby Jane giving birth to another were. He was huge. He was the werebeast who'd attacked me in my yard. Lilith forced him down on his back, climbed on top of him like he was a man, and rode herself on him. She came, and then the were shifted into a human form and mounted Madelaine Sauvage.

I recognized him.

CHAPTER FORTY-SIX

"Ovsanna, get off her! She's on fire!" Flames had moved up one of the mannequin's clothes, melting its torso and flaring when they reached the acrylic wig. The form toppled over onto the hind legs of the dead werewolf, and its fur caught fire. Ovsanna had her teeth buried in its neck. She seemed to be in a daze, not aware of the heat or flames. I forced open her jaw, grabbed her by the shoulders, and pulled her off. She had blood running down her chin, her mouth was covered with it. She bared her fangs, snarling at me. Her eyes had turned; they were glowing red. There was no recognition in them, just rage. And something else—a primal urge to attack. I yelled her name again and they flickered, and I saw her humanity come back into them. If that's what you call it. I saw understanding return, a realization of who I was and who she was—all in a split second.

"Peter—," she said, wiping the blood off her lips.

The flames had spread to a second dummy. The clothes were burning, but whatever the mannequin was made of, it was melting instead. I grabbed an iron poker from the fireplace set and rolled the charring mess into the hearth. "Cover that one with that rug," I yelled, and Ovsanna did, stomping on the embers that escaped from under the purple flokati.

That just left the werewolf. It was blazing in the middle of the room, but the floor beneath it was concrete slab, so nothing else was on fire.

"I can do this!" Ovsanna said, and she took two more tools from the set and began to push the burning body toward the hearth. I grabbed a spaghetti pot off the kitchen counter, filled it with water, and doused everything that was still burning. It took a couple of trips, but by the time Ovsanna had the carcass all the way in the fireplace, the danger was over. Except for the smoke and the smell. Like driving past the dairy farms on the way to Pacheco Pass.

Talk about a mess. I'm a cop, goddamn it, and there I was helping to kill my second—what, victim? perp? beast?—in two days. Less than two days, if you want to be exact. Cyril Sinclair had been alive on the beach, attacking Ovsanna, just the night before. Now he and his girl-friend were both dead. At least we didn't have another body to ex-plain. Nothing was left of Madelaine Sauvage but a pile of sodden ash in the fireplace.

We opened the remaining windows to let out some of the stench. Aside from the charring on the concrete and the burned rug, the fire hadn't done any noticeable damage. The mannequin popu-lation had diminished, but unless the cops got a good friend of Mad-elaine's to examine the room, they wouldn't know that.

I went outside and hunted around in the bushes until I found my gun. Made sure I had all the pieces of the shoulder harness. Ovsanna filled a garbage bag with most of the ash, and we burned another small log to mix with what remained. She said there wouldn't be any human DNA in the pile, but I didn't want any signs that a body had been burned at all, regardless of the species.

We were both bloody, although most of the blood on Ovsanna was from the werewolf and not her. What had dripped on the floor had landed on the rug, and the rug had burned with the dummy, so there was no blood to clean.

That left a little charred concrete and the broken window. With a dishcloth, I picked up Emilie's martini shaker—Jesus, I was calling the mannequins by name now—and threw it through the window. It landed in the ice plant outside. Let the investigators think Madelaine had gotten drunk and let it fly. Hell, let them think whatever they wanted; there was no body, no sign of a break-in, nothing but a fire in a fireplace that may have gotten out of hand and a window broken out from the inside. Maybe she threw herself a raucous going-away party and then left town.

The neighborhood was empty. No one seemed to have noticed the commotion. I slipped quietly out to my car and grabbed gloves from the evidence kit I keep in the trunk. Even though I could explain I'd had to interview Sauvage because of her relationship to Cyril Sinclair, there was no sense leaving our prints anywhere. Ovsanna mopped the concrete while I wiped down the window latches, the coffee table, and the fireplace tools, feeling more and more like a perp myself. Then we started a search of the rest of the house. I was looking for anything that would explain Madelaine Sauvage's link to Cyril Sinclair or to the paparazzi-cum-boxenwolves or why Ovsanna had been attacked.

There were two bedrooms upstairs, a bathroom, and a small office. And more dummies. One sat on a high stool at the end of the hall, in a tight black sheath with her legs crossed at the ankles, her knees swaying to the left and her toes pointed to the right in one of those fifties coquette poses. Her face was covered with a black veil attached to a wide-brimmed black hat. Another shy one, it looked like. I wondered what her name was—Gigi, maybe? Or Sabrina?

Two more mannequins stood on either side of the master bedroom closet, with their arms motioning to the door the way Betty Furness used to in those refrigerator commercials. They were nude except for aprons around their waists. Creepy. I imagined some guy in the middle of screwing Madelaine looking up to see those two figures pointing like that. He'd probably jump out the window.

There was a cell phone on the desk in the office. I made a note of the number to compare it with Smooch's incoming calls. His name was number two on the speed dial. The only other name I recognized was the guy Sauvage said she had worked for, the head of WorldWide Talent, Mick Erzatz. He was number one on the speed dial.

There were pictures of him and Madelaine in an album she had on a shelf in the closet. Pictures of Smooch and Madelaine, too. And Madelaine and several other guys, dating back fifteen years or so from the looks of the clothes and haircuts. She looked lovey-dovey with all of them. So maybe Mick Erzatz had been more than her boss. I wondered if he preceded Smooch or if she was screwing them simultaneously. From all the stories I'd heard about Erzatz, I was guessing she didn't have much choice. He got off on having power. Rumor was if you wanted to work for him, you had to audition on tape. He had videos of every woman he'd hired giving him head. A lot of the actresses he represented, too.

Ovsanna found one wolf-pelt collar. It was in a drawer with Madelaine's lingerie, under her bras and panties. There was definitely a connection between her and the boxenwolves.

We took the collar with us and put the garbage bag with the ashes in my trunk and tossed it in a Dumpster on Herkimer Street, where Ovsanna had parked her car. Then she followed me back to my house. She wanted to clean up before she went home to Maral.

CHAPTER FORTY-SEVEN

Driving away from the woman's house, following Peter, my body shivered with excitement. I wanted to tear off my clothes, free myself of anything touching my skin. Feeding on that werebitch had left me desperate for release. I rubbed my free hand across my breasts as I drove, barely able to concentrate on the road. My nipples were hard and warm, and each time I touched them, I got closer to the edge. I still had the were's blood on my arms. I licked it off, reveling in the rich resin taste. It wasn't until I parked next to Peter's Jag that I forced myself to calm down and pull back from the passion that was threatening to bring on a change. He didn't need a full-blown vampyre awakening the neighborhood. I sat in the car for a minute, breathing slowly, letting the energy flow away from me. Letting my nerves relax.

It was the first time I'd seen his house. I concentrated on that. It was charming—a three-bedroom Spanish bungalow in a canyon off Beverly Glen, with a hot tub and a lap pool and a guesthouse in the back. While he was looking for something for me to wear, I walked through the rooms. He'd turned one of them into a combination office and workout space; free weights and a treadmill had been set up in front of a flat-screen TV, with a computer desk and bookshelves across from it. The other bedroom looked as if it was reserved for guests. And ironing. A full-size ironing board with an iron on it stood in the middle of the room. Made me smile; no wonder he always looked neat.

We met up in the master bathroom. He'd removed his leather jacket and bloodied shirt. His blood had soaked through and was drying on his face and chest. The smell roused my need all over again. Forget oysters. Blood does it for me every time. He had a black terrycloth robe in his hands and he was turning on the shower.

"Here," he said, handing me the robe, "I'll go over to SuzieQ's and see if she's got something you can wear to go home in. Her car's here but her shades are up, so she's probably out on a date. She won't mind if I borrow something for you."

"I can wait, Peter," I said. "Let's get that glass out of your hair before we do anything else. You've got a bunch of cuts we need to clean."

He shook his head over the sink and slowly ran his fingers through his hair to flick out any remaining slivers. Then he opened the medicine cabinet and handed me a bottle of Bactine and some Q-tips. He leaned against the counter, watching my face while I dabbed each of his cuts with the medicine. His blood was still flooded with adrenaline from the attack. I wanted to lick off every drop. I said, "You know, the last time you cut yourself, it was all I could do to keep from jumping you." It was the first day we'd met: I'd scratched him with my claws and convinced him it was a *shurikan* he'd cut himself on. I could probably tell him the truth now that he knew I was a vampyre.

"Really? Well . . . if I'd known that," he said, "I'd have been using a dull straight razor to shave with. Ouch!" I pulled a tiny sliver of glass out of his forehead. "Are you doing that to *make* me bleed?" he teased. "'Cause I'll be happy to oblige the jumping me part without any more cuts or slicing."

I looked in his eyes. He was smiling, but he wasn't teasing any longer. "All right," I said. I put down the Bactine and the Q-tips, pulled my sweater over my head, and stepped into the shower in my boots and bra and black leather pants. He could do the rest. I turned around and stared at him. His chest was broad and muscled, with a layer of flesh that made him look solid and strong, not cut like a gym rat. His skin was smooth, just a trace of dark chest hair. I wanted to lick the strands that curled around his nipples.

His eyes never left mine. He unbuckled his belt, pulled off his shoes and socks, worked his pants and briefs down over his body, and joined me.

There was a tile bench along the back of the shower. I sat on the edge, arching my back against the wall, stretching my legs out straight under the stream of water. He straddled my hips, his cock hard and huge, inches from my mouth, and then he bent forward and reached around to unhook my bra. I scraped his chest lightly with my nails, circling his nipples. We kissed, our mouths only, while his hands moved down to unzip my pants. It took a while to peel the wet leather down my legs, especially since he'd buried his face in my body, but neither of us minded. The heat from the shower coupled with the heat from his flesh made it hard for me to breathe. I kicked the shower door open to let the cool bathroom air temper the steam. He put my pants and my boots on the rug outside the door. Then he knelt in front of me, and I stopped paying attention to anything else.

CHAPTER FORTY-EIGHT

I hadn't fully trusted Ovsanna until I'd pulled her off Madelaine Sauvage. She'd seemed at the height of her full-blown vampyre self right then—completely instinctual and bloodthirsty—yet when I'd called her name and she looked at me, she came back from whatever she was, and she knew me. And I wasn't fodder. That's when I knew I was safe with her. I didn't realize it at that moment, but that was the last piece that needed to fall into place for us to come together.

Standing outside the shower, knowing we were finally going to make love, made me so hard—and huge, even if I have to say so myself—that I had trouble getting my shorts over my cock and off my body. I stood staring at Ovsanna in her black bra and boots and skintight leather pants. I felt like I'd walked through the screen into one of her movies. Nothing about it seemed real. Her skin, when I reached my arms around her to unleash her breasts, was as smooth as travertine and just as cool, in spite of the hot water pouring down on us. I wanted to get inside her to find out if she was cool there, too. I wanted to get inside her as deep as I possibly could. Not just to feel her body around me, her muscles sucking me in. No, I wanted to get all the way inside her, into her core. Connect with her, so I wouldn't be able to tell where I stopped and she began. So it was all one. I didn't even know what that meant; I just knew I had to get to her. It was an urge unlike anything I'd ever experienced. I mean it. And believe me, as a single man in urban L.A., I've had my share of experiences. Especially when the *Times* profiled me as a "hero" for saving that kid from drowning in the L.A. River—I had women throwing them-selves at me for months. I didn't throw too many of them back.

But none of them was like Ovsanna.

Of course, they were all human. That could be the difference.

This vampyre scraped her nails over my chest, around my nip-ples, and I thought I was going to explode right then and there. Any ideas I'd had about going slowly or being tenderly romantic went out the shower door along with the steam. I concentrated on getting her pants peeled off and then lost myself in her, my mouth on her body. She thrust forward and met me, guiding my tongue. She set the rhythm and I followed, tracing the outline of her as she swelled, dipping inside her as I licked. And yes, she was cool inside. Cool like the water off a Caribbean island. Cool like the Santa Anas blowing in December. Cool like I didn't mind a bit.

She was on her knees with my cock in her mouth when the hot water ran out. I was trembling so hard I could barely stand up. I turned off the faucets. We dripped water all the way to the bed, and then I was inside her. We pounded against each other, driving to the brink, our mouths locked together. Then she wrapped her fingers in my hair and pulled my face away from her. She held me there, star-ing in my eyes, watching my reaction as her fangs unsheathed. "Please, Peter," she whispered. I lifted my head in acquiescence and she slid her teeth into my neck.

It was three A.M. when I looked at the clock. Ovsanna was lying on her side, tracing her nails lightly down my chest. Her nails, not her claws. Her fangs were nowhere in sight. And thank God, because I was spent. I couldn't have come around again if my life depended on it. Not for another hour or so, at least. She brought her lips to my neck and licked the spot where she'd fed.

"You realize," I said, "you give a whole new meaning to the term *suck me off*."

She laughed and kept on licking. It had been less than an hour since she'd bitten me, but the cuts were barely visible. She'd licked my forehead, too, and the wounds there were almost gone.

"How does that heal so quickly?" I asked.

"It's my saliva. It closes the wound and fills in your cells to speed their regeneration. But I have to work at it. Some of my kind take great pride in leaving their mark, as though they are branding a pet. 'You see what I can do?' they seem to be saying, like humans geld their horses or chop off their dogs' tails, 'because you belong to me . . . and there's the proof.' I hate that."

"So they're not all like you, even though you are their . . . what do you call it . . . chatelaine? Their boss?" I ran my hand down the curve of her body.

"No. They're members of my clan, the Vampyres of Hollywood, because they came here after I did, and they owe fealty to me as the one who was the first to establish myself here; but we don't all share the same traits. Those of us who were born vampyre are from different parts of the world; hence Orson is Strigoi Vui, Douglas is Blautsauger, Theda Bara is Azeman, I am Dakhanavar. It's sort of like you being Italian and Welsh, but you're also an Angeleno because you live here. And then if I turn someone, he or she becomes like me, with my Dakhanavar instincts and capabilities."

"So you mean Rudolph Valentino and Jason Eddings and Mai Goulart and Tommy Gordon—all people you turned—they all could do what you do? Touch people and get images, see things so clearly, hear better, do that heat thing you did to me? And my aunt Adelaide, you did something to her, too, didn't you? Some kind of mind-control thing? Could the others you turned do that, too?"

"Well, Rudy, maybe. He was older. We get more powerful as we get older. My attorney, Ernst Solgar, is Clan Obour born, more than nine hundred years ago. You should see the things he can do. Just with his tongue. And you definitely don't want to go up against him in a contract dispute. He gives new meaning to the term *bloodsucker*."

"But you're not like that. I mean, I don't see you laying waste to people just because you're thirsty."

"I try not to. That's the reason I'm not going to sleep here tonight. I've learned to control my urges, but if a change comes on me while I'm sleeping—and sleeping next to you, that could very well happen—I can't be certain I won't latch on to you and not let go until it's too late."

"You knew me when I pulled you off Madelaine Sauvage. I watched you come back to me. You killed her, you were just as much a beast as she was, but when I called your name, you changed and you didn't attack. Which, I have to tell you, I'm very glad about, because I didn't have my gun and I don't know what would have happened."

She sat up quickly on the bed. "I saw something when I touched her, Peter. I just remembered. I know why Maral and I are being attacked. And you, too." She had one leg tucked under her and the other crossed over it in a yoga pose.

Just for the record, vampyres don't get bikini waxed.

"Did you hear me?" she asked.

Just barely. I was staring at the wetness we'd left glistening in her curly black hair. "Yes. Why? What did you see?" I didn't miss the bikini wax at all.

"She was an alpha female, Peter, and she was using Cyril Sinclair and his boxenwolf friends to attack us."

"Us? Why?"

"Because she's Lilith's progeny. Her mate, the alpha male, a true were—the were that attacked me last Saturday night—came directly from Lilith. They both did. I saw Lilith birthing her, and him. I also saw Lilith fucking him. She always was a twisted old bitch. I think he wants revenge for her death. I think that's why he's after us."

Chapter Forty-nine

I didn't tell Peter I'd seen the alpha were shift and I'd recognized him. I didn't tell him Lilith's avenger was Mick Erzatz, former head of what used to be one of the largest talent agencies in town. Telling him would have meant admitting I had been chatelaine of the Vampyres of Hollywood for nearly a century and Mick Erzatz had managed to avoid exposing his true nature to me in thirty years of that time. I was reeling from the implications.

It all made sense when I thought about it. None of my clan had ever signed with him as an agent. There are fewer than two hundred vampyres here. Those who were stars in the early days of cinema live in anonymity; others, never in the public eye to begin with, change their names and their histories as the decades pass. Erzatz had come on the scene as an agent long after Douglas and Mary and Theda and the rest of my original clan had stopped working. They wouldn't know him. And the actors that we'd turned, most of them major A-list players now or on their way to becoming such, are repped by CAA and William Morris Endeavor. I didn't take over Anticipation until the late 90s, several years after a scandal involving two of Erzatz's underage clients had forced him into early retirement. Seems he pimped a set of fourteen-year-old twins to a network producer to get them cast in the "tween" series *I'm So Thirteen*. The producer had his fun—well, as much as he could have with his limp-dick reputation—and then cast two eighteen-year-olds instead. He didn't want to deal with SAG working conditions for minors. The girls' mother went ballistic. Not because the producer tried to screw her daughters, but because they didn't get hired. She sold the story to the trades.

Mick Erzatz was one of the most hated men in town, but in the eighties and nineties he'd been one of the most powerful. Every studio head had had to suck him off in one way or another to get their deals made. My favorite story about him was when he was flying home from the Telluride Film Festival on a private jet, paid for by his company. There wasn't enough room in a G5 for all his luggage and the pet ocelot he'd bought there, so he hired a G2 just to bring the bags. Then when he found out the tail number on the G5, which was on its way from L.A. to pick up him and the cat, he had it sent back to Van Nuys and another one flown in. Because the first one had leopard-skin sofas and he didn't want to upset the ocelot.

Erzatz and I had attended some of the same fund-raisers and industry events, but we'd never had reason to be alone together. I'd never been near enough to him without other people around to mask his scent—and I hadn't ever had reason to pay attention.

Well, now I did. And I needed some time to think about what I should do before I got Peter involved.

CHAPTER FIFTY

Ovsanna wouldn't spend the night, and I didn't push it. I figured she'd had four hundred years or so of getting to know herself, and if she said it was dangerous, it was probably dangerous. Besides, I needed some sleep. I took a fast shower and threw on some sweats, then went out to the guesthouse, knocked to make sure SuzieQ wasn't there, and slipped in to borrow something for Ovsanna to wear home. Suzie must have found a date who didn't mind snakes; it looked as though she'd had a pretty wild party in the house. She'd stripped the sheets off the bed, and her room was messier than usual. One of the snake cages was lying open and upended on the bathroom sink. I found a Dallas Cowboys sweatshirt and a pair of jeans in a pile on the floor. Ovsanna would have to roll up the cuffs.

My cell phone was ringing when I came back. Three thirty in the morning only means one thing. I opened it, expecting to hear the Captain's voice.

"Peter?" It was SuzieQ.

"Suz?" She sounded strange. "Where are you?"

"I'm at the duck pond in Franklin Canyon. Can you come here . . . by yourself? I need your help." The phone went dead.

What the hell was she doing at the duck pond? Not feeding the ducks, that's for sure.

"Another case?" Ovsanna asked. She'd showered while I'd been in the guesthouse, and she was waiting for me to hand her Suzie's clothes. I didn't realize I was still holding them.

"No. It was SuzieQ. Something's wrong." I pulled off my sweats and grabbed my jeans and a pair of hiking boots. "She wants me to meet her in Franklin Canyon."

"Car trouble?"

"I don't think so. She wouldn't have called me for that. She said she's at the duck pond, but that doesn't make sense; she can't drive her car into the park at night. She must be in the parking lot. I don't know . . . maybe it's a guy. Somebody gave her trouble on a date or something. She asked me to come alone, so whatever it is, she doesn't want anyone else to know. Will you be okay?" I had my gun and my keys and my jacket, and I needed to go. Ovsanna followed me into the living room. She was nude. I didn't want to leave.

"I'll be fine. I'll talk to you in the morning."

"Okay. The front door locks automatically, so make sure you're dressed before you walk out the door."

"Yes, Officer. I think I can remember that." She reached up on her toes and kissed me. "And if I don't, it really won't be a problem. Bats, remember?"

That made leaving a little easier.

The streets were empty. A heavy fog had settled in, and the Jag's headlights barely cut through it. I put the flasher on the ragtop and kept my speed down to forty on the curves up Beverly Glen, then opened it up a bit on Mulholland. Franklin Canyon covers more than six hundred acres on the edge of Beverly Hills, but the entrance near the duck pond is on the north side, closest to the Valley. It was four o'clock in the morning. The park was gated closed. The more I thought about it, the less I thought it was a date gone bad; SuzieQ is far from naïve.

I was about a mile away when my cell phone rang again.

"Suz?"

"No, sir, this is Dispatch. Detective King?"

"Hey, Amanda, yes, I'm here. What's up?"

"I just got a call from Patrol. They've got a sighting on that city-wide you put out this evening. Car's parked and empty in the Three Hundred block of Saint Cloud. Anything you want them to do?"

I nearly ran off the road. "Not if it's empty. Thanks, Amanda, I'll take it from here. Thank the guys for me."

The 300 block of St. Cloud. That's two blocks from my house. Maral McKenzie's black BMW, the one DeWayne Carter had been driving, was parked two blocks from my house. I thought about the mess in Suzie's bedroom, and suddenly it didn't seem like the aftermath of a hot date.

I pulled up received calls on my cell and hit redial for Suzie's phone. A recorded voice said the customer was out of range. Then I tried calling Maral and got her voice mail. Ovsanna didn't answer, either. Three women I wanted to talk to and I couldn't reach one of them.

You can take Franklin Canyon Drive all the way through the park from Coldwater Canyon at the north end to Beverly Drive at the south. Both ends of the road are residential, but where the park starts, a few blocks in, gates prevent access. The gates are open from sunrise to sunset and then closed and padlocked shut. But they're just gates running across the road. No walls or fences on either side of them. All you need to do, if you're intent on getting into the park after dark, is walk around them.

SuzieQ's SUV was parked by the side of the road, in front of the locked gate. It was empty. I pulled in next to it and shut off the lights. The duck pond was about a mile away.

I called her name but got no answer.

I couldn't see ten feet in front of me, even with the flashlight. If there was a moon, I couldn't tell; the fog was too thick to let any light through. Felt like walking into wet cotton candy. I concentrated on the dirt path that led around the gate and joined up with the road on the other side.

Fifteen minutes later, I was at the duck pond. I called Suzie's name again and heard a pounding from the far side of the water. I unholstered my gun and slid down to the water's edge. Using the pond to guide me along the bank, I aimed my flashlight into the tall reeds that covered most of the slope. I could hear ducks splashing, but I couldn't see them.

The fog distorted the direction of the sounds I was hearing. Twice I started back up the slope, thinking that's where the pounding was coming from; then the direction changed, and I slid down again and headed toward the trees farther to my right.

That's where I saw her. Bound in strips of a sheet and lying half in the water. Her mouth was gagged. She was pounding her bound feet against a tree trunk.

I raced to her, stumbling in the mud. Whoever it was hadn't just tied a gag around her mouth, he'd shoved it halfway down her throat. I got it off and she started retching. I struggled with the knots in the sheets around her arms and legs. "Jesus, SuzieQ, what happened?! Are you hurt?"

"That fuckin' prick! He killed Dick Nixon! Oh, Peter, he killed Dick Nixon—I don't even know how he did it. And then he forced me into my car and made me drive here, and made me call you. That fuckin' prick!"

"Who? Did he hurt you? Are you all right?"

"Fuck me, no, he didn't hurt me. 'Cept for my pride. And killin' Tricky Dick! Fuckin' little no-neck weasel!" I got her untied. She picked up a rock and hurled it into the bushes.

"Who is it and what did he want? Why?" I put my arms around her to help her up. She was wet and muddy and starting to shiver.

"Hell, sugar, I don't know. He came lookin' for you! I heard somethin' in the bushes by the hot tub and I went out there thinkin' a coon was trackin' my babies. Instead there was this no-neck guy with pus all over his face, talkin' like a Florida cracker. He said

Maral McKenzie sent him to find you. I said it was two in the mornin' and he sure as shit better get off the property. That's when he jumped me. Do you know who he is?"

"Oh yeah, I know who he is." DeWayne Carter. Aka Vernon Cage. Maral's buddy and my prime suspect in the Graciella de la Garza case. "We haven't met, but I recognize the description. Let's get you out of here."

I wrapped my jacket around her. She was still shaking, but it wasn't from the cold. I wanted to get her back to the car before she went into shock.

Something rustled the bushes behind me, and Suzie screamed. I pushed her down on the ground and spun around to block her with my body. "Police! Stay where you are!" I yelled, aiming toward the movement. I couldn't see a damn thing through the fog.

"That's him, Peter! That's him! That dickweed! He killed my snake!" She picked up more rocks off the ground and fired them at the form that was barely visible coming through the sage. It was De-Wayne, all right. He ducked the rocks and kept on coming. I couldn't see his features, but the guy had no neck, just like the guy in the picture—his head just sat on his shoulders.

"DeWayne Carter? Get your hands in the air!" I couldn't see a weapon, but that didn't mean anything, I could barely see him.

"Hey," he said, "you're Peter King, ain'tcha?"

"Detective King, Beverly Hills Police Department! Now keep your hands in the air and get down on the ground!"

"Oh yeah, I kin do that. I jes' wanted to make sure you're who I was lookin' fer. I kin git down on the ground, no problem." He had his hands in the air, and they seemed to be pulling back into his body as he began to kneel. Then a sound came out of his throat, like a metal toilet tank flushing, and something happened to his face. It looked like it was cracking in half across his jaw. His chin pulled back toward his missing neck. His upper gums stretched forward, tens of teeth pushing out of them, flattening and elongating into the shape of an alligator's snout.

SuzieQ screamed and grabbed my arm. I couldn't control my gun.

DeWayne was growing a tail, huge and armor-plated. He whipped it from side to side and then rocked back on it, like a man sitting on a stool, and his legs split his pants as they changed into haunches— wolf haunches covered with hair.

"It's a rougarou, Peter!" Suzie screamed. "A rougarou!" I didn't know what the fuck a rougarou was, but I knew what it wasn't. It wasn't DeWayne anymore, and I wasn't going to worry about read- ing him his rights. I broke Suzie's grasp and fired, just as the thing lunged at me and clamped his jaw around my leg. My shot went wild. He got a mouthful of leather and Gore-Tex, my hiking boot, and I got pulled to the ground and slung into the water. I still had my gun in my hand.

He hadn't let go of my leg. He dragged me down and held me there, maybe twenty feet or so. My gun wasn't marinized; if I fired underwater, I could blow off my hand and blow out my eardrums. Instead, I jackknifed my body up and pounded him in the head with the butt, trying to get him to loosen his grip. I had maybe forty-five seconds before I needed air. This was how he'd killed Graciella de la Garza, drowning her before he chewed her up. I'd read somewhere that alligators can't chew, but this thing was something more than an alligator, some kind of hybrid alligator/wolf man with tiny little hu- man hands and a mouth full of razor fangs. That's what those prints at the Sportsmen's had been, this thing's hands. What the hell had Suzie called it—a rougarou?

I kept pounding, pulping one of his eyes. He released my leg, turned, and thrashed out with his tail. It caught me across the back and sent me surging upward. He followed me, coming at me with his jaws wide open. I raised my gun to fire—forget losing a hand— and saw SuzieQ through the water behind him. She was climbing onto a boulder above us, with a thick tree limb in her hand. Right in my line of fire. I hesitated. If I missed DeWayne, I'd hit SuzieQ. In that instant, she jumped off the rock and landed on his back, crashing the limb across his upper jaw. She had a strip of sheet draped on her shoulders. She whipped it over her head and wrapped it around his snout, tying those teeth closed momentarily. Man, she was fast. It was like watching a rodeo rider. He bucked her off, unable to open his mouth, his plated tail thrashing inches from her face, and I surfaced and fired with the gun out of the water. Two shots hit his neck and the third hit him right behind the eye. The fourth misfired, but it didn't matter; he was done. He thrashed for a few more seconds, and then his body began coming apart, separating into pieces of alligator and wolf and little bitty human hands. The pieces sank to the bottom and disappeared.

SuzieQ swam to the side of the pond where he'd first tied her and crawled into the weeds. She was shaking uncontrollably. I grabbed the second sheet, the one DeWayne had used to tie her legs, wrapped it around her, and held her close.

"It was a rougarou, Peter. A real one." She rocked back and forth in my arms. "I didn't think they existed for real."

CHAPTER FIFTY-ONE

I had a bad feeling about SuzieQ's phone call to Peter. It didn't sound right. He said she didn't want him to bring anyone with him, but that didn't mean I couldn't follow behind without either of them knowing it. Just in case.

I pulled on the sweatshirt he'd borrowed from Suzie and rolled up the cuffs on her jeans. My boots were still wet from the shower. I'd noticed Suzie's feet when she was dancing. She's a big girl; I couldn't borrow any shoes.

Peter had a pair of rubber flip-flops in his closet. I put those on and threw my boots in the backseat.

My phone rang as I was pulling out of the driveway. I didn't answer. Caller ID said it was Peter, and I didn't want to have to lie to him if he asked if I was on my way home. It was sweet of him to call, though. We'd only just parted, and maybe he was missing me already. I wouldn't mind that. I planned to follow him to the duck pond, stay out of sight until I was sure he didn't need my help, and call him when the sun came up.

Driving through the fog reminded me of being in Inverness in 1979, when I'd visited the set of *The Fog,* John Carpenter's film about the ghosts in Antonio Bay. And that reminded me I needed to get John on the phone. I had a project I'd been sitting on for two years, and now that the merger had gone through, I had the budget to make it the way it should be made. John would be the perfect director. I'd have Maral call him in the morning.

If she showed up at work. She'd left the office last night without saying good-bye, and she wasn't at home when I went there to change clothes. I needed to talk to her about DeWayne Carter. Why had she lied to Peter when she'd seen his picture with that alias? What was she doing in the cemetery? Why was she leaving a devil pod in her office? She could be in danger—and not only from a boxenwolf. The guy she'd brought out here to keep away from her brother could be more than a drug dealer. He could have killed that girl at the Sports-men's.

Peter's car wasn't hard to find; it was at the entrance to the park. I hid mine around a curve up the street and walked down and stood by the gate in the wet darkness, letting my vampyre senses flare. I could see, just barely, maybe eighty feet through the fog. More, certainly, than any human, but not enough to discern anything save reeds and trees on either side of the road leading down the hill. I knew where the duck pond was, though; I'd filmed there several times. Anyone who'd ever watched *The Andy Griffith Show*'s opening credits would recognize the area. Or *The Creature from the Black Lagoon.* I started walking into the blackness.

I was still a quarter mile from the pond when I heard the sound of ducks in the water. And something pounding against wood. Peter must have found SuzieQ because I picked up his scent and a female scent close by. And something else—farther away; something putrid and briny. The way Maral had smelled when she came home with DeWayne Carter.

The pounding stopped and I heard voices: Peter's and SuzieQ's.

I couldn't understand them at first—she was talking about killing President Nixon—and then Peter shouted, "Police!" That briny smell flooded my senses. In an instant, I was at the water's edge. I knew Peter and Suzie couldn't see me—the fog was impenetrable—but I moved behind a copse of live oak just in case. I didn't want them to know I was there. Peter had already gotten pissed when I suggested he might need me to deal with the female were, and it probably hadn't helped that I'd been right. I didn't want to challenge that male ego again unless I had to, to save his life. And I definitely didn't want to expose my true self to SuzieQ.

The briny smell was coming from DeWayne Carter. I watched while he came out of hiding in the bushes and Peter ordered him down on the ground. And then I realized what it was I'd heard when I touched that dead girl's body in the Coroner's office. It was the sound of an alligator in a death roll. Now it was coming from DeWayne.

SuzieQ screamed at the same moment I recognized DeWayne for what he was—a rougarou.

Peter fired at him as DeWayne started shifting. The bullet missed DeWayne and grazed my elbow. Damn it, how would I explain that when I gave SuzieQ back her sweatshirt? I barely felt it, but by the time I looked up from the wound, Peter and the rougarou were underwater. SuzieQ was racing towards a huge rock on the side of the pond; she had a sheet in her hands.

I waited. Rougaroux aren't really vampyre and they're not werebeasts. They can be killed as easily as a human, and Peter had a gun. If he'd just use it. What the hell was he waiting for? How long could he stay underwater?

Suddenly, SuzieQ was jumping on the back of the roug and tying his snout with the sheet. Then Peter fired, and fired again and again, and the damn thing was finished. I was glad I'd waited. I knew he could do it. And I didn't really want to get in that water.

More than that, I didn't want to expose myself to either one of them. SuzieQ wouldn't know what to think, and Peter would think I didn't trust him, which wasn't entirely true. I trusted Peter enough to tell him what I really am; enough to make love to him. I just didn't trust him to be able to handle anything nonhuman by himself. That's like asking a piranha to go up against a bear. No matter how sharp his teeth, the fish is going to need help.

CHAPTER FIFTY-TWO

SuzieQ calmed down a lot faster than I expected. I wanted to get her to the car and turn on the heater, but I had to make sure there were no signs left of that glob of screwed-up DNA. All I needed was an early-morning hiker to find an alligator tail growing out of a wolf's leg. I mean, come on . . . I was still learning the terms for some of the things I'd seen—boxenwolves and loup-garoux and weres—but this creature wasn't even one identifiable thing! "What the hell is a rougarou, SuzieQ? And how do you know about them?" I'd moved down to the water's edge and was searching for body parts. "And how did you know to tie his snout like that?"

"Well, he's part alligator, ain't he? My daddy used to work summers in Brazos Bend State Park and he was always talkin' about gators. How you could keep their mouths closed with your two hands 'cause they have real weak muscles for openin' their mouths. He used to wrap duct tape around their snouts when he was trappin' 'em. I just figured the sheet could do the same thing."

I couldn't see anything in the water. Whatever was left must be twenty feet down. All of a sudden it struck me: Here I was with another murder solved, another perp dead, and no fucking way to explain it to the Captain. What was I going to do, tell him the guy who killed Graciella de la Garza was lying in pieces at the bottom of another duck pond—and oh, by the way, they were pieces of a man-wolf-alligator? Fuck me a duck. "But that DeWayne thing was some kind of aberration, SuzieQ—some fucking supernatural monster. That's like seeing Sasquatch or something. Bigfoot. What do you mean, you didn't think it was real? How do you even know about it to begin with?" I couldn't tell her this was one in a long list of *Island of Dr. Moreau* escapees that I'd suddenly discovered existed—just in the last month since I'd met Ovsanna.

"I'm a Catholic girl from the South, Peter. Everybody knows 'bout rougaroux, especially Ovsanna's friend Maral. She's from the bayou, right? Hell, the rougaroux come from the bayou. I just never believed they really existed. I thought it was a tale the old people made up to scare us kids, just for the hell of it. Like a bogeyman. A rougarou's a man who breaks the rules about eatin' during Lent, and that makes him change into an alligator and a werewolf and a vampyre all rolled into one. He roams around at night, tormentin' folks he runs into. Only this guy wasn't roamin' around at random. He was after you. He came to your house snoopin' around, and when he couldn't find you, he grabbed me to use as bait. That sure wasn't random. He told me Maral McKenzie sent him lookin' for you." She stood up and squeezed some of the water out of her pajamas. They were pale blue flannel, a western motif with rattlesnakes and armadillos and wooden rail fences printed on them. She was so tall, they ended two inches above her anklebone.

"There's a lot going on, SuzieQ, and I can't tell you most of it. Maral McKenzie brought him here from Louisiana, supposedly because she wanted to get him away from dealing drugs to her brother. That's all I know for sure." I didn't tell her he was probably the perp in the Sportsmen's Lodge murder. The less she knew about him, the better.

"Well, I can tell you somethin', sugar. I think Ms. McKenzie wants you dead. I told you, didn't I? Weeks ago, when you were thinkin' she was the Cinema Slayer? I told you to be careful of her. She's got the hots for Ovsanna Moore and you're movin' in on her territory. And she's from the South, Peter. You know southern women will do just about anythin' to keep their man. Or in this case—woman."

CHAPTER FIFTY-THREE

Once again, I could smell Peter's blood. The rougarou had sliced his back with its tail spikes, and what hadn't washed away in the pond was drying under his torn T-shirt. I could use my saliva to heal the cuts, but I'd have to wait until he told me what happened. Instead, I stayed hidden long enough to make certain he and SuzieQ were all right.

I heard SuzieQ talking about Maral, and finally I understood what was happening. SuzieQ was right. Everything she told Peter about DeWayne and Maral made sense. Maral hadn't been using magick to make DeWayne go away. She wanted Peter out of my life. That's what the spells were for. The animal hairs on his walkway; the pinholes in that candle stub in Thomas's wastebasket. That's why she was burying that pepper-covered candle in the cemetery. And when those hadn't worked, somehow she'd found out what DeWayne was and she'd arranged for him to attack Peter. Maral had arranged for Peter's death.

Rage flooded through me. I felt the change coming on, anger taking control of my body. If I didn't calm down, I was going to

have to drive with my fucking claws out and my fangs in place, seeing everything in shades of gray and having to concentrate on which
traffic light was lit. Instantly, I shifted to my car, way ahead of Peter
and SuzieQ. I sat hidden in the dark, breathing slowly and deeply to
keep myself from changing. It took all my concentration to drive
back to the house.

Maral was asleep when I got there, her red hair fanned out on
her pillow like an Avedon photo of Suzy Parker from the fifties. I'd
pounded up the stairs, intent on pulling her out of bed and throwing
her against a wall.

She looked so innocent sleeping there in her pale pink nightshirt. I watched her soft breath, her arms flung open atop the sheets,
her wrists exposed. Those pale, slender veins throbbing under the
flawless skin; not a sign of the hundreds of times I'd pierced her in
the decade since we'd met. I loved running my tongue up and down
the inside of her arms, brushing my lips on her skin ever so lightly
before penetration. I'd been feeding on Maral for nearly nine years.
She'd been my confidante, my assistant, my lover, and my life's
blood. It had never been an equal partnership, but it had always ful-
filled each of our needs. It worked for us. Until now.

I thought about what she'd tried to do, and my anger intensified.

"Maral," I said, my voice so cold that I didn't recognize it,
"wake up."

She opened her eyes. When she saw the look on my face, she
pulled away to the far side of the bed, holding the blanket to her
neck as if it could protect her.

"You tried to kill him, didn't you," I said. My words came out
strangled.

"Who? What are you talking about?" Her face, already pale
from morning sleep, drained of all color. The red began leaching
from her hair, and I knew I was changing. The whites of my eyes
filled with minuscule threadlike veins; soon they would be glowing
red.

"You fucking bitch!" I growled, and this time I did throw her
against the wall. My talons dug into the muscled flesh of her upper

arms and I heaved her from the bed, pinning her to the full-length
mirror across the room. I looked past her for a moment and saw my
snarling face reflected back at me, lips pulled open, fangs descend-
ing. Talk about a money shot—it was a shame I couldn't use that on-
screen. "Don't pretend you don't know what I'm talking about, Maral.
You've been using hoodoo to get Peter out of my life. And when that
didn't work, you used DeWayne Carter. DeWayne Carter killed that
girl at the Sportsmen's Lodge and you knew it and you sicced him on
Peter!"

"I didn't know he was a rougarou when I brought him here,
Ovsanna. I swear it. I just wanted to get him away from Jamie. I didn't
figure out what he was until I saw that picture of him that Peter said
was the killer. And then I thought about what you saw when you
touched her body—about how she'd been killed like a gator would—
and I figured it out."

"And what . . . once you realized what he was, you decided to
put him to work? Are you fucking nuts? Maral—he tried to kill Peter
King!"

"I know that! I convinced him to do it! He was ranting about
that girl being a dealer and trying to charge him street prices, even
though they had the same supplier, and how he got so pissed off he
'let the ol' rougarou out and they took care of business.' He said sometimes it pays to have a curse on you, and I said, Well, now he had the
cops on him, and if Peter King showed up to arrest him, he could
kiss his movie career good-bye. And that's all I had to do. I just gave
him Peter's address and went home and put on my black bustier and
crotchless panties to wait for you."

"Why?!" I could barely speak, I was so enraged.

"Because I tried everything else. I used his business card and the
ring you gave me, and I made a Breakup Spell and a Come to Me
Spell. I left the animal hairs with the pins and nails at his doorstep. I
prayed to the Little Cajun Saint, because that's the only saint I know
besides the football players. I poured breakup oil on a candle and
pricked it with a rusty nail and threw the pieces far away from each
other. I even poured hyssop tea on myself. Nothing I read about

worked! He's taking you away from me. I can't let him do that. I won't. You're my whole life. Please, Ovsanna, you have to under-stand!"

I lost it. What little control I had once I'd changed was gone. Maral was squirming in my grasp, blood flowing from the rendering my talons had made in her flesh. The sanguinolent perfume was overwhelming. Coupled with my rage, it drove me to pure instinct, and I watched in the mirror, like I was watching one of my own horror films, as I drove my fangs deep into Maral's throat.

The blood flowed out faster than I could swallow. I must have pierced her jugular, but I didn't care. She writhed and bucked and begged me to release her, but I reveled in her juices—rubbing that rich red viscous liquid all over my face and eyes and throat. Sucking as hard as I could. Drinking as fast as I could. Swallowing as much as I could.

Minutes passed and her body quieted.

"Ovsanna," she whispered.

I pulled my mouth away and looked in her eyes. Those beautiful gray-green eyes. She was dying. Blood pumped from her throat, even without my lips there to draw it out.

"I'm sorry, Ovsanna. I love you. I didn't want to lose you."

My rage had abated along with my Thirst. What the hell was I doing? I didn't want to kill her. I couldn't forgive her and I couldn't trust her, but I didn't want to kill her. In the mirror behind her, I barely recognized myself. Ovsanna Hovannes Garabedian of the Clan Dak-hanavar of the First Bloodline was there. Ovsanna Moore wasn't. I stared at myself for a long minute, thinking back to the Turkish massacres in my homeland at the beginning of the last century. I had slaughtered indiscriminately until then, the first 350 years of my life, whenever I needed to feed; but seeing the brutality leveled against those Armenian villagers had overwhelmed me. Hundreds of thou-sands of them raped, tortured, and butchered or forced into the desert to die of starvation. Children. Babies. I couldn't face being a part of that. It left me searching for a way to control my nature. And eventu-ally I learned.

But the vampyre I was seeing in the mirror had forgotten what I had learned.

I stared at my reflection, willing myself back in control.

"Maral, listen to me. Can you hear me?" Nothing I could do would stop the bleeding. This wasn't a simple puncture wound that I had made; I couldn't close it and heal it with my saliva. There was only one thing I could do. If it had been anyone else I cared for, I wouldn't hesitate, but no one else I cared for was as unstable as Maral had become. Would I be able to control her if I saved her? Look what happened to Rudy when I turned him. How much more unbalanced would she be?

"Maral, can you hear what I'm saying?"

She didn't answer. Her eyes were closed and her breathing was thready. She looked so innocent. So helpless.

"I'm not going to let you die. I can turn you. Do you understand?" I wouldn't do it without her agreement.

She opened her eyes and stared at me.

"Do you understand, Maral? Will you let me turn you? You will become one of my kind. It's the only way I can give you your life."

She nodded and moved her lips. I bent closer to them, her blood dripping from my mouth to her cheeks.

"Turn me," she whispered.

CHAPTER FIFTY-FOUR

I held Maral in my arms as best I could while she underwent the transformation from her genus to mine. As angry as I was at her betrayal, I still wished there were some way I could lessen the violent agony brought on by the change.

I couldn't. The pain was excruciating, I knew. I'd held Rudy and Ty and several others when they turned, watching them writhe and buck as they sucked on my nipples, with their insides ripping apart and rearranging themselves. It starts like the burn you get when you've been working out—that feeling of hardness, of muscles expanding. Only it isn't just the muscles, it's everything inside pushing out. Like that moment before orgasm when you know you're going over the edge, you're going to explode, and there's no pulling back. But with the turning, there's no release, there's no explosion. Just a consistent swelling, until the fullness becomes pain. An aching at first, throbbing, then sharper, a rolling pain that moves like waves through the body. And burns. Ty described it as a white-hot flame searing him from the inside out. Rudy said he felt as though someone were tearing his organs from their membranes, moving them around, scrambling them.

Enkindling him from within. The only thing that lessened the pain
was the sucking.

It was hours before Maral's body stopped seizing and she lay
limp in my arms. I slid out from under her and went to her closet for
a robe. The French doors were open. A sharp December breeze tossed
the curtains around, but Maral's skin was unblemished by the cold.
Just like mine. I covered her and moved across the room to sit. She
opened her eyes.

"You're alive," I said.

"What happened? What did you do to me? The pain . . . is it
over?"

"Yes, Maral. The pain is gone."

"Am I . . . am I like you now?" She'd begun to shake.

"You are. You are vampyre now. You were dying—it was the
only way I could save you. And you agreed, do you remember?"

She wrapped her arms around herself to lessen the tremors. She
nodded. "You asked if you could turn me, didn't you? I was moving
toward a great brightness, but I didn't want to leave you, and I said
yes. I remember that. How long ago was that? What time is it, is it
Friday afternoon?"

We both looked at the clock. It was one twenty. I expected Peter
to show up at my door any minute with an arrest warrant for Maral.

She rose from the floor, pulling on her robe, and went to her
closet. She had her back to me. "You have a meeting with Solgar this
evening. I need to take care of things. I need to take a shower and
get dressed to go to the office." The shaking hadn't stopped completely. She reached for a hanger and knocked several to the floor.

"No, Maral. You're not taking care of things any longer. I don't
want you back at the office. Now turn around."

She wouldn't. She bent down to pick up the clothes that had
fallen and then stayed there, kneeling on the floor with her shoulders
hunched, clutching her robe around her. I could tell she expected to
cry, wanted to, probably, but she couldn't. She never would again.
My kind don't.

"I don't want to talk about this, Ovsanna. I just want things to be the same. I don't . . . I don't want to know anything else. I'll just . . . be whatever you say I am and do whatever you tell me to do, but please, please don't send me away. Please. I asked you to turn me so I could stay with you. You can't send me away now. I do everything for you. And if I'm like you now, I can do even more."

I'd had enough. I pulled her out of the closet and over to the bed. "You don't have a clue what you're talking about. You betrayed me, Maral. I almost killed you because of it. I can't keep you with me any longer. I can't even let you stay in Los Angeles. You are one of mine and there is much I'm supposed to help you with, to adapt to your new existence, but I will not."

"What do you mean? What do I need to know? What will happen to me?"

I pushed her down on the floor and held her face close to the dried blood on the carpet. "Smell that," I said. "What do you feel? What do you want to do?"

She twisted her hair out of my hands. Her mouth was on the rug. She began licking the blood. Tentatively, at first, but then the more she licked, the more she wanted. She used her nails to scratch off flakes of it and shove them in her mouth. In seconds she was scrabbling across the dried puddle, tearing at the bloodied wool. I grabbed her by the hair to pull her up, sat her back down on the bed.

"There. You see? You're a vampyre now. Everything you knew about yourself is no longer valid. Your body doesn't work the way it did. Your hunger, your sex, your strength, your needs—all different. There are a thousand things you need to learn: how to control your appetites, how to use your abilities, how to live among humans without being discovered. And later, how to temper your emotions. Later still, how to deal with watching the people you care about age and die while you have to move on to someplace where you won't be recognized so you can't be questioned. Living in anonymity, or living as someone else—or something else—entirely."

She grabbed on to me. "I can do that, Ovsanna, I can do that, but I need you to teach me. I need you. You can't send me away."

"You'll go to New York, Maral. I want you as far away from

here as possible. For your own sake as well. Peter knows you tried to have him killed. I don't know what he intends to do about it, but he's a cop, remember? I've already called Theda and Charles. They'll take you in and guide you. Maybe you can work for them in one of their businesses." Theda and Charles own a chain of boutiques specializing in Goth clothing and makeup. It would be a perfect place for Maral to begin to learn about herself.

"But I love you, Ovsanna."

"That will change now, too. As a human, you loved me. You've loved me because I completed something in you; I provided whatever it was that you wanted in yourself and couldn't find. Fearlessness, maybe, or self-esteem. Stability. Emotional strength. Worthiness. The caretaking you needed. You're vampyre now. Vampyres don't need caretaking. We don't need anything—except blood. We don't need others to give us a sense of worth; we don't need attention to make us feel valuable. We don't need 'things' to show others what we've achieved. We don't need like humans do, and so we don't love like humans do. You'll see."

"But you've kept me with you all these years. You must love me."

"It's a word, Maral. And whatever it means to you, it's not something I'm capable of. I can use it to mean I have enjoyed being with you, I have trusted you enough to expose myself to you. I would rather have had you in my life—close to me—than be alone. My life was easier with you in it, and I took pleasure in caring for you. If you want to call that love, then fine, you can use the word. But I'm telling you, and you will come to know this on your own, vampyres are ultimately solitary creatures. What humans classify as love doesn't translate to our existence."

"But Ovsanna—"

"You need to bathe and dress and pack. Now. You're leaving for New York."

Maral wouldn't need to feed for several weeks, but I didn't want her around people until she'd had time with Theda and Charles to adjust to her new self. She was going to have to come to terms with a lot, not the least of which was living without me. It's one of the reasons I so rarely turn anyone. Helping a newly made vampyre find his way in the world is a greater responsibility than raising a baby. At least with a baby no one's comparing the way things are with the way they were. Newly mades are not tabula rasa; they've got a whole list of expectations based on their past life. Like making plans for dinner. Well, she'd learn soon enough not to do that anymore.

I called Sveta and had her order a car to take Maral to LAX and then charter a Citation to get her to New York. Vampyres hate flying commercial jets—all those horrific human odors in a confined space with recirculated air. It's torture. No need to expose her to that so early in her creation. I would continue to pay her living expenses until she no longer needed my help. "You'll be fine, Maral. Theda is Azeman, and Charles is one of mine. I turned him years ago. He'll know what you're going through, and they'll both be able to help you."

"Will I see you again?" she asked. Already her emotions seemed subdued.

"Of course you will. You're Dakhanavar now. We have a lot of years ahead of us."

She handed the limo driver her suitcases, took one long, last look at me, and left—just minutes before Peter arrived.

CHAPTER FIFTY-FIVE

I drove SuzieQ home in the Jag. She showered and washed her hair while I cleaned up the mess in her bedroom. Dick Nixon was in pieces in the kitchen. I used a pair of barbecue tongs to drop him down the disposal. I was just going to hit the switch to grind him up when Suzie came into the room, wrapped in a towel, and saw what I was doing. She screamed, dropped the towel, and shoved me across the room. I landed on my ass, staring up at this six-foot-tall naked Amazon who was pulling chunks of dead snake out of the plumbing and wailing uncontrollably. She didn't calm down until she'd laid out all his pieces on the counter and then rearranged them in the proper order, so they formed a sort of ragged-edged dead snake jigsaw puzzle. By that time, she'd stopped crying and was crooning James Taylor's "You Can Close Your Eyes" to the chunks. At least it wasn't "Black Snake Moan." She covered them with a tea towel embroidered "Mondays Are for Ironing," wrapped the whole thing in the towel she'd been wearing, and walked outside naked to lay him in the garden under the pansies. I've got to say she was quite a sight, especially from my vantage point on the floor. Especially when she bent down to deposit him. Then she came back in, put on pajamas and a robe, checked on the remaining reptiles, and walked with me to my place. I didn't want her to be alone.

The sky was lightening. SuzieQ made decaf while I took a shower. She insisted the cuts on my back needed attention, so I let her play doctor with a box of Band-Aids. We stood in the kitchen drinking coffee and talked about what we'd just been through.

"What're you gonna do, sugar? You can't tell anybody 'bout what happened. Can you?"

"No, SuzieQ. Nobody would believe it. And you can't, either."

"Hell, Peter, who'm I gonna tell? You're the only person I talk to in this town with any degree of trust, and I sure as hell ain't gonna tell anyone back home. They think I'm nuts the way it is. 'Sides, rougarou or not, we killed someone, didn't we? How do we explain that?"

"We don't. Whatever that thing was, nobody's going to miss it. Except maybe Maral McKenzie. And I have a feeling she's not going to want anyone searching for it, either."

It was seven o'clock Friday morning by the time I fell asleep. I'd set Suzie up in my guest room and we both slept until one. So much for my day off. She made French roast espresso while I made mango smoothies. We took them with us when I drove her back to Franklin Canyon to get her car. After she left, I walked to the duck pond. There was no sign of the attack. No body parts floating on the water. No shredded clothes lying anywhere. Nothing.

I called Ovsanna at the office, but her receptionist said she hadn't come in yet. Neither had Maral. I didn't bother to call the house; Ovsanna would either be home or she wouldn't, and I didn't want to broadcast my arrival.

Graciella de la Garza was on my mind while I was driving. Maybe she'd gone to the hotel to sell DeWayne his drugs and he hadn't liked the deal. Whatever it was, he must have shifted and drowned her and torn her apart. That would explain those tiny handprints on the ground. And what I thought were a large dog's paw prints. Not dog at all. Wolf. Well . . . werewolf, Louisiana style.

"Peter?" Ovsanna must have been watching the monitor. Her voice came over the intercom before I pressed the button at the gate. I had to turn down the iPod to hear her. Robbie Robertson singing "Somewhere Down the Crazy River."

She was waiting outside the front door, the way she always did. I couldn't tell if she'd slept or not; she never looks bad, no matter what. She'd changed clothes, though. No Dallas Cowboys sweat-shirt or rolled-up jeans. She was barefoot, in cutoff jeans and a man's white shirt, the sleeves turned back.

She reached out for me. I wrapped my arms around her and kissed her and momentarily forgot what I was there for. I lifted her off her toes, our mouths still together, and carried her inside the foyer. Her fingers found the Band-Aids on my back.

"What happened?" she asked.

That brought me back to my job. "Where's Maral?"

Ovsanna didn't answer my question. She shook her head, took my hand, and led me back to her library, the same room we'd been in on Christmas Eve when I'd freaked out and left. That was six days ago. It seemed like months. This time she sat next to me on the sofa. She said, "I know why you're here, Peter. I know what Maral did."

"She told you?"

"No. I followed you last night. Now, don't get mad. I was wor-ried about SuzieQ. I had a feeling it was something more serious than a date gone bad and I wanted to see for myself."

"You wanted to see for yourself. You didn't think I could take care of it, huh? Whatever *it* was. Whatever it was that she had asked me to come *alone* for?" I was getting angry, and not just at Maral. "So you know what happened and you're lying when you ask about the bandages. What the hell, Ovsanna? Why didn't you just show yourself? Sweep in and save the day? You're a vampyre. You've got superpowers. What the hell do we need the police for, anyway? We've got Ovsanna Moore!" I was off the sofa and yelling at her.

She didn't raise her voice. "I'm sorry, Peter. I didn't show myself because I knew you could handle it. And you did. But think about it. Think about what you've seen in the last month. You know now that there are things out there that are out of your control, things you can't possibly go up against by yourself. We're being stalked, Peter, and it's not just your garden-variety attacker. If DeWayne Carter had been a true werebeast and not just a rougarou—if he'd been one of Lilith's kind—you wouldn't have had a chance in hell. You saw what they can do, in Palm Springs. And you know what you can't. This isn't about strength or training, or even marksmanship. It's about reality— and your reality has just expanded way past anyone around you. We've got to stay together on this."

"Yeah? Well, I don't think our staying together is what Maral had in mind. Where is she? I'm taking her in."

"For what? What can you arrest her for?"

"I'll think of something. How about she tried to have me killed? How about she hired a fucking alligator to kidnap my friend and drown me? Conspiracy to commit murder by beast? You know that thing killed the woman at the Sportsmen's Lodge, don't you?"

"Yes, I know it. And you know you're not going to be able to arrest Maral for hiring a fucking alligator to do anything. They'd have you committed before the ink dried on her fingerprints."

"She can't get away with this, Ovsanna. She's unbalanced and she's dangerous. Now where is she?"

"She's gone. I took care of it. She's not going to be a problem any longer."

"What do you mean, gone? Gone like DeWayne Carter is gone? Like the rougarou is gone? What did you do, Ovsanna?"

CHAPTER FIFTY-SIX

I didn't tell Peter what I'd done. Not exactly. I told him I'd sent Maral away and she wouldn't be coming back. I started to say she'd never eat lunch in this town again, but he wouldn't get it. He didn't need to know I'd turned her. Not then, at least. We were already having issues about trust. I didn't want him worrying he was next in line.

It took some time, but I calmed him down. "You don't have a dead body; you don't have any evidence. You can't charge Maral with anything without sounding like you've lost your mind," I told him. I convinced him she was no longer a problem for us, and then I convinced him we had better things to do than worry about Maral.

I took him upstairs, and we did them.

It was different this time. Maybe because I knew Maral was gone, maybe because I'd almost lost Peter to the rougarou. The need was different. Not driven by lust or Thirst. We took our time, exploring, exposing ourselves a bit. A different kind of intensity. A deeper pleasure. I never dropped my fangs until the very end.

———————

My reaction to Maral's departure didn't hit me until after Peter left. A wave of sadness washed over me when I walked into my office and saw her abandoned desk. I had to sit down for a minute.

She'd cleared off her papers. Her laptop was gone. The scripts she kept piled on the floor were missing. That corner of the room was bare. She'd removed the black-and-white candid Helmut Newton took of us on the set of *Dying to Meet You* and a publicity still of the two of us Santa D'Orazio shot for *Vanity Fair*. I could replace the *Vanity Fair* shot, but not the candid.

I couldn't replace Maral. I wasn't even going to try. She'd been working for me for ten years, living in my house for nine. She did everything for me. She was my Alfred. Not just at home, in my business as well. I guess as much as a vampyre can feel love, I loved her. It wasn't any deep, wrenching pain settling on me—the kind I had to use my imagination for to write my screen roles—but it was a true sorrow. I missed her.

And she was my blood. My life source. I'd drained so much of her, I wouldn't need to feed for a month or more, but I would eventually need to drink again. I thought about Peter and how our lovemaking had been this second time. I'd kept my fangs sheathed until the last minutes when he'd slid inside me, and then I'd only nicked his skin. I didn't want to drink; I wanted to suck. I wanted to suck on him while he was inside me, pounding harder and harder until we both lost control. As intense as it had been, there'd been a tenderness there and the merest hint of vulnerability from both of us. Maybe because we trusted each other a bit more. I wondered what would come next.

CHAPTER FIFTY-SEVEN

By the time I left Ovsanna's, it was almost five. I was drained. Not literally this time, but I definitely needed some nourishment. I drove over the hill to see if my mother wanted to feed her favorite son. I didn't have to ask. She saw my car in the driveway and the braciole was on the stove before I opened the screen door. She had pizza dough resting on the granite counter. While we talked, she formed a half dozen calzones and slipped them onto the baking stone in the oven. I grabbed some bagged lettuce, cherry tomatoes, chi-chi beans, and avocado and made a salad. My dad came in to set the table. Start to finish, the food was on the table in fifteen minutes.

"So I've got a question," my mother said. "What the heck did Ovsanna Moore do to my sister on Christmas Eve?"

"Aunt Addie, you mean? Why, what's wrong with her?"

"There's nothing wrong with her. That's what I'm asking you about. She hasn't been this easy to get along with since she ran for homecoming queen in twelfth grade."

"I don't know, Ma. Ovsanna's just got a way about her. She can be pretty persuasive."

"Yeah? Has she persuaded you into bed yet?"

"Ma!"

"Well, I wanna know. She's a big-time movie star and a Holly-wood producer. And she's got to be at least ten years older than you, although she sure doesn't look it. I wanna know what's goin' on. Are you sure you can take care of yourself?"

"Ma. What's next? You're gonna tell me to make sure I go to the bathroom before we leave the house?"

"Well, are you using protection, at least? You know what they say on those commercials—you're not just sleepin' with her, you're sleepin' with everybody she's ever slept with. And she's been around a long time."

You don't know the half of it, Ma. "Ah jeez, Ma, I skeeve when you talk about stuff like that. I'm a grown man. Just trust me. I know what I'm doing."

And thank God, I thought, you don't.

Chapter Fifty-Eight

Peter left a little before five P.M. I hurried to shower and change clothes, missing Maral even more when I had to drive myself to Beverly Hills. Goddamn her and her jealousy.

At six o'clock in the evening on Friday, December 30, it was eleven in the morning the next day in Japan. Solgar and I had a date to meet at my office to fax the signed merger papers to Takeyama-san, Yoshiri-san, and Ito-san. The three gentlemen, waiting in their office in Tokyo on New Year's Eve, would then sign them and fax them back. I would have new partners, and Anticipation Studios would have a lot more money. I was excited. I'd started the company ten years earlier with my own money and a 20 percent investment from a private equity firm. Initially, I was making low-budget horror films with limited theatrical release, aimed straight for the home entertainment market, but when *The Milk Carton Murders* and *What the Orderly Saw* grossed a hundred million each, I bought the production facilities in Santa Clarita and brought in Thomas DeWitte as my head of development. Once Thomas came on board, we started making six to eight features a year, along with several television films and a series pilot. Now I could push that number up. And not only could I do the deal with John Carpenter, but I'd be able to pursue George Romero and Sam Raimi and some of the hot young directors who'd been making a name in the genre, like Alex Horwitz. For years, I'd been wanting to film George R. R. Martin's *Fevre Dream*—one of the few novels about my kind that I really loved—and I thought Kim Newman's *Anno Dracula* would make a great cable series. Now I would have the money to do it.

As long as Mick Erzatz didn't kill me first.

Solgar was waiting for me in my office. He'd accepted Sveta's offer of a drink—to make her comfortable, I suppose; he's such a gentleman—and a demitasse sat untouched on the coffee table in front of him. I knew he couldn't stand the smell any more than I could. I closed the door and dumped the espresso onto the Australian fern in the corner.

"Sorry about that, Ernst. It was very gracious of you to say yes to Sveta."

"She took me by surprise, Chatelaine. It's usually Maral who shows me in, and she knows not to offer me coffee. Where is she?" He stood up and came towards me, reaching out with both hands to show me he wasn't holding his *kirpan*. He air-kissed me on both sides of my face. That was fine with me. I don't like getting too near his sucker-tipped tongue. Just seems so unsanitary.

I sat down at my desk, where Ernst had stacked the papers for signing. One by one, I began initialing each page.

"Have you heard anything, Ernst? Is there any talk on the street about someone wanting me gone?"

"No, Chatelaine, and I don't understand it. No one knows more about what goes on in this town than I. You know that. I take great pride in that. I have probed and queried and listened—discreetly, of course—and I have heard nothing. I am sorry to be letting you down, but no one in town is talking."

"Well, I think I know why. My stalker isn't welcome in this town any longer. He's living in his pseudo castle in Montecito, surrounded by his sycophants and Michael Jackson's leftover menagerie."

"Mick Erzatz?"

I nodded.

"You think Mick Erzatz is a were? The wolf that came into your yard to attack you? Why would you think that?" He was so taken aback, he sank into the chair in front of my desk.

I explained to him what I'd learned when I'd laid hands on Madelaine Sauvage. How I'd seen Lilith birthing Mick Erzatz. And fucking him.

When I finished, he looked away for the longest time. I could see his mind working, thinking back to incidences that would support my belief. Finally he nodded, his lips pressed together in the flattest of smiles. "Mick Erzatz is a were. Forgive me, Ovsanna, I should have known. His behavior all those years when he was head of WorldWide: preying on young girls, ruthlessly stealing clients from other agencies, slashing at his associates' reputations . . . of course, now it all makes sense."

"We both should have known. But now we do. And I'm going to have to deal with him. Soon."

I'd finished the individual pages, all thirty-six of them, and started autographing the lines Solgar had highlighted. I hit the intercom.

"Sveta, would you get the Japanese gentlemen on the line, please? And then once we're connected, you can go home. Have a happy New Year." She was taking Monday and Tuesday off; it would be a nice long weekend for her. A pain in the ass for me with Maral gone, but I didn't want to disappoint her with a change in plans. I answered Solgar's earlier question.

"Maral became a problem, Ernst. I lost control."

"It never really works, does it, Chatelaine. Humans and vampyres. When I think of all the young men I've had to ignore. I must say I'm surprised she lasted as long as she did. But she was special to you, wasn't she?"

"I didn't kill her, if that's what you're thinking. But I lost control of her, and then, of myself. I had to turn her to save her life. It's not what I would have chosen had she not backed me into a corner."

"But that's fine, then. She's one of us now. Although I suspect you'll have to keep an eye on her for a while, until you see how her nature develops. Why isn't she here?"

The intercom rang. "Because if she were, she'd be in jail. Can you imagine a newly turned in a cell full of tattooed veins?"

It took almost an hour to get everything faxed to Japan and back. The machine jammed several times, and Solgar went on a rant about outsourcing electronics manufacturing and how nothing ever worked when you needed it to. I'd been at the Great Exhibition in London in 1851 for a demonstration of one of the first telefax machines. I was just glad technology had come this far and I didn't have to go to Japan to finalize the deal.

The last sheet came through, and I dialed Tokyo once more to let them know everything was in order. After we all wished one another *domo arigatoo gozaimasu* and *kanpai* many times, I hung up. Immediately, the intercom rang.

"Yes?"

Sveta said, "Ms. Moore, I'm sorry to bother you, but there are people down here."

"What are you doing in the office, Sveta? I thought you went home."

"Well, I was just locking up when that lady came to the door. You know, that one that was here the other day?" She lowered her voice to a whisper. "With the weird outfit and all that makeup?"

"Mary? She's downstairs?" In the background, I heard another voice. It sounded like Orson.

"Yes. Although her hair is different. And she's not alone. Several people have arrived, and they all seem to know each other. I didn't want to interrupt you while you were calling Japan, but one after another they came to say they wanted to see you. One of them is the handsome man from that TV show *Lost*."

I turned to Solgar. "Mary and Tyrone and Orson are all down in the lobby, Ernst. Do you know why?"

"I don't. Unless it's to congratulate you on signing the papers. They all called to ask when you were doing that, but no one said anything about coming to see you. I assumed they wanted to send flowers."

I spoke into the intercom. "You can send them up, Sveta. And then go ahead and go home. I'll be fine. And thank you. Have a happy New Year."

I neatened the stack of merger papers and gave them to Ernst to copy and keep on file. Then I opened the door to my office and watched Tod Browning, James Whale, Mary Pickford, Tyrone Power, and Orson Welles walk up the stairs. Five of my Vampyres of Hollywood.

Chapter Fifty-nine

"How the hell are you, Chatelaine? I didn't know you'd have all this company. Hey, I brought you a present to celebrate the merger." Tod handed me a small ceramic figurine of an Asian girl in a kimono with a parasol. She looked like Anna Mae Wong.

"What is this, Tod?" All of my clan have their eccentricities; it goes with the species, I suppose, although I don't think of *myself* as eccentric. But Tod leads the way. He became such a recluse after directing *Miracles for Sale* that *Variety* accidentally published an obit for him in 1944. That did make it easier to keep his true nature hidden. That, and the fact that he stopped speaking completely until after he'd "died." Even now, his voice sounded scratchy and unused—a hundred years of smoking Lucky Strikes will do that to you.

"It's from my collection. If I remember correctly, it's an original. The studio passed them out in 1923 when *Drifting* was released." He removed his bowler hat and laid it on the back of my sofa, his arm resting there behind Mary. I saw her hand go up to her necklace, and I knew what she was thinking. Tod had a reputation for stealing jewelry right off the necks of his women friends. Even though Mary had turned him after that terrible auto accident, she knew better than to trust him completely.

"I'll bet I can make it disappear," said Orson. "In fact, hand me your hat, Tod, I think there's something in there." And before any of us even knew what he was talking about, Orson leaned over Mary, practically suffocating her with his girth, grabbed Tod's hat, and pulled a rabbit out of it. The damn thing immediately started peeing on my rug, liquid splashing everywhere because Orson had him by his neck at arm's height. "Well," he said, "what do you know. I found a rabbit."

"Oh, for God's sake, Orson," I spit, "what the hell are you doing?"

"Just a little magic, Chatelaine, just a little magic. I so seldom get a chance to show off anymore. You know, no one ever asks to see magic tricks."

"Well, there's a reason for that, dear boy," said James. "Especially if it involves urine and furry animals." He was using a giant candy cane as a walking stick and he quickly moved to the opposite side of the room, out of dribbling distance.

"Oh . . . this isn't really magic. It's Charlie."

"Charlie? Chaplin?"

"Yes. He didn't want to take a chance on being recognized, but when I told him why I was coming, he said he wanted to tag along. Worked like a charm, didn't it?" Orson put the rabbit—Charlie—down, and he hopped over to the sofa and jumped in Mary's lap. Thank God Pola wasn't here.

"Oh, for God's sake." I walked out of my office into my bathroom, ran a hand towel under the tap, and came back in with a shaker of Comet to wipe up the spots on the rug. Ernst took the towel from me and began dabbing.

"I've brought you something, too, darling," said Mary. "After I left Neiman's the other day, I had my driver stop at the video store— where, I might add, no one recognized me—and I picked up my latest DVD collection for you. *Mary Pickford: Signature Collection.* And honestly, Ovsanna, the salesclerk didn't even recognize me—with that photo of me right on the cover in front of him! I really don't think it's going to be a problem." She was right about that. She'd changed her hair and her outfit once again. This time she was wearing a wig I swear I'd seen on Tina Turner at the Fillmore East in 1969. It was such a huge Afro, I don't know how she fit through my office door. And the outfit was something out of *Braveheart*. Green plaid kilt, red wool knee-highs, lace-up Doc Martens, and a blue velvet blazer over a frilly white blouse. Douglas Fairbanks wouldn't recognize her.

"A problem for what, Mary?" Tyrone asked. "What are you worried about? What are you doing here, anyway?"

"Well, I want Ovsanna to bring me back into the business. I think I'm perfect to replace Thomas as Head of Development at Anticipation."

Charlie hopped off her lap onto the floor and turned around to stare at her, his front paws covering his mouth.

"You?" said Orson. "Oh, my goodness. Well, you would be good, my dear, although you'd have to hire someone to dress you, but I've already talked to Ovsanna about that job. I *know* how to make movies, it's not even creative with me, it's instinctive. Who better than I?"

By now, Charlie was hopping up and down like he was auditioning for *Dancing with the Stars*.

"Wait a minute. Wait a minute. Is that why you're all here?" I asked. "Ernst—"

"I'm sorry, Chatelaine. I truly didn't have any idea."

"I don't know about Orson and Mary, but of course, we're here to congratulate you, Chatelaine. This merger will be great for Anticipation." Tyrone was riffling through his carrying case. "But you're going to need more help running the studio. And I know I can do it. Your concerns about my appearance are unfounded. Look at this picture." He handed me an eight-by-ten black-and-white of a very attractive young man, dark hair, thick lashes, the same bone structure as Ty's.

"Is this you?"

"There. You see? Another actor who looks so much like me you have trouble telling us apart. His name is Danny Pino, and he's on that television series *Cold Case*. But before that he played Desi Arnaz. My point is, Ovsanna, I won't be recognized as Tyrone Power. No one will figure out the truth. I can do the job."

James left his candy cane in the corner, skirting around the stains on the rug, and used my Rigaud candle to light his cigar—without asking. "Look," he said, "all three of you are too recognizable to be in the public eye again. Well, maybe not you, Mary, if you insist on dressing like Cyndi Lauper whenever you leave the house. But what you're not taking into consideration is what Ovsanna wants to accomplish. From my considerable experience, I can state positively that horror pictures are much harder to produce successfully than the straight narrative films you all have done. Where's your *Frankenstein,* your *Bride of Frankenstein,* your *Invisible Man?*"

Tod croaked. "Oh, come off it, Jimmy. I wrote the book on horror films with *Dracula*—six months before your *Frankenstein* saw the light of day. Are you going to watch *Freaks* and tell me I don't know the genre? I had Lon Chaney playing a transvestite ventriloquist, in a silent film! Nobody can do what I do. Remember, I 'know how to create images that defy the power of time'!"

"My God, man," said Orson, who'd managed to light his pipe when I wasn't paying attention, "do you actually have your reviews memorized? What are you doing with your time these days—poring over old copies of *Variety?* Did you see your obit? You've all been out of touch way too long. Ovsanna needs someone who's kept up. Tyrone, you're down there in Mexico, playing with your bulls. Mary, God knows what you've been doing—certainly not reading fashion magazines. When's the last time one of you actually saw a film that wasn't one of your own? Ovsanna, I only need a little more financing—for sound facilities and an editing bay, primarily—and Anticipation could release *The Other Side of the Wind*. Do you know what a coup that would be?"

Charlie was in paroxysms on the floor. His front paws kept flapping up to hit his chest. His nose was twitching to the left, and his ears were crisscrossing each other. Either he was having trouble shifting back to human form or the thought of the other Vampyres of Hollywood taking Thomas's job was causing him some sort of seizure. I hoped it was a seizure. I didn't want to see him shift. Seeing Orson nude had been more than enough.

"If the two of you," I said, turning on James and Orson, "don't put out that cigar and that pipe, the only coup I'm going to care about is throwing you both out the window. Then we'll see who gets recognized, splayed on the cement on Beverly Drive!"

"Sorry, Chatelaine," Jimmy said, "I truly am. I simply got excited at the prospect of working again." He doused his cigar in the wet bar, which only added to the god-awful stench they'd both made. I kept my mouth shut while he went on. "And you know how rare it is for me to get excited over anything. I hate this time that just passes and passes. It's depressing. The only time I've felt alive recently was fighting Lilith and her minions in Palm Springs. And how often do we get to do that?"

That was the second time one of my clan had said the same thing.

Solgar must have read my mind. "Perhaps you can do it sooner than expected. The chatelaine is in danger again. Tell them, Chatelaine. They were there for Lilith's death; they are most likely in danger as well."

I told them what had been happening: how I'd been attacked in my yard by a were and then again on the beach by the paparazzi-turned-boxenwolves.

"Peter shot one of them and he died in human form. We were able to trace him to the alpha female who'd sent the pack to kill me. When I touched her, I got vivid images of Lilith and Mick Erzatz, the agent. Ex-agent. I believe he's born of her, he was sleeping with her, and he wants revenge for her death."

"Mick Erzatz?" said Orson. "That putz. He tried to get me to sign with him back in the seventies. Wouldn't leave me alone. Until I finally convinced him I wasn't interested, and then he turned vicious and tried to blackball me. Tried to convince people I was too drunk to work. Imagine, trying to blackball *me*. Me, about whom Mankiewicz said, 'There, but for the grace of God, goes God.' Nasty little putz. Erzatz, I mean, not Mank. Oh, definitely, let's go take him apart."

Mary stomped the floor with her Doc Martens. "I despise that man. He may be a were, but he acts like a pig. A chauvinist pig. Some of the things I've heard him say about women are just reprehensible. He actually called Marlene Dietrich a lesbian!"

"How long have you been alive, Mary?" Tod said dryly, doing a take only he and Bea Arthur could master.

James said, "He's a homophobe, too. You should hear some of the things he's said about Truman and Andy. I agree with Orson. If the business couldn't finish him off, the Vampyres of Hollywood can. When do we start?"

"It might not be that easy," I said. "Since the industry turned on him, he rarely leaves his home in Montecito. He's got a thirty-eight-room fortress on twenty thousand acres up in the hills there. He probably has his other weres with him. I'd have to lure them all down here without letting him know I realize what he is."

"I have a simpler solution, Chatelaine." Solgar reached into his attaché case and pulled out an engraved invitation. "Would you like to be my guest at a New Year's Eve party tomorrow night? I hadn't intended on going, but I think now I must. Our host is none other than the reclusive Mick Erzatz."

CHAPTER SIXTY

"I'm not going to let you take your life in your hands without me. I don't care how many years you've been around and how capable you think you are just because you're a vampyre. You're telling me this Mick Erzatz is related to that fucking monstrosity we got rid of in Palm Springs? I saw what you had to do to kill her. If I hadn't been there to help, you would have been vampyre sashimi."

"Peter—"

"And you're not going to show up there to kill him, Ovsanna. I can't let you do that. You don't even know for sure if he's the one who's after you. Talk to him, fine. Check him out, see if he's what you think he is. But you're not going to kill him. That's a premeditated murder charge."

"Oh, so it's okay if you shoot the guy attacking me on the beach and okay if I kill Madelaine Sauvage and okay if you kill DeWayne Carter, but I can't kill Mick Erzatz? Even though he sent the guy on the beach and that bat-shit woman to kill me?"

"Those were all self-defense killings, Ovsanna, and not one of them was a human being when they attacked. For all we know, this guy is nothing but a has-been agent, which may not classify him as a human being, but it doesn't mean you can walk into his house and open fangs. I'm going with you to this party. End of story. Do I need my tux?"

He's so friggin' Italian, isn't he? Oh well, I just had to make sure the members of my clan didn't discuss our specific plans in front of him. Once we got to the party and I was certain Mick Erzatz was the were who'd come into my yard on Christmas Eve, all bets were off. Peter could play good cop all he wanted, I was out for blood. He didn't need to know that.

Not only did Peter own a tux, but he looked so good in it when he showed up at my house, I wanted to tear it off and ravage him right then and there. I would have, too, if Orson and the others hadn't arrived while we were standing at the front door, embracing. I was wearing my silver Narciso Rodriguez strapless, which I'd chosen because it was short and I could move in it. I wasn't sure my breasts would stay covered if I had to do battle, but what the hell. Nude breasts might distract a werebeast or two, and I'd use any advantage I could get. I showed Orson and the others into the living room.

I don't know where he found one to fit him, but Orson had traded his cape for an actual limo driver's uniform, complete with a leather-visored chauffeur's cap, gloves, and a sixteen-rib umbrella. He looked very professional. Enormous, but professional.

James, Ty, and Tod were dressed all in black. Ty had on another cashmere sweater, a turtleneck this time, which didn't seem very practical to me in the event he might have to shift in a hurry. It matched his cashmere jogging pants. He hadn't been with us in Palm Springs; he was probably expecting a nice, neat kill, maybe like his bull-fighting days. Well, if we all came out of this in one piece, I'd buy him more cashmere.

Charlie, ever the showman, was wearing camo pants and a camo jacket. He'd covered his face with green greasepaint. On his five-foot-five-inch frame, he looked like a head of hair resting on a short bush. I had to give him credit, though; if he stayed outside, he'd never be noticed.

Mary looked like she should be singing folk songs with Peter and Paul. Flat bangs on a long, straight brown wig and a tie-dyed caftan with a multihued crocheted shawl. All she needed was a guitar with a capo on it. It took a while, but I finally convinced her the outfit would only make people stare at her and she'd eventually be recognized, regardless of the Judy Collins impersonation. She went up to my bedroom to change and came down as a toy Pomeranian, having agreed to let Solgar carry her into the party as the pet he never wants to leave home alone.

The plan was to have Orson drive all eight of us to Montecito in the limousine. Solgar, Peter, and I would attend the party, with Mary in Solgar's arms, while Jimmy, Charlie, Ty, and Tod stayed hidden behind the privacy screen in the limo.

After Orson dropped us off, he'd find a place to park the car and stay with it as the chauffeur. The fellows would slip out onto the property and hide until I needed them, if I needed them. I couldn't go into specifics with Peter there, but they already knew from our conversation in Solgar's office what my real intent was. They were going to have a lot of acreage to explore. Erzatz had an Olympic-size pool, a regulation basketball court, two tennis courts, a boccie court, and a private lake just beyond his back gardens. If I wanted to get a message to them, Mary could jump down and scamper away to find them. An electric train ran on tracks from the house to the vineyards and on up into the hills, where Erzatz had fenced in 250 acres for a wild animal preserve. He told everyone he had helped Michael Jackson by taking Michael's menagerie when Neverland Ranch went into foreclosure, but now that I knew his true nature, I suspected there were sentient creatures on the property who bore little resemblance to delightful zoo inhabitants. I was pretty certain the hills were crawling with werebeasts.

Mick Erzatz had deigned to do an episode of *Cribs,* which is how I knew so much about his home. I'd been fascinated seeing this short, pudgy-faced man wearing a martial arts uniform with his paunch hanging over his belt—albeit a black belt—pad through his house in his zoris while he name-dropped all the Hollywood stars he'd represented.

He'd made a fortune off his stars and his movie deals, and he'd spent it building a reproduction of a Japanese castle in the mountains overlooking the Pacific, above Santa Barbara. On camera, it looked impressive. The main building was five stories high, with two adjoining three-story structures. He had original copper and clay roof tiles imported from Hokkaido, along with stone fish and crane sculptures. Inside one of the smaller buildings was a media room, a dojo, a tanning salon, a bowling alley, a dry cleaners, and a room reserved solely for wrapping presents. That was the smaller building.

New Year's Eve traffic was bad, especially where the 101 narrows to a single lane. It took us two hours and fifteen minutes to make the ninety-minute drive to Montecito. Erzatz had been one of the lucky ones when the Tea fire swept through the area. His property was above the devastation. From the 101 we drove another forty-five minutes up a charred, winding road into the mountains. By the time we saw the lights surrounding the estate, it was after ten. My kindred were chomping at the bit. They knew we were going up against Mick and his clan, even though no one was talking about it in front of Peter. James seemed almost happy, and Orson was bellowing out the theme to *Star Wars* as he drove. I spent some of the time telling them what I knew about the layout of Erzatz's house and grounds. Solgar told us what he knew about the guests we might see there—the celebrity wannabes and junior agents who still thought Erzatz could be their ticket to fame and fortune. And the star fuckers who just wanted to be able to say they'd spent New Year's Eve at a "Hollywood" party. Mick Erzatz was trying to reestablish himself with the power elite, but from what Ernst had heard, most of the studio heads and A-list actors didn't believe he was worth driving ninety miles to party with.

The castle was built on a twenty-foot-tall stone foundation, with walls that slanted thirty degrees from the leveled peak of a mountain. We drove up a long dirt road, barricaded on either side by round wooden spikes, and came to a stone gatehouse. Female valets dressed as circus performers waited to take the car, while a dozen paparazzi crowded in front of them, ready to get shots of us as soon as the doors opened. I stared through the darkened glass, searching for collars on their necks. If any of them were boxenwolves, I couldn't tell. They were buttoned up in jackets and scarves. Orson rolled down the front window level with his visor, just enough to tell the valet he wanted to park the car himself so he could stay with it. She waved us through to another gatehouse and then down a road to the right, where sixty or seventy cars were already parked. Maybe Ernst was wrong about the guest list. A valet waited there in a golf cart to drive us back to the castle. She was also dressed as a circus performer. That seemed to be the theme of the evening.

It was borne out by Chinese acrobats forming a human pyramid at the bottom of a long flight of stone stairs. I wondered if this was the act Madelaine Sauvage had hired. We had to climb the stairs to reach the front entrance. "Who decided on a double-coated Pomeranian?" Solgar asked in ancient Armenian, indicating the mass of fur in his arms. "If I'm going to have to carry her all night, she could have at least shifted to a Chihuahua." Mary barked at him, and one of the acrobats midway up the triangle started to sneeze. I was sure the girl at the top was coming down, but somehow she managed to keep her balance. Solgar held Mary's nose closed to shut her up. She tried to bite him.

"Goddammit, Mary," I whispered, "if you don't behave, I won't even consider hiring you for Thomas's job. I need your help here. Now shut up and act like Ernst is the best owner a dog could ask for. And for God's sake, Ernst, carry her under her butt!"

A mime stood at the front door, indicating he wanted to take our coats. It was a Southern California winter night, with a temperature in the high fifties. I could smell rain in the distance. I gave him my black velvet Monique Lhuillier wrap and wondered if I'd see it again. I didn't think the mime was a thief; I just didn't know if I'd survive the night.

"This is incredible," said Peter under his breath. "I knew this guy had money, but I didn't know how much. Look at the gold leaf on the turrets. Are you sure he's the one trying to kill you?"

"Trust me, Peter. I'll *make sure* before I do anything rash. But let me get near enough to smell him and I'll know if he's human or not. That's the first step."

Seconds later, I knew. Mick Erzatz was definitely not human.

I suppose it's like pheromones between a man and a woman. To vampyres, humans give off a specific scent. Maybe it's the blood running through their veins, just below the skin. It's subtle and easily overshadowed by the tanning lotions, moisturizers, perfumes, soaps, and deodorants, or lack thereof, that color a person's hygiene. But it's always there in humans, whether they stink of body odor or wash in Chanel. Vampyres don't have it. *Dhampir* don't have it. Werebeasts don't have it.

Mick Erzatz didn't have it.

Mick Erzatz, despite the orange-vanilla candles burning everywhere and the Royall Spyce cologne he'd lavished on himself, smelled slightly pungent and feral. Just as he had the night he'd attacked me in my backyard.

As far as I was concerned, it was one more confirmation that he was the one who wanted me dead.

"Ernst, you old queen," he said as he approached us, looking first at Solgar and then at Peter and me. He did a double take when he saw me but recovered quickly. "Give me a hug, Ernie baby. I am fucking surprised, and I am feeling the love. You'd better fire that twat you've got working for you. She declined my RSVP."

"It wasn't her fault, Mick. I had a change of plans at the last minute and I didn't think you'd mind."

"I know what happened. You heard about my New Year's resolution. Everybody loves a comeback, right, Ernst? I am back in business, and I'm gonna be bigger than Kozakura's tits. Come on, man, let's hug it out." Mick stepped forward to put his arms around Ernst, and Mary let out a growl. Mick backed off.

Ernst continued without missing a beat. "I didn't want to leave the puppy home alone all night, so I decided to bring her with me.

And I've brought two friends along, too. I know your parties, Mick, the more the merrier, right?"

"Right as rain, my man. Especially when it's the beautiful Ovsanna Moore of Anticipation Studios." He leaned forward and gave me an air kiss. "Hey, did the paps get your picture? You haven't aged a bit, sweetheart, are you rubbing cum on your face? They say that gets rid of wrinkles. I'm not seeing any scars, either. You really haven't had any work done, have you? How do you explain that?"

He was asking for it. "I don't know, Mr. Erzatz. I guess it's just my DNA." I could play the game, too. "This is my friend Peter King."

"Ovsanna—sweetheart—you've gotta call me Mick." He looked Peter up and down. "And you, you're the detective who caught the Cinema Slayer. You're a fucking miracle worker. We oughta call you Annie Sullivan. You really closed on that deal, didn't you? Come on in. What's your poison?"

We entered a candlelit foyer, and the first thing I saw was a print of Hokusai's *Dream of the Fisherman's Wife*. Two octopi going down on a woman. Made me wonder if any of Mick's werecreatures were aquatic. There was Japanese erotic art on all the walls. The floors were a beautiful polished black slate. As crude as his language was, he had good taste in décor. Or else a talented designer. The rooms were all post-and-beam construction, with low ceilings and minimal furniture. It looked like he'd brought in tables and chairs and decorations just for the party.

Off to the right of the foyer was a huge banquet hall, with a bar running the length of one side and a disc jockey setup on the other. Black stone pots with white orchids surrounded the dance floor, and on the far side of the room were the food stations. There were cocktail tables dotting the perimeter, all with candles on them.

The rest of the lighting came from above. Hundreds of tiny ceiling lights that changed color constantly. Made the orchids look even more beautiful. Didn't do much for the guests, though. Especially not the green.

The party was in full swing, people crowding the dance floor.

The disc jockey, a six-foot-two-inch transsexual dressed like Wonder Woman, moved back and forth between two turntables, keeping the music going, loud and fast. Maroon 5's "Wake Up Call" was playing when we walked in. S/he followed it with Shakira's "Hips Don't Lie" and Lady GaGa's "Bad Romance." By the time Enrique Iglesias's "Bailamos" came on, I couldn't stop myself. I took Peter's hand and pulled him to one corner of the dance floor.

I grew up dancing. I've never met an Armenian who didn't, man or woman, human or vampyre. My earliest memories are of the men in the village forming a circle, each holding on to one end of a white handkerchief, stomping and kicking and dipping as they snaked around a fire pit to the sound of the dumbek and the oud. Even my father came down out of the mountain when he heard the music. He wouldn't dance with the others, but for hours on end he'd leave the valley unguarded while he twirled around by himself in the shadows. Then my mother would join him and they'd disappear back into the trees, satisfying urges the music gave rise to. Music affects me the same way, almost as much as the Thirst. The right music. Primal . . . minor . . . a driving beat. It sets up a longing in me, an aching, a need for release that only gets satisfied by movement. Or coupling. Someone's hands on my body, down my breasts, between my legs. That's what the right kind of music does to me.

"Bailamos" did that for me. I turned my back on Peter and moved my hips against him, keeping beat to the music with my ass against his groin. He kept the beat right back. I danced away so I could turn around and watch him. The man could move, even in a tuxedo. If it hadn't been for Frank Sinatra, I might have ravaged him right on the dance floor. But Wonder Woman changed CDs, and Ol' Blue Eyes started singing. I calmed down. Frank Sinatra doesn't do it for me.

Peter likes him, though. He took me in his arms and we finished "Bewitched, Bothered and Bewildered."

"Mick Erzatz is definitely a were, Peter. I can smell him. And all that dialogue about me not aging. He knows exactly what I am," I said as the DJ segued into Nickelback. We stood there embracing each other without moving.

"Look, Ovsanna, you still don't know if he's the one who's trying to kill you. These fucking things are multiplying like rabbits. The rougarou, the boxenwolves, the woman we torched. They're all over the place. You don't know for sure he's the one. Just enjoy the party and we'll see what else we can find out. "

I could feel Mick watching us. He was by the bar, talking to a short brunette with huge breasts and a huge ass. I blocked out the music so I could eavesdrop.

"I'm telling you, Kimmie, you gotta release another tape. Your STARmeter's dropping. You can only get so much mileage outta the breakup with the boyfriend. Believe me, I got plenty of clients who'll be willing to bang your brains out on camera. Then we fake the tape getting stolen and file a lawsuit and you'll be right back on 'Page Six,' and your show's guaranteed another season. You just let me handle the details."

I stopped listening.

The invitation had said black tie. Most of the men were in tuxedos, except our host, who was wearing a brown kimono over silk pajama pants. All the waitstaff were dressed as circus performers. That's what some of them must have been, because a fellow in a harlequin outfit came tumbling across the floor to present me with a rose. A green rose, under the lights. He took our drink order. Five minutes later, a clown on a unicycle delivered Peter his Guinness.

There was a seminude woman covered in silver body paint and black feathers, sitting at a harp to the left of the bar. She played when the disc jockey took a break. The waiters, passing trays of hors d'oeuvres, and the chefs, standing at the food stations serving designer pastas, lobster salad, and individual filet mignons, were dressed in red-and-yellow unitards. They looked ready to tightrope walk at a moment's notice.

I left Peter waiting at one of the food stations and walked from the banquet hall into a long, low-ceilinged corridor that had rooms opening off both sides. A woman stepped out of the first one, leaving the door ajar. She was dressed like the Philip Morris bellhop from the Hotel New Yorker, and she had a cigarette tray in her hands. Inside the room, I saw two men and a woman on a bed. One of the men was tying off his arm. He looked familiar, an actor who'd walked off that show *Celebrity Rehab,* claiming his faith in God was all he needed to get straight. He must have stopped praying. The other man was licking cocaine off the woman's nipples. She raised her head to look at me and smiled.

"Would you like some enhancement for your festivities this evening?" It was the cigarette girl. She turned so I could examine her tray. There were cigarettes nestled in a black-lacquered bowl, next to a matching bowl of cocaine. A small mountain of cocaine. Three more bowls held what looked like ecstasy, oxy, and acid-laced sugar cubes.

Vampyres are immune to the effects of alcohol or drugs. But if we take blood tainted with either, we feel it. I fed on Rimbaud once when he was drunk on absinthe. We were celebrating his birthday in Abyssinia. Over a hundred years ago and I still remember how ghastly I felt. One of those times when I wished I could vomit.

The Philip Morris girl was feeling no pain; she'd obviously been sampling her wares. She wasn't going to see the new year if she kept it up. I put both my hands on either side of her face and stared into her oh-so-tiny pupils. Blocked out the images I got before they became too clear. Someone had burned her as a child; I didn't want to see it. She closed her eyes and sank to the ground, quite gracefully for someone so loaded. I took the tray from her and proceeded down the hallway, trying doorknobs. Two of the rooms were locked; I could hear the sounds of sex coming from within. The third was a meditation room, complete with altar and jade Buddhas. There was a fire in the fireplace. Perfect. I tossed the pills in first and then a few cigarettes at a time. On the altar, a dish of sand held sticks of incense. I replaced some of the sand with the cocaine, mixing it to disguise the color a bit, and stood the sticks up again. Set the empty tray on a low table, decorated it with a candle and one of the Buddhas, and stepped into the hallway.

"Oh, Ms. Moore, I'm such a fan!"

She was a tall blonde in a short dress, with feet big enough for a circus clown. I couldn't think of her name. One of those skinny girls who are always in the gossip magazines. There are two or three of them who seem interchangeable to me; I can never keep them straight. Celebutantes. All wealthy, all cadaverous, all completely devoid of talent. But incredibly successful, if you measure success by notoriety. Her picture is everywhere, even on a DUI report. *She's* everywhere. Of course she'd be at this party.

"I can't believe you're here, that is just so cool," she continued. "Are you getting a kickback from the paparazzi? Mick didn't pay you to come, did he? That lady, Madelaine, who works for him? Told me I was the only celebrity he could afford, and then I showed up and I can't believe it, Tori Spelling's husband is here. I wonder what he's getting paid. I haven't seen Tori, though. Are you actually a friend of Mick's? You must be. Oh, I know, I'll bet you were his client when he was big."

CHAPTER SIXTY-ONE

I found Ovsanna in a hallway, with the cigarette girl stretched out on the floor in front of her. The girl had that same dazed expression my aunt Addie had on Christmas Eve after Ovsanna took her outside to talk to her. I wondered what was going on, but I didn't take the time to ask. Instead, I guided Ovsanna farther down the hall and through an open door into some sort of meditation room. It smelled as if someone had been in there, smoking.

"Charlie just called me," I said. "I was waiting at the seafood station. The chef there has peacock feathers attached to his crotch. You ought to see him trying to sear tuna."

"Where was he?" Ovsanna asked.

"Next to the smoothie station with the papayas and bananas, which is where he should have been to begin with—with his feathers away from the flames. Whoever designed these costumes didn't have cooking in mind."

"No, I mean Charlie. Where was he when he called? Did you just have another Guinness?"

"Yes. And you don't have to worry. I'm half Welsh, remember.

We have saints who turned water into beer to cure the plague and feed the multitudes. And my other half is Italian. I was drinking watered-down wine when I was nine. Believe me, I can hold my own."

"Peter! What about Charlie?"

"Charlie said he and Tyrone and James had gotten to the wild animal preserve. It starts about ten miles up the mountain. They took an electric train that circles the property. There was no one else on it."

"Are they still up there?"

"No. He couldn't get phone reception on the mountain. They came back down about halfway and they're exploring the property around the castle. He said to tell you Erzatz has all kinds of beasts on the preserve and some of them aren't human. I mean, they aren't mammal. You know what I mean. Some of them are werebeasts."

"I suspected as much. They're probably the surviving weres Lilith had with her in Palm Springs. We killed a lot of them before she died, but once her gooey body dribbled into the pool, the remaining weres and *dhampirs* disappeared into the desert. You didn't get there in time to see that."

"I saw enough, believe me. I don't ever want to see anything like that again. Olive Thomas, nude, with snakes coming out of her skull and goat haunches for legs, is an image I'll never forget."

Chapter Sixty-two

Peter and I went back into the ballroom to tell Solgar what Charlie and the others had found out. Ernst had set Mary on one of the cocktail tables with a bowl of water in front of her for verisimilitude. It's one of the reasons he's such a good lawyer, his attention to detail. I didn't expect to see Mary lapping at the bowl, though. When we shift to another form, we don't necessarily take on the needs of that being. I can become a bat, but I won't spend my time searching for insects.

I wanted to get away from Peter. What I really wanted was to get Mick Erzatz off by himself so I could confront him, but Peter must have known that—he was on me like white on rice. He wouldn't leave my side. He kept me with him while he got a bite to eat, and then we went downstairs to watch the female mud wrestlers battle it out in the nude.

We ended up outside by the pool, watching six synchronized swimmers in abbreviated fish costumes do an Esther Williams extravaganza. Mary jumped out of Solgar's arms, landed in the pool, and, before we could stop her, peed in the shallow end. Fortunately, no one noticed. It was almost midnight and most of the guests couldn't see through a ladder.

"Ah, here you are." Mick Erzatz approached us with a young woman on his arm and a paparazzo in tow. I looked for a talisman around the pap's neck, but he had on a hoodie and I couldn't tell what it might be hiding. The woman looked slightly familiar. She had short orange hair, truly orange, like a Satsuma mandarin. Her top was cut loose and low, and without a bra, when she leaned forward to shake my hand, I could see both breasts and her stomach. That's what I recognized. She was the girl from the threesome I'd seen in the bedroom earlier. "I've got a client who wanted to meet you. This little hottie is Nicky." He turned to Miss Tangerine. "Say hello, sweetheart."

"Oh, Ms. Moore," she said, staring at Peter the entire time she spoke, "I've been watching you since I was a kid. And I can't believe you're here with the detective who solved the Cinema Slayer case." She turned to Peter, offering both hands and an even better view of the previously cocaine-laden nipples. "You're Detective Peter King, aren't you? You saved that boy from being drowned last year. Oh, my God, I can't believe I'm meeting a real-life hero. Could I have my picture taken with you? Oh, please?"

I stepped to the side, like the chopped liver Miss Nicky obviously thought I was, and the paparazzo moved forward to snap a couple of stills. Nicky had her arm around Peter for the photos. Somehow she managed, with her free hand, to pull a business card out of her purse and hand it to the photographer, begging him to e-mail them to her as soon as possible. She never let go of Peter, just kept flirting her little heart out.

"Jeez, I think she's gonna offer to blow him right in front of us," Mick said, pulling me away from the two of them. "Let's get outta here, I want to show you my pets."

He was my attacker, all right. As soon as he touched me, I saw an ancient old woman with dessicated skin and a short black tongue, her teeth worn down to nubs by thousands of years spent devouring human flesh. It was Lilith, the Night Hag. In my vision, Mick was fucking her.

I pulled my arm away from his hand and followed him outside.

CHAPTER SIXTY-THREE

I couldn't get away from the orange-haired girl. She pulled off her top and insisted I sign my name across her heart. Swore she was never going to shower again. By the time I caught up with Ovsanna and Mick, they were boarding the electric tram. I wasn't going to let them go anywhere without me. Ovsanna had her own agenda, and I knew it.

Mick had the same paparazzo with him. He introduced him as Blink. Mick said he wanted a photograph of Ovsanna for his office wall, posing with his giraffes. Blink was along to take the shot. I checked his neck for a collar, one of those boxenwolf talismans, but I couldn't tell; he was wearing a hoodie.

The tram was designed like a San Francisco cable car. Two open-air cars with wooden benches running back to back lengthwise, seating six on a bench. The cars weren't attached to each other. I guessed Mick took one up at a time and left the other at the house in case someone needed to follow him.

Solgar and his Pomeranian were right behind me.

"May we join you, Mick?" he said. "I've heard so much about your vineyards and your animal preserve, I'd love to see them for myself."

Mick pressed a couple of buttons on a control panel and the tram started up the mountain. He kept up a running commentary as we made the climb, peppered with *fucks* and *bitches* and *jerk me offs*. The guy must have had a lot of power to be able to get away with running a business using that kind of language. No wonder when he fell, he fell hard. He was an easy man to dislike.

The higher we climbed, the more we could see of the castle. It was twice as large as I'd originally thought. Mick pointed out the *on-sen*—the hot baths. "You put your dick in there and you don't need any bitches to make you feel good," he said. There was a group of men near it, setting up fireworks for midnight. We passed the tennis courts and a lake, and then we were out of sight of the house. The terrain was high mountain, rocky, covered with chaparral and oaks, pines, and sycamores. The Pacific Ocean spread out in the distance like a roll of black velvet.

After about ten minutes, we came to the vineyards. Mick had low-wattage solar lights running down every row, so even without the moon and the stars, which were hidden by rain clouds, you could see all the vines. He didn't have a lot of acreage planted, but what I could see looked healthy and thriving.

Ten minutes later, we came to the end of the line. Another station to match the one below, this time with a restroom attached. Beyond it, a chain-link fence, twenty feet tall.

"This is my fucking beautiful baby," Mick said. He pressed a few buttons to shut down the engine and then stepped off the train. He must not have known about Ovsanna's ability to read people when she touched them, because he offered her his hand to help her down. She didn't take it, and I stepped between the two of them. I don't think he noticed. He was at the fence, unlocking the gate. The five of us walked through.

There were peacocks roaming the preserve, dozens of them. They weren't shy. They came within feet of us. Spider monkeys hung from the blue oaks. Nasty little buggers, hissing and spitting. One of them jumped down from a tree, squatted over his hand, and threw a steaming lump of feces at Solgar, just missing his tuxedo. Mary went nuts.

She jumped out of Ernst's arms and ran at the thing, teeth bared, snapping viciously. The monkey raced back up the tree, making that high-pitched monkey bark sound, and the rest of the monkeys joined in. Mary took off through the gate and raced down the hill, out of sight. Ovsanna caught my eye. I figured Mary was on her way to let the other vampyres know where we were.

"Sorry, Ernst," said Mick, "I didn't expect that. Good thing the little cocksucker can't pitch. Blink, will you go after the dog? See if you can keep it in sight, at least. And call someone down below when you get in phone range; have them come up on the other tram to find it. You three come with me. I've got a herd of llamas to show you, and giraffes, bison. . . . I've even got an elephant. I get hard just thinking about him."

Ernst took two more steps and got hit with another wad of shit.

I had to give him credit; he stayed a lot calmer than I would have.

"That's it," he said, backing away and staring at the brown glop running down his chest. "I'm not going any further. I don't give a damn about seeing a bunch of animals. I've already seen their shit. I am going back to the restroom and I'll wait for you on the tram." With that, he walked through the gate and closed it behind himself, with a lot more dignity than I would have had. I clamped my lips shut to keep from laughing.

CHAPTER SIXTY-FOUR

Good. That just left Peter and Mick and me. And a collection of wild animals, none of whom appeared to be of my kind. I was certain I was right, though. These mountains were home to Lilith's offspring. Mick might be showing off his lions and tigers and bears, oh my, but the real werebeasts were waiting in the wings.

I could smell them.

We walked about a half mile, down one hill and up a second, out of sight of the train station. The path was dimly lit, but my vision made it easy to see the zebras in the distance, drinking at a small vernal pool.

Suddenly the sky was filled with exploding red lights. Fireworks. The zebras spooked and ran. I heard the bellow of an elephant, and then the monkeys drowned it out with their howling. More explosions rocked the night and the sky turned white.

Mick screamed over the cacophony, "It's midnight, bitches! We're celebrating New Year's! Top o' the world, Ma! Happy fucking New Year!"

Green and gold fireworks topped each other, lighting the mountain like daylight. The noise was deafening. I turned to Peter to give him a kiss, but he had moved closer to the pool to watch the zebras. He was thirty feet away from me.

And tracking towards him, through the grasses and the underbrush, was a Bengal tiger.

I turned on Mick. He was smiling. "What the fuck, Ovsanna . . . are you frightened? It's just a pet."

"Peter!" I screamed, turning back to him.

He couldn't hear me. The fireworks were too loud. Another display shot into the sky, the lights forming a blue champagne glass. At that, Peter started towards me, grinning and yelling, "Happy New Year!"

I had already begun the change. My eyes were red, my fangs in place. "Your gun, Peter!" I screamed. "Behind you!"

The cat was running. Five hundred pounds of death speeding towards Peter at forty miles an hour. This wasn't a werebeast, this was one of Mick's *Wild Kingdom* menagerie—the most powerful killer in the animal world. I shifted to put myself between Peter and his attacker. The Bengal was in midair when I appeared before him. He wrenched his body and his front paw swiped past me, mauling Peter's shoulder, taking him down. I heard the crack of Peter's skull against the rocks beneath him.

He moaned and rolled on his side. I couldn't believe he was still conscious. His tuxedo was shredded from his collarbone to his ribs. His right arm looked useless. I knew his gun was trapped beneath him. He was trying to raise his body enough to get it with his left hand.

"Don't move!" I yelled, and leapt over him to keep him behind me. The cat had landed fifteen feet away and turned to face us. He was growling at me. Pacing. He wanted to get at his prey, wanted to get his teeth into the neck of the two-legged creature on the ground, snap its spine, and carry it away to devour at leisure. But I was in the way, and he didn't recognize my scent. I wasn't like anything he'd ever tracked before. I stood with my talons ready and my fangs ready and I watched his mind work. Peter had stopped moving. He was silent. Probably unconscious. I couldn't take my eyes off the tiger to check.

I called out to Mick, "A pet, huh? Are you going to do something?" He hadn't moved from the spot he'd been standing in when the fireworks began. He was thirty feet from me, with the Bengal pacing between us. But the animal wasn't interested in Mick; he was facing Peter and me.

"Oh yeah, bitch. I'm going to do something. I'm gonna pull out the big guns." He pinched his lower lip between his thumb and middle finger and sucked in sharply. The air split with a deafening, high-pitched whistle. "I gotta lotta pets, Ovsanna. You met them in Palm Springs, remember? And you killed one of them in Silver Lake night before last—one of my favorites. They're gonna make you fucking pay for what you did to Lilith."

From out of the trees, Mick's other menagerie began to emerge. Werebeasts—that hybrid race of vampyre that can only change into a specific beast shape. I was surrounded by Lilith's progeny: hyenas, foxes, a dog, wolves, even an ape. There must have been twenty of them, at least. They were misshapen, grotesque looking, which told me they were old—so old, they could no longer change out of their beast form. But not so old as to be less of a threat. Weres grow more powerful as they age.

If Mary had reached my clan and if they got here anytime soon, we might be able to take down all of Mick's beasts, but I wasn't sure. We'd have to do it fast. Peter needed help. I could smell his blood draining into the dirt.

It was the Bengal tiger I wasn't sure I could survive. He'd stopped pacing and was crouched, ready to spring.

The hyenas started whining, making that peculiar laughing sound. Mick yelled over them, "Don't you need to take on another form, bitch? Like you did with Lilith? Maybe put on a strap-on? Well, forget about it, you could turn into Sasquatch and the Loch Ness monster and you wouldn't survive. What a shame your Vampyres of Hollywood aren't here to watch you die, you slimy cunt!"

"Language, old man, language! I wouldn't talk to our chatelaine like that, if I were you."

Orson appeared behind Mick, just long enough to be recognized, and then he was shifting to his favorite form. A werebull, twelve hundred pounds at least, with huge curling horns and iron hooves nine inches wide. Trust Orson to choose girth over fangs. The man who once said, "Ask not what you can do for your country. Ask what's for lunch."

The tiger saw the werebull and turned rabid. He sprang for me. Instead of leaping to meet him, I shifted out of the way—so fast that he landed off balance, inches from Peter's head. He stumbled on his front paws and Orson came crashing down on his back with his hooves. I heard bones cracking as Orson jumped off him, away from the deadly swipe of his paws. His front paws, only. Orson's attack had crippled his hind legs. He struggled to lift himself and only managed to roll over onto his back.

Mary came racing to Peter's side. She'd changed to her she-devil form, with a gargoyle-shaped skull and the haunches of an emu. She grabbed what was left of Peter's tuxedo jacket and pulled him out of reach of the Bengal's flailing claws.

I had one split second of pity for the animal. He was beautiful, a regal beast with gorgeous black, white, and orange markings. And he was helpless. This wasn't his fight; he'd just been following his nature. Mick Erzatz had penned him, in a parody of domestication, and then used him to try to kill me when Mick and his boxenwolves and his alpha female had failed. I wanted to put the tiger out of his misery. If I could use Peter's gun . . .

But I didn't have time. Ty and James and Charlie and Tod had all shifted. They were attacking the weres that Mick had gathered around him. Ernst had a *kirpan* in both hands and he was slashing at an ancient red werefox. The fox was fast, but Ernst was faster. Chunks of red fur scattered around him. He was using his sucker to toss pieces of cut flesh. Ty had morphed into a sleek black jaguar—twice the size of a real one and just as beautiful as you'd expect him to be. Leave it to a leading man to make sure he looked good in battle. Charlie, on the other hand, understood the value of special effects. He'd shifted into a monster with bat wings and a pig's snout, his skin layered and crusted like a mangy Shar-pei. His black tongue was covered with spikes, and he had four sharp three-inch tusks protruding from his mouth. Ever the showman.

He was using them against an ape—a giant weregorilla who must have weighed four hundred pounds. The ape fought with its hands and its feet. Charlie locked his jaw around the beast's leg, breaking its tibia with his tusks, and severed its tendons. The ape's scream was unearthly.

Mick had backed away. "You should have signed with me, bub-aleh!" he yelled at Orson. "I never would have let you make those wine commercials!" He scrambled onto a low boulder and made that whistling sound again.

James, half man and half bear, and Tod, a werejackal, tore into the beasts that surrounded them. Their fighting took them farther away from me, up the hill. I saw James crush the head of a massive dog and fling the entire carcass across the mountainside.

The noises the weres made belonged in Dante's *Inferno*. Howling and shrieking and screams raged even louder than the fireworks. Mick whistled again, and this time I heard another sound, human voices whispering a mantra. And rubbing. The sound of flesh rubbing fur. Mick Erzatz had summoned the paparazzi who'd been waiting at his front door hours ago. The paparazzi with the wolf collar talismans hidden around their necks.

I was fighting alongside Ernst, chewing off a werehyena's ear, when the pack of boxenwolves attacked. They cut me away from my clan the way an Aussie herds sheep. I was suddenly by myself, and I was surrounded.

CHAPTER SIXTY-FIVE

I needed to help Ovsanna, but I was in trouble myself. I'd cracked my head open, I knew that. I'd heard the sound it made when the tiger knocked me down. Now I needed to open my eyes. There were noises—explosions and screaming—and I needed to open my eyes to see what was going on. But when I did, I saw Ovsanna on the beach, attacked by paparazzi-turned-werewolves. I closed my eyes again. My eye sockets throbbed with a white, shooting sharpness. I touched the back of my head and my hand came away wet. I struggled to open my lids. Everything blurred in front of me.

I could barely make out animals fighting thirty or forty feet away. No, they weren't animals. They were grotesque, monster versions of dogs, wolves, and foxes. They must have been those fucking werebeasts Ovsanna said Mick had on the preserve. The hyenas had giant jaws and no fur, just slimy, pinkish gray skin with yellow spots. Their hindquarters were twice as tall as their front legs. They looked as though they should be stretched out on a prayer rug. The ape was ancient, with patchy white hair and pustulating tumors on his back and haunches. He was huge, though, and he was being torn apart by a half-pig, half-bat apparition that could only have been one of Ovsanna's clan. I was guessing Charlie Chaplin.

Ovsanna was away from the others, closer to me. And she *was* being attacked by werewolves—this wasn't a déjà vu. My heart started pumping, but my mind slowed down, the way it always does when I'm dealing with danger. I saw everything I needed to do in slow motion. I'd promised Ovsanna I'd take care of her; I wasn't going to let anything hurt her. I didn't want to lose her.

I tried for my gun, but my arm wouldn't move. The right side of my body was numb. I reached my holster with my left hand and freed the Smith & Wesson. From my right, I heard a pain-filled, high-pitched barking sound. Fireworks lit the sky, and I saw two werefoxes and something that was part woman and part ostrich. That had to be Mary, with a gargoyle skull. The foxes had her down; they were going for her neck. I fired. One fell away from her. Snakes shot out of her mouth and attacked the other. I turned back to aim toward Ovsanna. The sky was dark again, rain clouds blocking out any moonlight. I could just make out the pack of wolves blurring into a black mass around her silver dress. I wasn't worried about hitting her, I'd seen her recover from a lot worse, but it took all my strength to raise my head and pull the trigger a second time. Nausea hit me like a tidal wave. My vision dimmed. I fired once more before I couldn't see anything. I puked and the pain seared through my head. I knew what I needed to do, but I couldn't keep my eyes open to do it. I dropped my face in my vomit and everything went black.

CHAPTER SIXTY-SIX

There were five boxenwolves circling me—none of them as big as Mick's alpha female friend, and not nearly the size Mick had been when he'd attacked me in my yard. That didn't mean I could survive them all in a pack, though. If they took me down, I'd never get up again. And I had to get up. I had Peter to take care of.

The first one came at me low. I kicked him in the side of his head, smashing him against the boulders off to my left. He stayed down. Two more sprang at me from either side. I grabbed one by the throat and ripped open his chest with my fangs. Head-butted the other, his mate's lung and bones dripping from my teeth, and twirled out from under him as he went flying over my shoulder, slashing my back with his hind paws. So much for my silver Narciso Rodriguez. I still had my hand around the second one's throat. I spit out his ribs and pulled him to my face, took his heart in my mouth, and tore it from his body. This time I didn't spit. The taste was too seductive. I was chewing and swallowing even as the last two boxenwolves took me down.

One sank his teeth in my neck, the other tore at my stomach.

The third, the one I'd thrown over my shoulder, came at my legs. I kicked him off and sliced the claws of my toes across his jugular. Even as his life's blood spurted into the air, he tried one last time to hamstring me. Again I kicked him away while I struggled with my hands to pry the first wolf's jaws from my neck. If he bit any deeper, I wouldn't survive. The wolf at my stomach had backed off to devour the flesh he'd torn from me, but already my body was healing itself. It was my neck I had to protect.

I was gushing blood. Losing strength. The wolf's snout was buried in my throat. If I took my hands from his jaws, he'd clamp down deeper and I'd die. I tried raking him with my toes, kicking him off me, but I couldn't get purchase. I felt my strength draining. I'd been right about my evening wrap. I wouldn't be wearing it home.

I wasn't ready for my life to end. Not when I was just beginning a new relationship. And not when Peter needed me to save him. Fuck Mick Erzatz and his fucking zoo beasts. I struggled harder to break free.

Two gunshots fired. The wolf with my stomach in his mouth never stopped chewing. The wolf with his teeth in my neck let loose, his jaw went slack, and he collapsed on top of me. I pushed him off and leapt after the gourmand. He was so busy dining that he didn't know I was there until I ripped off his collar.

"You're a fucking piece of shit, Diego!" Mick raged over the explosions. In the light of the fireworks, I saw the boxenwolf begin his shift back to human form. I grabbed him by his forearm and flung him over my head, impaling him on a tree branch. He looked like the Scarecrow in *The Wizard of Oz*. Mick screamed at his spasming body, "Do I have to do everything myself?!"

And instantly, Mick shifted. It was so fast, I barely saw the transformation. One minute he was a short, fat ex-agent in a brown kimono, smelling slightly feral, and the next he was the rabid werewolf that had attacked me in my yard a week ago, foaming from the mouth with acid saliva, and smelling so rancid that my eyes began to burn.

He advanced on me slowly, snarling, his orange eyes glowing

with hatred. His body was muscle and power, but his head was grotesque, with its double row of yellow fangs and mangled muzzle. My vision was so heightened, I could see the veins in his gums, even in the darkness between fireworks. He was no longer Mick Erzatz, but a frenzied beast driven by ancient intincts. He wanted to eviscerate me, disembowel me. To feed on the vampyre who had obliterated his progenitor, the creature who birthed him—the mother of all evil.

It's not easy to kill a vampyre, especially if we've fed recently, and God knows I'd done enough of that in the last few days. Drowning, staking, dismemberment, and decapitation will do the trick. This Mick-turned-werebeast wouldn't be able to drown me or impale me, but he could tear me apart.

I needed my clan. In the distance behind me I heard them rending flesh, bodies crashing against beasts, teeth crunching bone. Howling, raging, ungodly screams rent the air. The Vampyres of Hollywood had their hands full with the rest of Mick's weres; they wouldn't be coming to help anytime soon.

I sprang at him as he crouched to leap. He was stronger than I was, more powerful, but I was faster. I raked my nails across his face and his left eyeball split in two, viscous liquid draining down his snout. I landed to his left, and he had to turn his whole body to track me past his newly blinded eye.

We circled each other, with him lunging in to snap at me and pulling away before I could strike or kick. If I could get my teeth into his neck, I could pierce his jugular, but to do that, I needed to come at him from behind. His snout was too long for me to rush him head-on. One second I was facing him, and the next I took myself to his blind side and prepared to spring.

I felt a searing pain in my calf. The boxenwolf I'd kicked in the head and sent flying against the boulders had slunk in to help his master. He looked dazed and disoriented, but he had his teeth clamped on my right leg. I was wearing chain-link Giuseppe Zanotti ankle straps with four-inch metal heels. Not the best choice for someone who anticipated a battle with beasts, but they worked with

my dress, and come on, what's more important? The advantage was
that the ankle straps had kept them on my feet. I slammed my left foot
down on the boxenwolf's head. My heel smashed through his skull
like a steel spike. He was dead instantly, my shoe sucked into his brain
matter so deeply that I couldn't withdraw my heel. So when he went
down, so did I. I had to push against his skull with my right foot to
free myself.

And by that time, it was all over. Mick was on top of me, his front
legs pinning my shoulders to the ground. We locked eyes. There was
nothing human left in his, only animalistic rage and the foreshad-
owing of a kill. He raised his head and howled in victory.

I was going to die. Too young for a vampyre. Too young for me,
Chatelaine of the Vampyres of Hollywood. Who would look out for
my clan? Who would take care of Maral? And what had I done to
Peter, brought him into the lion's den to be killed?

I heard a loud crack and tore my eyes away, searching the sky for
the fireworks, the last image I would see in my 450 years of life. The
sky stayed dark; I was losing my vision. A second sound exploded
past me and that's when I realized Peter was firing again. His second
shot grazed Mick's shoulder.

Mick pulled away from me, a chunk of my breast in his jaws, and
hurtled towards Peter. Peter fired a third time, missing Mick but hitting me. That was twice he'd done that. If I didn't know better, I'd
think it was Freudian. We'd have to talk about that—if we lived to
talk. Pain burned through my arm as I focused my sight on the space
between Peter and the were. Mick was twenty feet from him. Peter
would be dead in two seconds.

I am Clan Dakhanavar of the First Bloodline. Our nature—my
father's and my ancestors'—is to guard and protect. At that moment,
450 years of instinct flooded my being. I've never been so strong or
so fast. I was on top of Mick in an instant, reaching around to tear
off his gonads. He writhed and bucked, and I rode him like Debra
Winger in *Urban Cowboy*. Then I sank my teeth in his neck and used
my claws to rip out his heart. The last of the fireworks exploded.

So much for Mick's New Year's resolution.

CHAPTER SIXTY-SEVEN

At one thirty in the morning on New Year's Day, the skies over Montecito opened up and flooded Mick Erzatz's wild animal preserve with torrential rains. By that time, most of my clan had disappeared, leaving behind them the minimal remains of fifteen or twenty werebeasts, all of which were conveniently washed away in the deluge. They wouldn't have been identifiable anyway, just bite-size pieces of hyena skin and ape bone.

Ernst had stayed with me, helping me get an unconscious Peter into the tram and down the hill and then calling the police and EMTs once we got into a phone service area. They were waiting with an ambulance and a medevac when we got back to the castle. The party was still going strong. Nobody seemed to realize their host was no longer alive.

The rains brought flash floods in the mountains. Unfortunately for the investigating officers, they wiped out any sign of the vicious tiger attack that had taken the lives of celebrated agent Mick Erzatz and his photographer friend Diego. I described to the Santa Barbara Police what I thought had happened, but I don't think I was very helpful. I said I'd been quite a ways away when the big cat had gone crazy and devoured the two men. One minute we were celebrating New Year's, and the next my escort was being mauled. I didn't see the attack on Diego or Mick; I was too busy trying to help Peter. All I knew for sure was that if Peter hadn't regained consciousness and killed the Bengal, we probably would have been his next course.

It was an award-winning performance. I know they believed me.

The doctors did surgeries on Peter's arm and chest and shoulder. They put him in traction. I was alone with him in his hospital room when he came out of the anesthesia. He stared at me for the longest time, and then he smiled.

"Hey. Happy New Year," I said. "I'd give you a kiss, but the doctors don't want you to move your head. How do you feel?"

"Like I must be on pain meds. I'm not feeling a thing. How are you?"

"I'm fine. Not a mark on me. And no more werebeasts to worry about. I'll tell you all about it when your head is clearer."

"I don't remember much. I hit Mick Erzatz, didn't I? Did I save your life?"

I nodded. I was grinning. "You helped. That's for sure."

"You see, I told you you couldn't go there without me. There are times when being a vampyre just doesn't cut it—you need a cop, with a gun. Anyway, it was a hell of a way to celebrate New Year's."

"Oh, I don't know. We got rid of the bad guys and we got to dance. What else could you ask for?"

"Well . . . how about mad, passionate vampyre love? Which I'm developing quite an appreciation for, by the way. That would have been a nice capper to the evening. So what are you doing for Valentine's Day?"

"We're not going to have to wait that long."

"We're not? With me in traction and a body cast? I don't see it happening anytime soon."

"Well, you're forgetting one thing," I said, tossing off his sheets.
"What?"

"There's always your toes."